DEADFALL IN BERLIN

DEADFALL IN BERLIN

by

R. D. ZIMMERMAN

DONALD I. FINE, INC.
New York

Copyright © 1990 by R. D. Zimmerman

Library of Congress Cataloging-in-Publication Data

Zimmerman, R. D. (Robert Dingwall)
Deadfall in Berlin / by R. D. Zimmerman.
        p.   cm.
        ISBN 1-55611-222-X
              I. Title.
        PS3576.I5118D4   1990
            813'.54—dc20
              90-55019
                CIP

Manufactured in the United States of America

10   9   8   7   6   5   4   3   2   1

For my brothers,
Chip, Scott, and Jamie

A writer sits in a corner and makes up things, but in order for a book to work, the story must be credible. With that in mind I'd like to thank Dr. Don Houge, not only for offering his expertise in the field of hypnosis, but for making me so many hypnosis tapes for writing. Peter Petzling generously shared his vast knowledge of German history and his native Berlin, and I'm indebted to him for his help. The very friendly people of Berlin were of great assistance, too, directing me to various archives, various sites, and, among other things, helping me read menus.

Also, my writing group, The Suspenders, heard every high and low, and offered invaluable advice and friendship. And, of course, thanks to my editor, Susan Schwartz, for the dare.

Chapter

1

BERLIN

FEBRUARY 1945

When I heard my mother's scream rise through the ruins of Berlin, I froze in the mountain of rubble that had once been the apartment building where Herr Schulenberg, his wife and children, and seven other families had lived. All that remained was now beneath my feet—bricks, plaster, shattered beams, and buried somewhere below, the two Schulenberg boys who still hadn't been found after one recent night of heavy bombing.

Standing there in the moonlight—me, blond, blue-eyed, disarming smile, and rather tall for a ten-year old—I held a bucket of water. I had a helpless, desperate look I could put on in a second and that always worked to my advantage, especially if I smeared my face with dirt. But for once that look was genuine. Fleeing the Gestapo, we'd been in hiding all evening.

I heard the voice of my mother, the chanteuse, and at

first it didn't occur to me that she was begging for her life. I stood there atop the rubble and looked up through the faint light at Frau Schulenberg's piano, which sat on a narrow ledge of what was once the fourth floor. We had an upright like that in the bar Mother operated beneath the charred ruins of our little Berlin *Pension*. A bar that was in a cellar three levels down and that was almost as safe as the Zoo Bunker and much more popular, for when the bombs started plopping, those in the neighborhood much preferred to smoke and drink and listen to my mother's husky voice than cower in a concrete tomb.

It was only when Mother's voice shrieked out again that I realized she could be in danger. Just once before had I heard her cry out like that, lungs squeezed, face red, mouth open like a ghoul's. That was when my little brother Erich was killed. Now, fearing the worst, I started to run through the night. We had lived through Hitler and bombs and intrigue and fear. And we were preparing to flee Berlin. Our friends were planning it all. We hoped to leave tomorrow, perhaps even escape all the way to Switzerland.

"Mama!" I called, hauling the bucket of water.

I was as adept as a mountain goat at making my way through the ruins, and I clambered down the backside of the rubble, desperate to hear my mother say, "Willi, is that you? No, don't worry, everything's all right." But she didn't call out, didn't even sing, and I charged through a maze of charred beams and nearly emptied the bucket of precious water as I climbed through a window with no glass. If only I could make it to our little hovel, a secret hole carved in the ruin of a building.

"Mama!" I shouted.

She cried in response, her deep, hoarse voice now jagged with fright.

It was dark and chilly, and I shouldn't have left her alone.

I was supposed to protect her, take care of her. But instead of going directly to the broken water main and back, I'd poked into several ruins, scavenged and spied. I must have taken too long, and while I was gone someone must have discovered her, taken her by surprise, and was beating her or stealing our cigarettes or chocolate or coffee. Things we could trade for potatoes.

I spilled the last of the water, let the pail drop and clang, rushed around the corner. I flew against a sheet of metal that was our door, shoved it aside. Nothing. There was no one in the faint glow of the spirit lamp, just our blankets, a suitcase, and a cigarette. A priceless cigarette smoking on its own.

"Mama?"

Charging back outside, I turned right, clambered over a pile of bricks, searched and pleaded. Then in the skeleton of the building next door I spotted something twisting and struggling. It was my mother in the arms of the head Gestapo guy, the one who'd been pursuing us. He glanced at me over his shoulder and laughed, then pulled my mother closer in his arms and kissed her neck. She cried out, rallied somehow at the sight of me, and tried to push that scum of a man away.

I grabbed a brick and heaved it at that eel. Then I flew at him, me, less than half his size, punching and kicking. He twisted sharply, and I spotted his gun as it tumbled to the ground and clattered on the broken stones. I lunged for it, stretched out my desperate, skinny, little arm but couldn't reach it. The man grabbed me and hurled me through the air and into a wall and I dropped to the ground just like a robin that had slammed into a window. I shook my head, couldn't see. Suddenly I sensed someone else. There was shouting and yelling, and then a huge explosion sent tremors through my heart and shook my entire body. My mother screamed. My eyes opened and I shrieked for sight. I pawed in blindness across the rubble. What was happening? Who else was here?

"Mama!" I sobbed.

A second explosion blasted my ears. What was happening, an air raid? Were we being bombed yet again? A man screamed, first low, next long and high like a dog that had been half-smashed by a car. I turned vaguely saw someone holding a gun. The eyes, they were deep and crazy and—

I scrambled to my feet. We had to get out of here. Little by little my vision was returning, and I scanned that pit of death for my mother, then spotted her for the very last time. She was motionless on the ground, a bullet hole having carved a simple red eye in her forehead. Not far from her lay the Gestapo man, a pile of flesh and bones in a swelling puddle of blood.

"Ah!" I screamed.

I wanted to rush to Mother, but I glanced over my shoulder and saw a huge dark figure coming after me, arms outstretched, eyes glaring. I was to be killed, too. That much was clear. Turning to run, I tripped over a brick, clambered back to my feet, and started running. Running. Outside I ducked around a wall, charged on. I twisted around.

"No!"

Bursting from the ruins and into the night, this monstrous person clawed out, shouted after me. In the dim light I couldn't tell if it was a man or a woman. I only knew I'd be killed if I were caught. Scrambling through the remains of a bank, I didn't know where to go, where to hide, but then the sirens started to cry and moments later came the planes. Hundreds of British bombers swept over the city, dumping destruction upon us. As Berlin exploded, I checked behind me, could no longer see my would-be assailant, and so I dove into some pit and covered my head and opened my mouth, just like I'd been taught. When it was over, when I emerged into the hellish smoke and fire, there was no one around. I wiped away my tears and stumbled on, going and pushing, which was the beginning of my trip to America. A trip that did not include my mother, the chanteuse, for she lay dead like so many others in the ruins of Berlin.

Chapter

2

CHICAGO

JUNE 1975

I was staring at a flat white ceiling, had been fixed on it for God knows how long. Finally my eyes drifted to the side and I saw a white formica dresser and my little color portable. On the other wall hung a print of the 1893 Chicago World's Fair and a Kandinsky poster. That's right. Chicago. That's where I was. In my one-bedroom apartment not far from Lincoln Park. A little place at the top of a three-flat with lots of white walls and shag carpeting and a good amount of exposed brick and a sleek kitchen. That was why it cost so much. Avocado-colored appliances always jacked up the price.

I reached over, groped on the bed, touched a plastic box. My tape recorder. Yes, I had listened to my hypnosis tape again. I was scheduled to shoot a commercial tomorrow morning, me as some suburban dad with his son at a ballgame enjoying and sharing a particular brand of wiener—

which brand I couldn't just now remember—and I always used hypnosis to step out of myself and into a role. You gotta have a gimmick, and hypnosis was mine. This afternoon, though, I had done something different. I had been about to go under and imagine myself as the all-American guy, but then I veered. All day I'd been thinking about her voice, that beautiful, smoky, lyrical voice. That was all I wanted. So that's what I'd done. Listened to my induction tape and not pictured myself at Wrigley Field. No. I'd taken myself back.

But, Christ, no matter how real it felt, despite the salty streaks of dried tears on my cheeks, I hadn't really gone anywhere. I was still here, still in America. I had been brought here thirty years ago, a scrawny little *steppke*—street urchin—and adopted by a nice man and woman who already had a little girl some five years younger than me. They were all nice, America was nice, our near-north suburb was nice, and I left me, Wilhelm-known-to-everyone-as-Willi Berndt, behind, and became William Walker who, thank God, became not Bill but Will. My mother tongue was forbidden, and I was silent for my first three months. Then I started speaking and I don't think I've shut up since. Forget. Forget.

I tried to leave Berlin behind. I was happy in the fifties, and Dad and Mom and little sister, Cathy, and I took trips to the Grand Canyon and California. I did what I've always done best: pretended. I smiled and I laughed, and I tried to think of other things as we drove our blue Ford along new concrete roads that were called freeways not *Autobahns*. I got a dog, had friends, went to school. Never once beat up on my kid sister. War scares me, and in the late fifties one of my first psychologists secured my exemption from the draft. I had seen too much, of that everyone was sure. Later, I embraced the sixties and organized the first demonstrations, dabbled in drugs, and slept with Jean and Susan and Margie and someone I never knew the name of yet who I keep thinking I see on the streets. Going. I kept going. Running. Pushing away. Trying to forget. I became an actor. Did two aspirin commercials, a soap, a handful of sit-coms, but actually I'm not yet the star I thought I'd been ordained to be. Oh, and the up-coming wiener ads.

I pushed aside the tape recorder, rolled over, and sat on the edge of the bed. Me, Will, forty and here in Chicago. Will, the actor, dark blond hair, balding (just a bit), blue eyes, oval face, broad shoulders. All of that was in this bedroom. How was that possible? How was it possible that I was here when I was so sure I had just been there?

Everyone except my string of therapists thought I was just Will, kind of handsome and someone who tried so hard, so ridiculously hard, to be nice. Well, it made me want to puke. No matter how nice and sweet (my two least favorite words in the English language) I was, I obviously still couldn't forget. Deep, deep inside me it was all still there. That's why I couldn't go on. I'd tried to leave Berlin behind but it kept creeping back.

I touched my eyes. I had actually cried. Amazing, I thought, as I rose and headed in the bathroom. I splashed my face, slid back the mirror, then slugged down a couple of aspirins. I was supposed to be good Will, sweet Will, and that was such a burden. Glass of water in hand, I stumbled into my living room, plunked down on my tweedy couch, looked up her number, and dialed.

"I need to speak to Dr. Brenner," I said into the phone I tightly clutched. "It's Will Walker calling."

In her usual flat, dry voice, the receptionist informed me the doctor was busy, but I insisted. Sounding as unpromising as possible, the guard of the office then parked me on hold. I had to listen to almost an entire string version of "Strawberry Fields" before Alecia picked up.

"Will," began my dear doctor, "I'm glad you called. I wanted to talk to you."

Not giving her a chance to elaborate—I feared she wanted to change an appointment—I quickly blurted: "I have an emergency."

I tried to picture her—long brown hair, thin face, narrow nose, a big warm smile. I was, I knew, in love with her. But I shouldn't be. Big taboo. Alecia was my shrink, and even though I'd had an hour with her just yesterday, I was desperate for another appointment today.

Her voice came through, deep and concerned. "Is everything all right?"

"No. I can't remember my mother's voice."

"Go on."

"She had this dreamy, rather dreary voice that your ears sort of inhaled. While Berlin was crumbling, we were down in the bar. I knew every song she did."

Alecia was silent, which didn't really surprise me because I was aware that she thought I was dramatic; in my last session she'd barely batted an eye when I'd told her I thought someone was following me. My present pain, though, was as real as it was awful. I choked, coughed once. This would get her full attention, wouldn't it?

"My mother died thirty years ago and I can't remember her voice."

Alecia cleared her voice. "You can't remember?"

"No, nothing. Not even a little peep. You see, I was supposed to forget everything. That's why I can't remember how to speak German and that's why I can't remember much about Berlin. But I didn't want to forget my mother's voice. That was all I had of her. Now that's gone too." I took a deep breath, clutched at my courage. "But I have to remember. Not just Mama's voice. Everything."

"And that's what you've been working on," said Alecia, clicking into her role. "It's going to take some time, but you will get to the point where you'll be able to remember all that you need to. I'm sure of it, Will."

I glanced out the window and into the sunny, quiet street. "'You know, I've come to realize that forgetting is like lying. It's like a sin of omission."

"What do you mean?"

"Truth is like acid. If you hide it inside you, it eats away at you slowly, very slowly. Destroys everything, you know."

I told her I'd lain on my bed, flicked on the tape recorder, gotten ready to transport myself to wiener heaven. She understood all that, of course, for it was Alecia's voice on my induction tape; she'd been making tapes for me for over a year now, tailoring trances for specific parts. You know, Matt on one of the soaps. Or Shakespeare, which I did last summer up in Wisconsin.

Tonight, thought, I'd used just the vanilla-plain induction tape and had slipped into my normally deep state. I was good at hypnosis, maybe because I used my imagination so much in my work, maybe because Alecia had taught me so well. Whatever, I could roll up these blues of mine until there was nothing but the whites, listen to her chant, and POOF. I was gone.

"So I went back."

Suddenly I knew I had her full attention.

Alecia said, "Will, we talked about that. I told you that age regression was something best done only under my supervision."

"So I found out."

Silence.

I loved pissing off my shrink. I loved showing her that I had a will of my own, that I wasn't going to do everything when and how she wanted. I didn't want to be her nice little client and do it all her way.

I gazed at the huge oak out front. "So you want to hear about it or not?"

Silence.

She was pissed. She was often quiet when she was mad.

Once, though, I had her so steamed she wouldn't shut up. I just laughed. Even back then I wondered if she knew I loved her.

"So I went back. To Berlin, I mean. It was innocent enough, I suppose." I explained how I'd been moping around, thinking how the images of my mother had been slipping away, fading like photographs taken out too many times into the light. "Then all of a sudden it just struck me: I had forgotten her voice. It just wouldn't come. My memory was deaf." I took a deep breath. "So I put on the induction tape and took myself back. Just to hear a song or two. Just to hear the husky voice of my mother, the chanteuse. But I didn't hear a nice . . ."

All the muscles in my neck went crooked. I couldn't speak.

"What did you hear, Will?"

"My mother's . . . my mother's scream."

My eyes broke. I clutched the phone and suddenly I was sobbing like I hadn't in over thirty years.

"Will?"

"It's useless."

"Will, what are you trying to say?"

"My mother didn't die in an air raid like I thought, like I told you. She . . . she . . ."

"Go on."

Alecia's voice was calm, unruffled. But this would get her.

As if I were jabbing Alecia with a red-hot poker, I blurted, "My mother was murdered."

Pause. "Murdered?"

"Yeah. I was there. I went to get water, but then I heard her screaming and I ran back. There was this disgusting Gestapo agent kissing her."

"My God."

"I threw a brick. There was a fight. I was hitting this guy, this Gestapo man. This is where it gets all fuzzy. He hit me. No, no, he threw me against a wall and I kind of blacked out. But I kind of didn't, either, because someone else came running in."

"Who?"

"I . . . I don't know." I closed my eyes and recalled more. "Then there were gunshots—two, maybe three of them. Very close, very frightening. And then this person started chasing me, you know, coming after me. I ran and—"

"Will, I—"

"Wait, there's more." Yes, this was the ghastly part, the bit that was killing me. "Somewhere inside me I know who did it. I can't picture the face. I mean, my vision was all screwed up, but I know I looked right into the eyes of the person who killed my mother."

I took a deep breath. This was the source, the artesian well of anxiety and self-hate within me: I had never revealed my mother's murderer.

"Will, I'm glad you called," she said, having professionally reined in her shock. "I have an opening at four. Can you make that? There's something else we need to talk about, too."

I looked at a clock tacked up on one of the brick walls. It was not quite two.

"Sure, but you know what? I'm afraid to remember it all. I'm really afraid."

"I understand, but you have to keep in mind that these events took place thirty years ago, Will. That was World War II."

Out of nowhere I started to cry again. "I know, and I've been afraid so long." I clutched my eyes. "God, you just don't know how afraid I've been."

"Afraid of what?"

"I don't know. There was a circle of people that all turned against my mother and went after her. They might still be alive, they might come after me." I blew my nose. "Oh, God, I don't know."

"Will, just calm down. If you want, do a light trance to relax. Don't do an age regression. Just cool off and then come down to my office. We'll talk about everything then."

"Okay."

I plunked down the receiver, wiped my eyes. I stared at the phone, almost picked it up again to make another call. But that wouldn't help. We'd been through it several times. My adoptive parents, now living cozily in Sun City, knew nothing of my former life. Neither did little sister now with three kids out in sprawling Schaumburg. They didn't know anything. Toledo, let alone Berlin, was out of their realm of consciousness. That's why over a month ago I'd fired off a handful of letters to Europe. Didn't anyone—genealogy service, adoption agency, old friend—know anything about my real family? So far, without a response, it seemed no one did.

I stared at my one hanging fern, turned to my four packed bookcases, then my bike and a long stack of records. I couldn't stay in the apartment. It seemed suddenly cluttered. Grabbing my keys and wallet, I headed out, bounded down the stairs, pushed open the door, and rushed down to the street, Lincoln Park West. A small, one-way passage, it traversed the heart of the Old Town Triangle, and was lined with brick townhouses and tall wooden houses built by German immigrants in the 1870s. Plus a few relatively more recent three-flats like mine. Beyond trend, this place was fashionable, had been so for decades.

The air was summery thick and steamy. Like stew. Eyes flitting, hands rubbing, I quickly headed toward Wisconsin Avenue. My appointment with Alecia seemed days not hours away. What was I to do in the meantime? Cup of coffee? Walk? There was, I realized, enough time to hoof it all the way to the Loop. But did I want to arrive at Alecia's

with anxiety beaded on my forehead? No. Just take it easy,
I told myself. Coffee in an air-conditioned diner. That would
do. Then I'd bus it.

Wisconsin was empty and I started across. Images of
Berlin rubble were creeping into my mind. Siam, my elephant friend at the zoo, was long dead, I was sure, but I'd
heard that Knorke, the hippo, was alive and proliferating.
How odd, I thought, that some creature could bridge those
thirty years from my youth to adulthood, and—

Out of nowhere I heard tires peeling and screeching.
Crude and determined, that's what they screamed. I looked
to the left. A big blue car was barreling toward me, gaining
speed and proximity with each second. At first I wondered
why the driver didn't see me, why he didn't slow. Then I
realized he did see me and that's why he was going faster
and faster. Yes, he was looking right at me. And I now at
him. I stood deerlike-paralyzed in the street as I studied the
figure behind the wheel. It was a man, a black patch over
his right eye, and my entire body went rigid as if I were
looking at some monster that had stepped right out of a
recurring nightmare.

I stumbled backward, determined as I moved to get a
clear look at the face. Then, however, a streak of light
bounced across the windshield, hid him behind a glaring
reflection. I turned to flee, but my heel struck a sewer lid
and I felt my balance slipping away. I started to fall, heard
the engine of the blue car roaring down on me, looked at
the vehicle and saw little black dots of death on its grill.
Bugs. Someone started screaming desperately. Then hands
were poking out, grabbing, yanking. I felt myself jerked
back to the curb, next crashing and rolling to the ground in
a mass of arms and legs. I untangled myself from someone,
a young kid with long hair, scraggly beard, and tattered bell
bottoms.

"Jesus Christ, man," said the stranger who'd just rescued me. Quickly on his feet, he stared after the car, pointed, waved his arms. "What was that fuckin' idiot trying to do?"

I pushed myself up, brushed my hands, and calmly said, "Kill me."

Chapter

3

The clinic where Alecia worked was on the fifth floor of a building on Madison, just off Wabash. A very sixties kind of building, boxy, with lots of glass and a receptionist to match. It all felt very professional down here—and it was—and that was the atmosphere at my shrink's as well. Clinical, from the professionally maintained plants on up.

As I followed Alecia from the waiting room—why did I feel like a naughty schoolboy every time I traipsed behind her to her office?—I wanted to blurt it all out, tell everyone about the blue car. I held myself in check, though, even as she stopped at her door, turned, and motioned me in. She offered me not her usual grin, but something restrained, serious. I stared at her long face, into her brown eyes. What, I wondered, is it? What's the matter? I was suddenly more afraid. She wasn't quitting, moving, going off some place where I couldn't follow was she? I wouldn't be able to bear that, for Alecia was everything I desired. Tall, thin, beautiful, of course. But also smart, insightful, and more effusive than any shrink I'd ever encountered.

I proceeded into the office, a square room with tan walls and a Kandinsky poster just like mine. Her standard issue desk was against one wall, then three chairs—two normal straight-backs and one that was heavy and bulky and looked out of place in downtown Chicago. It was a La-Z-Boy, the thing she used as a hypnotic launching pad, and I sat in it, studied her, admired that silky brown hair I'd wanted so much to touch.

"Is everything all right?" I asked. "You're not going anywhere, are you?" Oh, shit, I thought, she doesn't have *more* vacation, does she? "Not another Club Med cruise?"

"Six of us went sailing, Will. We rented that boat."

She looked at me, grinned, I knew, at my jealousies, but said nothing more. Christ, it was harder than hell to get to know her. I could spill out my guts and more, and all she'd say was that she'd had a "nice" weekend at a friend's or a "nice" vacation down south. While she was coming to know every ugly detail of my mind, it was all one way. I knew that she was single, very dedicated, dressed somewhere between suburban and frump, drove a gray Mazda, and jogged. She did a marathon not too long ago, which undoubtedly was why her legs, now summery brown, were so trim and tapered. Once I squeaked out of her that she'd almost been married; otherwise she was very keen at keeping her private life private.

"Everything's basically fine," she said, "but there's something we need to discuss. Will, I—"

"Wait," I blurted.

I looked over at the ivy plant on her windowsill; she, not the plant company, took care of that one and it wasn't doing so great. I'd calmed down, but the vision of that blue car was still cruising through my mind.

"I need to tell you something, too," I said.

"Fine. Go ahead."

"Well . . ." What was she going to say about this one?

What could she? "I went out after we talked. You know, to get a cup of coffee. As I was crossing the street, someone tried to run me over."

"What?"

Her long face stretched longer, and I was pleased to hand her the story and have her shock confirm and legitimize it all. As I spoke, I plucked at some loose threads on the recliner and found myself having to repress a smile of sorts. I'd always wanted to be special, particularly in her eyes.

As soon as I was finished, she looked away, a very dry expression on that thin face of hers. She took a pen and started rolling it in her fingers.

"Will, I must admit I'm not quite sure what to make of this. Did you get a license plate number or anything?"

I shook my head. "There's not much that can be done, is there?" I shrugged. "Oh, well, it was probably just some old drunk bastard." I looked up, and asked, "So what was it you wanted to tell me?"

"What? Oh." She took a deep breath as was her habit when trying to appear calm. "Well, it's something almost as disturbing—the clinic was broken into last night."

My body tensed. This was my territory now, a place that over these past few months had become a haven of solace. Most important, from this spot reigned my Alecia, doling out love and hope to my needy soul. So was the clinic now soiled and no longer safe, ruined by some transgressor?

"That's terrible," I responded. Had Chicago, to quote an English friend, finally popped its crust? Flipped out at last? "Was anything taken?"

"Unfortunately, yes." She looked right at me and raised her eyebrows. "A number of files were stolen, all with names beginning W. Yours was among them."

I bolted forward in the recliner. "What?"

"I'm sorry, Will, but your file is missing. It's among about a dozen that were taken." She gave a deep sigh. "I don't think there's anything for you to worry about. The police were here this morning, and the general thought is that it's related to a child abuse case. We've been advised, though, to alert everyone who could be affected."

Oh, shit, I thought. "How much was in there? How much had you written down?"

She looked at the floor. "A fair amount."

"Oh, man. I—" The idea of a stranger seizing my file and learning about me and my most inner neuroses horrified me. "This really bothers me."

"I understand and I apologize, but I don't think you have anything to worry about." She was silent for what seemed like hours. "The police are working on it, and I promise I'll keep you fully apprised of what we find out."

I rolled my eyes. "Terrific."

She asked, "Can we go on?"

"I suppose."

"We can talk more about this if you want."

"No." Groaning and moaning would never bring back my file. "It's okay."

I knew her fake smiles, and she gave me one. I could forgive her a couple of those because usually she was so right-on and perceptive. A mind surgeon whose favorite tool was hypnosis, she could split open my head and go right to the source of a problem. I wanted to say it was because she was so brilliant—she was terrifically smart— but I think it had more to do with chemistry. In an odd way that I never understood, there was something similar about us. Consequently, she knew exactly where to cut, when to stitch. Needless to say, quite often I was putty in her La-Z-Boy.

She said, "Regarding the age regression you did this morning—can you tell me more about it?"

"Sure."

I forced myself on, telling Alecia everything, just as I always did. And as I recounted this morning's trip down memory lane and all the way to Berlin, she sat there, totally focused, nodding, questioning here and there, probing for a true understanding.

Finally, she said, "Will, I'd like to put you into a trance. There're some nuances I'd like to check out. Some images. Would you be willing to do another age regression?"

"Only if you're steering."

She smiled, this time the real thing. "I promise it'll all be safe and I'll bring you back if it gets too rough."

"And none of that weird stuff?"

"No, none of it."

A few weeks ago she'd done a regression where she'd taken me back and I'd conversed with my eighteen-month-old self. In most ways it was an actor's dream, but I still didn't know how to identify it, fact or fantasy. Alecia had simply told me to trust in my imagination, that it had the power to take me where I needed to go in my unconscious.

"Okay, Will," began Alecia, "why don't you get comfortable."

I sat back, pulled the lever on the side of the La-Z-Boy. My head sank. My feet rose. Blast off time.

"That's good." She did her cue: a deep breath. "Just relax."

All right, I thought. Following her lead, I inhaled, exhaled. I knew that Alecia would enter a trance, too. Believing it gave them better concentration and keener insights, many hypno-therapists induced themselves along with their patients. And the thought of Alecia following me into my mind was thrilling, decidedly erotic. Never did I feel more close to her than in a trance.

"You know how to enter hypnosis, Will. Just roll your eyes up and then slowly, very slowly close your eyelids. That's it. Good. Good."

I did as commanded, for I was eager to get to that special place. Craved it, because there I was safe. I wanted to get away. Leave this world and rise upward toward the great unknown. I could see it now. My rising and rising until . . . until I was so high that I disintegrated altogether and was then pieced together in some totally new and all-embracing form. Well, that's kind of what hypnosis was like for me.

Her words slow, Alecia said, "Just breathe in and out. Relax."

But . . . but it wasn't coming. My mind felt cluttered, unwilling to slow down.

"I'm sorry," I said, "I can't stop thinking about some stranger reading my file."

"Let it go for now. We can discuss that later." She exhaled. "Just let all the tension leave your body."

"Okay, but you don't have to talk so loud. I'm right here. I can hear you."

"Will," she said, moving on and sinking her voice to a deep and seductive level, "for the next several moments concentrate on the tone of my voice, the words that I say, and your own physical sensations. Focus on them and allow them to build in a way that takes you into a very profound state of hypnosis. A state of hypnosis that you know well, for you are a good subject, someone who has all the senses at your command. You not only see things vividly in a trace, you hear them, feel them, taste them."

That's because I am who I am, I thought, lying there and sensing the foggy start of a trance. I'd always been able to set aside reality, picture myself elsewhere. I think fantasizing myself out of Berlin and into the tranquil Alps was how I survived the war. Even now, whenever I saw a movie it would seem real to me. I would become totally taken in by a film, would want it to go on and on, and would even be surprised when it ended. That's why I was a good actor, I knew. I could step out of myself.

"Will, just imagine yourself at the top of a staircase. I will count from ten to one as you go down the stairs and descend deeper and deeper into a very heavy state of—"

"No, I'm the one who gets lighter."

She said, "Sorry. Picture yourself at the bottom of that staircase. I will count from one to ten as you climb higher and higher, feeling lighter with each step. One."

"That's better."

"With each passing moment you feel the weights of the world dropping away. Two. You feel yourself lifting from earth, floating toward a state of hypnosis that is relaxing and calm."

As my dear Alecia continued her litany of the trance—her voice nurturing like a mother's, luring like a lover's—I suddenly felt an enormous rush of energy pulse through my body.

"Three."

I was like an enormous dirigible—no make that zeppelin—that had suddenly been freed of everything and anything that tethered it to here, now, a little office in Chicago. I was taking off, floating away.

"Four." Her voice was becoming increasingly dreamy, more and more mystical. "Five, you are halfway there, halfway to the top of the stairs. And with each step you take, you find yourself floating higher and higher into a trance. Six."

Yes, suddenly my arms and legs seemed to rise right off that La-Z-Boy. All my worries were like sandbags that fell from my body, dropped to the ground. As they tumbled away, I became lighter, flew higher.

"Seven."

I saw it. The swirling blackness of a truly wonderful trance. My heart quickened. I could feel hypnosis seeping over me like a magical mist that embraced me, carried me up and into the skies.

"Eight. You're getting near. Very near. Just remember, Will, you can trust this state of hypnosis because I am with you. And at the end of the session we can process all that you've learned. Nine . . ."

Suddenly I felt as if a mind orgasm was just ahead and I was rushing toward it faster and faster and feeling the pull and having no choice any more, like being on the edge of a vacuum, and suddenly I couldn't resist the pull and my whole being focused on that one little window and God I was so close and the pull was so strong and there was no going back and . . . and . . .

"Ten."

Chapter
4

"Oh," I moaned.

I was there, there on the other side. My entire being had flown like a starship to some distant universe. Inner space. I saw me, Will Walker, floating in black, no stars, no moon. Complete harmony where everything began and nothing ended.

"Alecia, are you still here?"

Into the blackness, her voice trickled, "*Yes.*"

"This is a good one." I grinned.

A smirk on my face, I lay there in my lightless universe and floated to the side. It was like a sea without water. A world without gravity.

"*Will, would you like to tell me more,*" she said, her words evenly spoken, "*about the age regression you did back at your apartment?*"

I was still there in this place without matter, but suddenly everything shifted. This was the issue that had been bogging me, smothering me all my life.

"My mother . . ."

"Yes, can you tell me what happened?"

I took a deep breath, bit at it. "She . . . she was murdered."

"Are you sure, Will?"

I nodded. Clenched my teeth. "Positive. Like I told you, someone killed her." In my inner darkness I knew that I could never deny that again. "All these years I've told everyone that she died in an air raid. But she didn't. She was murdered."

Alecia said, *"I believe you, Will. And I'm very sorry to hear that. It was a terrible thing—"*

"Yes, terrible."

"And I can understand how much it upsets you."

"Very much. Very, very, very much. You see, my brother was dead and my father had been killed in Poland five years earlier. He was a soldier. So when my mother died, I was all alone."

"I know." She paused, then asked, *"Will, you're a very observant person. And you were a very smart, wonderful boy and you loved your mother."*

"Yes!" My body was shaking. "Yes, I loved her!"

"Of course you did." She paused. *"Will, who killed your mother?"*

"I . . . I can see the shape of a face—but I can't make out anything specific." I tried to discern the nose, the eyes, the hair, but whatever was in front of me was hidden. "It's all black, so terribly black."

"Of course it is. Black is the color of fear and you were afraid."

"I am afraid. I still am."

"Will, you blocked it out because you needed to protect yourself, didn't you?"

"Yes," I confessed.

"And that was good. That was part of your body's defenses, part of your mind's defenses. To protect. What you

*witnessed was so horrible that your mind turned it all to
black so you couldn't see it. Your unconscious was taking
care of you. It also allowed the adult part of yourself to look
after you."*

"No one else was around."

*"I know. And you're alive today, Will, because you knew
how to take care of yourself."*

"Yes, there was an aspect of me that was very mature,
very capable." I heard a distant explosion and flinched.
"And now to help myself I have to remember everything."

Alecia hushed her voice. *"That's right. And you will be
able to recall it all through hypnosis. Once you've done
that, we'll work through whatever needs to be done."*

"I believe that." Good Alecia. Nice Alecia. I took a deep
breath. "I'm ready. To go back, I mean."

"I'm proud of you, Will."

I tripped on a doubt. Could I really return to Berlin? Of
course. I had just been there. Just this morning I had returned to 1945. I had stood atop Herr Schulenberg's flattened apartment house. I had felt the itchy, filthy wool
pants on my legs, scrambled across shattered bricks in
those old leather shoes I had torn from the body of a boy.
Yes, most definitely I had gone through a time warp in my
mind and returned to Berlin, beautiful, devastated Berlin.

I took a deep breath. "Let's start."

*"Okay, Will. You are already in a deep state of hypnosis.
You're a very good subject, and I'm going to guide you. I'm
going to direct you back in time, back through your memory. I'll be your guide and I'll always be here. If you need
anything or you want to come back, all you have to do is
say so and I'll help you shift your awareness back to 1975."*

I couldn't resist. "Yes. All I have to do is tap my heels
three times."

"Will . . ." An exasperated moment of silence passed before she said, *"Now let's think of life not as a linear expe-*

rience, not as something you pass through, leaving various events behind, events that become more and more distant and eventually forgotten. No, think of life as like the rings in a tree. A new ring for each year. A tree that is always expanding yet always containing what has passed before. Today you live at the outer ring. That is the present."

Her words splashed over me, filled me with hope. "Yes."

Could this be true? Could the foundations of my life not have been lost, not dribbled away? Perhaps. How wonderful it would be if all that I had once had was still within, if all the experiences had been gathered inside and held firmly and gently by the rings of the years. Some of it might be more densely hidden, but it might be there, able to be touched, sensed, and, yes, maybe experienced once again.

"To understand what happened a long time ago, Will, we are going to return to one of the inner rings. It is a part of you that continues to live within and is actually one of the integral aspects of your entire being."

Lying in my sunless universe, I suddenly knew, felt, believed with every ounce of my life that Alecia was correct. I accepted her thesis completely. Yes, I had already gone back to Berlin once. I could go back again. Yet as my passage through time was about to begin, I felt a blob of salty water bead up outside my inner universe and begin to roll. That's a tear, I thought. It formed in my eye and now it's rolling down my cheek.

"What's happening, Will? What's occurring to you?" asked Alecia.

"All this means that I didn't necessarily leave my mother behind thirty years ago, right?"

"Exactly. She's still within you. A part of your being."

"Thirty rings within?"

"Yes," said Alecia. *"A ring for each year."*

"I'm happy."

Whether my mother had died under the bombs or actually been murdered was one matter. That I had lost her so many years ago was an entirely different one. For so long I resisted growing old, hated it, because each year I aged meant that my mother was that much further left behind. It calcified the reality that she was never coming back. As an adult, I strived to look young. I picked the gray hairs from my head, covered up the little bays of baldness that washed upon my forehead, used creams to mask the wrinkles. Some thought it vanity, me the actor. It was, though, nothing more than an act of desperation: I didn't want to grow older because that implied leaving my mother further and further behind where she would appear as a fainter and fainter memory on some distant horizon. I feared, too, that a recent milestone—me age forty, Mama's death now thirty years back—could only mean that she would fall over my memory's horizon, disappear over the other side and be lost forever.

With but a few sentences, however, Alecia the Wise had given me an entirely new perspective. I had not begun at point *A*, then gone off in one direction, discarding people and experiences like Coke cans along a highway that was never to be traversed again. No, everything was all still within me. Mama, my brother, Siam the elephant, my rusty bicycle, and perhaps even my father, who had been barely around long enough to father me before being sent east and to his demise. My tastebuds began to swell with excitement. Even Frau Ruppenthal's apple strudel was baking in my mind, now decades later.

"Are you all right, Will?"

"Oh, yes. Yes."

"Good. Let's go back a few years at a time. Picture yourself as thirty again. Do you see anything?"

There I was. Thirty and anxious, desperate for work, fearful that I hadn't accomplished anything with my life. Just a droplet of an actor.

"No, no," I whined. "Not good. I didn't know if I was going to make it as an actor yet. I was a wreck at thirty. Let's . . . let's go back to . . ."

Suddenly I was twenty-four, lean and hard. Very hard because I was pressed up alongside a beautiful girl named Ellen who had this long, reddish brown hair and deliciously soft skin and enormous, I mean enormous—

"*Will?*" called my shrink's voice from far away.

Oh, shit. I, recently graduated and hell-bent on stardom, jumped out of Ellen's bed. Christ, said Ellen, what's the matter? Nothing, I responded. It's just that . . . that . . .

"*Will, where are you?*" asked Alecia.

Who the hell's that, asked Ellen, sitting bolt-upright in my imagination. Do you have another girlfriend? I shook my head, moaned. I can explain everything, Ellen, I stammered, throwing on my corduroys and a flannel shirt. Trust me. I can—

"*Will?*"

Suddenly I was out Ellen's door. I cleared my throat, and said, "Sorry Alecia. I was just remembering something."

"*You have a grin on your face. It must have been good.*"

My face pulsed like a hot beet. "Ah, yes."

"*You ready to go back further?*"

"Sure."

Under Alecia's orchestration, I left Ellen, passed through ring after ring, and my youth began to unfold right before me. There I was in college in Ohio. Me in a play. Dad and Mom and teeny Cathy. Spoofers my dog. A birthday party. Eighth grade. My best friends Tony and Matt and Pete. Yes, this was easy. Me, the actor. In an instant I could recall my youth, slip into it like an old pair of jeans. All so easy. Not half as much work as doing Shakespeare or a Tom Stoppard character or that stupid part on a soap. I just had to become a younger me that was still alive within the rings of my life.

"*Will,*" chanted Alecia, "*you're in a deep hypnotic state and we're going back. Back to Berlin. Take my presence and use it as the strength you need to block the side of fear. Just allow yourself to go very deep into hypnosis, to pass easily through the rings. And amazingly you are able to see so much while at the same time recognizing that it all happened thirty years ago. You can see and feel and experience everything, knowing that we'll be able to put it all into proper perspective at the end of our session.*

In a rush I went whirling past one inner circle after the next. There was a boat. The one I came over on and then ... then ...

A very familiar scent began to fill my nose. I stepped atop a pile of rubble. Took in a deep breath. The night air was good. Rich and sandy, the scent of distant loamy soils. And plush pine forests. Concrete. Beer. And *Bockwurst,* all boiled and garlicky.

"Will, what's happening?"

Yes, I thought, looking around. *Berliner Luft.* I'm home.

"Will?" said an airy voice.

I looked around to see who had spoken, saw no one, then craned my head up toward the dark sky. There perched on a slim shelf of a floor and clinging like a weed to a mountainside was Frau Schulenberg's piano. I was tempted to throw rock after rock at it, see if I could dislodge the thing or at least hit a key or two.

"Will, where are you?"

I craned my head around, searched the shadows. There was nothing. No one. Who was that talking? An angel?

"Ich heisse Willi. Ich wohne in Berlin." I gazed through the broken beams and shattered walls around me. *"Wie heissen Sie? Woher kommen Sie?"*

"I don't speak German. Speak English."

"Was ist los? Ich sprech kein amerikanisch."

"I understand that you're Willi now, but you've come back through age regression. You have your future talents

as well the perspective of a grown man. Willi, you can speak English."

"I can? Oh." The words coming out of my mouth startled me. "Smell the air? That's Berlin air." I took a deep breath and was pleased. "You're Alecia, aren't you? Where are you?"

Before she could answer, before I could see her, I became aware of a bucket of water hanging from my left hand. Water-schmater. Water? I looked down the mound of rubble and was abruptly filled with dread. Any moment a scream would pierce the still night.

"Oh . . . no. Something terrible is about to happen."

"Slow it down, Willi. Take it nice and slow. Tell me what you see."

My eyes lifted and followed the ragged edge of wall. "A piano. Up high." I looked up and into the clear night sky and saw a huge white orb. "And the moon. It's full tonight. Completely full. God, I've never seen such a huge moon before. The sky's a midnight blue, too."

Führer weather. We called it that because the weather was clear and perfect whenever the Führer held a rally. Of course, that was when he'd filled Germany with hope. Now there were no more rallies. Now the only things that came out during Führer weather were the planes. British bombers by night. The Americans by day. Clear skies, clear destruction.

"There's going to be a major raid tonight," I predicted, knowing I was absolutely right. "The Brits will strike Alexanderplatz and some factories to the north. Schöneberg—this district—will be hit some, but the piano up there is going to make it until the Russians start shelling the city."

"Willi, what else is happening? What else do you want to tell me?" gently called Alecia. *"Just let yourself feel it."*

Immediately there was a voice. No, voices. "Yes, I hear them. Talking."

"Okay, follow those sounds, Willi. Listen to the voices. Do you need to hear what they say?"

"Yes."

I looked behind me. The man-woman-dark-stranger's voice was coming from back there, rising from the ruins of another building. Carefully, I set down the pail of water, making sure it wouldn't tip, go bang in the night, and then I began creeping, one cautious step at a time. I mustn't let them hear me or they'll come after me.

"What is it? What do you hear?" called my guardian angel.

"There's a room. A little room in the ruins with all the windows blown out. They're in there, sitting around a candle."

"Who, Willi?"

"I don't know. There are three or four people. I recognize the voices, I think, but I can't look in or they'll know I'm spying on them."

"What are they saying?"

One of them was crying. "The countess is saying bad things about my mother. She hates Mama. She wants to kill her. And . . . and I think the man with one leg . . . is agreeing with her. He's saying how they're going to have to get rid of her. She's bad, he's saying. Beyond control. And they must . . . must . . ." His threat was so brutal that I started to shake. "And . . . and there's someone else in there with the countess and the man with one leg. The pilot. He's saying there's a way, a quick easy way to deal with her. Anton should be there as well, but he's not. He's Jewish and maybe he's already going after my mother. He hates her. He was friends with her but now he would carve her to pieces for what she did to him."

I fell back against the stone wall. Mother? They all hate her, want her dead. Oh, God. I have to tell her. I have to warn her. The ominous threats were slithering over bricks and stone, searching her out. I had to be quick, to reach my mother first. Maybe Anton was already on the way! Hurry!

I was crying. I wiped my eyes and looked up. The moon. So big and bright and white and innocent. Oh, God. Hurry, Willi! I reached out with my skinny leg and tripped on a brick and the brick went tumbling and banging downward.

Who's that? they all shouted out.

They mustn't see me! They mustn't know I'd overheard their plans to dispose of my mother. As quickly as I could, I tore back to my bucket and the pile that was Herr Schulenberg's house. Hurry, Willi! Hurry before they get her!

"Willi, are you all right?"

What was this all about? What was I going to say to Mama? How could I help her? Save her? How? I had to think quickly. I raced over the pile of rubble that was the massive grave of the two Schulenberg boys and lunged for my pail of water. But just as quickly I stopped. What could I do? How could I protect my mother, me, a scrawny kid?

I heard it then, the first scream. A high-pitched voice that crawled into the dark, stretched higher and higher. I looked up at the piano, at the full moon set against that rich night-blue sky. Then I heard her cry again.

"Mama?" I called. "Mama, are you all right?"

But I knew she wasn't, and it was obvious that everything was wrong, would never be right again. I clutched the stupid pail of water. No. Not my mother. Not her. I just wanted there to be no more bombs, no more soldiers, but someone was hurting her, beating her. Someone had reached her first, and I knew what was about to happen and I had to hurry to protect Mama! But I couldn't move. My feet were stuck and I couldn't move!

"No!" I cried, struggling to lunge forward.

"Willi! Willi, I'm going to count from ten to one and—"

Someone was about to kill my mother. One of those people. But it wasn't my fault! It wasn't my fault!

"Seven, six, five, four . . .

"Ah," cried my mother. "Ah!"

"Mama, Mama!"

I slid down a hill of bricks. Tripped, tried to scramble to my feet. The bucket of water dropped from my hand. Went clang, bang, smash. I looked up at the big moon. Someone's killing my mother, I shouted deep inside myself, and I can't stop it! I can't save her!

"I can't! I can't! I can't!" I screamed.

I tried to move forward, but couldn't. I cried out again. "MAMA!"

"Three, two, one." And then, "Will, it's all right. You're here. I'm here."

I rolled into her, lunged from the cushy chair and into her embrace. Alecia took me and held me, and I bawled and clutched at her like a lost child hysterically trying to find his way home.

Tears squirting out of my eyes, I sobbed, "It was one of those people." My mind clicked: the countess, the one-legged man, the pilot, Anton. "They heard me and followed me. Alecia, I think I led the killer directly to my mother!"

"It's okay, Will. It's okay," she said, holding me tight and rubbing my back.

I collapsed on the floor and kissed her knees with gratitude, so indebted was I. From the way she held me, I could tell. From her panicked grasp, her tight fingers. Yes, I sensed that at last, after all this time, someone other than I not only knew, but understood and felt, really felt, my pain.

Chapter

5

Frightened by what was hidden in my mind, I called my agent first thing the next morning and, dramatically feigning flu, finked out on the wiener commercial. He was none too pleased, but I assured him it would be even worse to have some vomity looking person sucking down a hot dog. Particularly in color. All right, all right, he said, and then mentioned something about a dairy council promo next month. Ah, I thought. The big time.

Alecia was booked that day but squeezed me in during her lunch hour. I took a cab directly there, wasted no time going up. When she collected me from the waiting room, I smiled for the first time that morning. Beautiful Alecia. Sexy Alecia. Today: blue glasses pushed up on her brown hair and a dress of some krinkly yellow cotton. Very summery, not very modern. Kind of bland. If only she'd let me help her. Never mind that I was just in faded jeans and a simple blue shirt. I had great taste.

"How do you feel today?" she asked as she shut her door.

"Like shit," I said, studying her green canvas shoes.

Really dull. "I'm a wreck and I slept terribly. Hardly at all." I lowered myself into the recliner. "So . . . what about yesterday? Was that real or what?"

Alecia pursed her thin lips, sat down at her desk. "Hypnosis is an honest tool, Will, that tends not to falsify past data. It's very good at giving you information that has been suppressed or forgotten. In fact, that's the only problem I have with it—hypnosis can give you access to information before you're ready to process it."

"Case in point."

"Well, I have to say that's why I was concerned when you did an age regression on your own. You discovered something quite terrible that you weren't able to deal with."

"Okay," I began, glaring at Miss Prissy. "But I don't have any choice now. I've opened the proverbial can of worms. If I don't find out what happened to my mother, I'll never have any piece of mind."

"That's right. So are you ready?"

"No, I'm not ready! I'm scared as hell. Really scared." I let out a deep sigh. "But I accept that I have to go back and look at some more things."

Alecia leaned forward, reached across that great expanse between us, and touched my knee. I shivered, wanted so much to take her by the hand.

She said, "I understand, Will. Just let me say again that I'm here to help and guide you. I won't let anything happen to you in trance."

I stared at that simple yet elegant face, admired the swell of her breasts, wanted to pull her close to me. Did she suspect? Oh, Alecia, I thought, the only benefit of all this is the surplus of time with you.

"Will?"

I tensed, dragged myself from my fantasies. Leaning back, I took hold of the La-Z-Boy lever and rocketed my feet upward. I was of the kind that never poked one's toe in a cold pool, but just jumped in. Fuck it.

"Let's go."

I settled back into the recliner, started on my own, ran ahead of her. One, I took a deep breath. Two, rolled my eyes up into my head while forcing my lids to remain open. Three, exhaled and slowly closed my eyes. I didn't really need Alecia's chant, for I was excellent at self-hypnosis. With a One, Two, Three and a roll of my eyes, I wouldn't be nervous entering a crowd of strangers or doing an audition or bouncing around on a choppy flight. I didn't know how it worked, only that hypnosis empowered me, tapped into more of my mind and enabled me to battle down the crud.

Alecia chimed in a few moments later, counting, "One."

Her soft, steady voice started ticking away the numbers, and I mellowed even more. Having her direct my trance was like getting into bed—I could do it on my own, but it was so wonderful being tucked in. Especially by her. I hooked on her voice, sensed my defenses softening, my knots of anxiety slipping away. As she beckoned to my subconscious—"feel the tranquility slipping into you, sense the weight dropping away, watch yourself float higher and higher—the fear and tension that gripped my soul began to grow lazy and flaccid, and soon . . . soon I heard her far in the distance count "Ten," and suddenly I was there in my own personal universe.

"Oh, I like this." I heard applause in my imagination. "Yes, this is very nice."

"*Good,*" she cooed.

I said it now honestly, calmly: "I have to go back to Berlin."

"*If this is what you want.*"

"Yes." Oh, absolutely. Without a doubt. "Not to that night, though. I can't. Not now. I'm too afraid. I want to go back to another day because there's something else that I need to remember. Have to remember." Yes, Mama's gift. The reason I had done an age regression back at my apartment. "My mother's voice. I just want to hear her sing again—it was so reassuring—but . . . but like I said, I can't hear it anymore. It's not gone forever, is it? I haven't lost it for good, have I?"

"Of course not, Will."

"Really?"

"Really. It's still within you, within the rings of your life. Don't worry."

I smiled. Trust Alecia. Trust yourself. It was in there somewhere. I knew what I wanted to hear, too. That song. I wanted to hear Mama's deep yet silky voice milk the words into music that captured both the sadness and the truth.

"I want to hear her sing *'Ich hab noch einen Koffer in Berlin.'* "

"What does that mean?"

" 'I still have a suitcase in Berlin.' "

Floating in my trance I was suddenly awash with . . . sentiment. Yes, I was a complete and utter sentimental slob. I cried at movies and I cried because I never told my mother I loved her. I guessed that's what kept my emotions as raw as a freshly scraped knee. You know, rich and bright and painful.

"There's only one thing," I admitted. "A little technicality. That's a song that came out after the war. Obviously, I never heard my mother sing it, but I always wanted to. When I was a kid here in America I prayed she'd come in my dreams and sing it to me. But . . . she never did."

"That's all right, Will. Just remember that your imagination is transformational. It has the power to alter and heal your psyche." Softly, she said, *"It would be very nice for you to hear your mother sing that song about Berlin, wouldn't it?"*

"Oh, yes."

No Freud here, I thought with a grin. Alecia was pure Jungian. Actual events took a back seat to creative visualizations and pretend dialogues—the fuel of the imaginal unconscious.

Oh, Mother, I thought. Not your scream, not your plea for life, but your voice in song. In melody. That's what my hungry spirit needs. *Ich han noch . . .*

"Are you ready to go back?"

"Yes, and I want to hear her voice."

"That's good, Will. Just focus on that. You are already in a trance, a good trance, so we can begin right—"

"But the song!" I demanded.

"Focus, Will, then make a simple request and trust in your imagination. Trust in your love for your mother. Now just go back . . . back . . . back . . . "

Trust? Love? Suddenly I became terribly nervous. Alecia didn't know the half of it. Wait! I wanted to shout. Stop! Hold everything! But . . . but . . . *burr.* I shivered. Trembled.

"Will, what's happening now?"

"I'm cold."

"What else?"

"I don't know. I don't know. It's just so chilly in here."

"Okay, let that build. Let that sense grow. Follow it. You're in a very nice hypnotic state. Trust that state of hypnosis. Let go of any fears behind it. Just let that feeling build very deeply, and as that builds it occurs to you that you've had that sensation before."

"Oh, yes."

"Of course you have. Now all you have to do is go back in time to when you sensed this before."

I felt my imagination building to warp speed. "Oh, oh my God!"

"It's all right, Will. You're doing very well."

That feeling. That chill. Cold. Damp. Dark. Yes, I knew exactly when and where. I felt myself hurling through space, through time, and then all at once my mind fixed on exactly one day, one place. The coordinates locked in, and all of sudden—Oh, Christ!—I was there.

"Oh."

I was cold because it was late winter and damp, and Mother and Erich and I had snuck into the ruins of the zoo and had been feeding Siam. Suddenly, the pre-warning sirens had gone off and everyone rushed to the shelters. A major raid. A thousand planes. American planes because it was daytime. There wasn't enough time to make it home to our underground bar, and so we charged out of the ruined zoo, past the Bahnhof Zoo, and on and on with the throngs toward that towering, massive castle of concrete, the Zoo Bunker.

"Willi, you're shivering. Is anything the matter?"

It's very dark in the bunker and my blue sweater is all wet. I can't see."

"Use all your senses. You have all of them within your power. You can feel and . . ."

It was as black as a cave in there because the first of the planes had already passed. Evidently they had struck something major, for the lights had flickered and died.

". . . see . . ."

An old man next to me struck a match and the shelter came to ghostly life. I gazed around. I sat on a wooden bench crammed into the first level of the Zoo Bunker with scores of people—mothers and children, mainly. Some older folk, too. Some soldiers—a few who were home on leave, many who were home permanently on crutches or in wheelchairs. Next to me was the old man who held the match and next to him was an old woman, both leftovers from the days of the Kaiser. In the flickering light, the old woman reached into a bag and took out two pots. One went on her husband's head, the other on hers. Make-shift helmets. And then the woman took out gauze spectacles for the both of them. I sat there, me much smaller, quite curious, understanding, staring at them. So they were expecting the worst. Phosphorous bombs. Did they also have damp rags to cover their mouths? But why? This was the Zoo Bunker. It was more than six stories tall and the concrete walls were meters thick. The windows could be sealed shut. There was a ventilation system. And there were even flak guns on the roof. If we weren't safe here, then—

Someone on another bench screeched, "Put out that match—it's using up the air!"

The old man with the pot on his head puckered his lips in an "O" and blew. The room was as dark as my worst dreams.

"Erich?" I called out into the nothingness. "Erich, where are you?"

I stood up, started to squirm and feel my way through the crowd. By the time Mother, Erich and I had made it to the bunker, there had already been a huge crowd queuing up. Mother had nudged my brother and I ahead, past the sea of parked bicycles and prams parked out front, and right into the mass of knees and skirts and purses and briefcases. But the crowd had been like a strainer, first catching our mother. Then me. And only allowing little Erich to reach the front.

"Erich?"

He must be downstairs. Erich with the miniature crutch who must have been carried along like a twig into the ground floor. I, on the other hand, had been pushed up the curving stairs onto the next floor.

"Young man, sit down," said a man's voice that rose out of the dark as if from a scratchy record.

I couldn't see a thing. My little brother didn't call back. All I could sense were feet, hands, parcels. Knees. And hot, moist garlicky breath.

The next wave of bombs churned toward us like a mighty storm that one sees rolling across a lake. Big heavy thuds. Huge things that fell from the sky and shook the earth. They were getting louder. Closer. But that was okay. If you could hear them, everyone said, you were all right. As long as you could hear the bombs, you were safe. The flak guns atop the bunker started their fire. ACK-ACK! ACK-ACK-ACK!

I heard a distant laugh and giggle.

"Mama?"

I knew she was in here. I turned my head in the lightless tomb. Where was she? Why didn't she answer? I shoved my way through the crowds.

"Mama!"

The thundering bombs were striking only blocks away. The noise seemed to be coming straight for us. Where was my brother? Where was my mother? There were people all around me, sitting unseen in the dark Zoo Bunker. Unseen, unknown faces. All strangers. When would the lights come on? Would the bombs get us? Siam! Siam the elephant was out there! Somehow he's survived that hellish night when the Brits had smashed the zoo and his world had caught fire. But this time, this time they might get him!

Just then I heard the vents being cranked shut. That meant there were indeed fires outside. Oh, Siam . . . ACK-ACK! ACK-ACK-ACK!

I heard a familiar laugh.

"Mama?"

I groped through the dark. Why couldn't I picture her? Why couldn't I remember the shape of her face, the sweet flowery fragrance of her skin? And her voice—Dear Lord, what did her voice sound like? Had I forgotten her? No, I thought. Don't let me lose her. Don't let me lose her!

"Mama, sing to me! Please!" I begged.

Suddenly a deep voice began to snake through the bunker, and we were all quiet. Yes, we were all brought to peace by this haunting thing: the silky-rough voice of a woman who had laughed too much, whispered too much, loved too much. I caught my breath, bit my lip. I wanted to cry, but held myself in check. No, I couldn't make a peep because all I wanted to hear was my mother! And it was her, and her tones curled over me, through me, into me.

She sang, *"Ich hab noch einen Koffer in Berlin . . ."*

The lyrics came slow and loved, pained and charmed, and did I there in the bunker hear not the bombs outside or the ack-ack of the flak guns but a muted trumpet, slow strings, and a twinkle of a piano? Whatever, I knew once again that my mother had told the truth, that they had in the early thirties flocked to the cabaret to hear her and see her long legs and swollen breasts. So many stories. So much champagne. She had lived Berlin to its fullest, a rising cabaret star decked out in sequins and feather boas and little else. But then . . . then He came to power, the cabarets were closed and my mother was put away like a nasty jar of decadent French jam.

". . . Doch ich denk, wenn ihr auch lacht, heut noch an Berlin."

Her chant continued—"Even if you laugh, I still think of Berlin"— lazy and mystical, and as she sang the charms of our Berlin, compared us to Paris and the Rhine, today's bombs rained over us, a forecast that any of us could have given. As Mama shielded us with her tune, the Ku-damm was hit hard, reducing ruin to rubble, while the Kaiser Wilhelm Gedachtniskirche—the memorial church—was cracked like a nut by three bombs, and Siam was spared. And as my mother sang in the Zoo Bunker and row after row of strangers sat silently drinking in her fresh song, the bombs passed by, whooshed overhead like the fiercest of thunderstorms that faded into the distance without having left a single deathly drop on us. Then all at once there was a surge of happiness: LIGHTS! We all cheered with the same thought: WE SURVIVED! We leapt to our feet. The all-clear signal blared away. Never mind that the Brits would come with the night. We were alive right now, right this minute.

I spun around and around. Where was my mother? I had heard her in the darkness. So where was she?

There. On the stairs. The curving stairs with their niches that cradled the lovers who kissed madly, wildly, while their city disintegrated around them. And perched next to my mother was today's lover, a soldier. An unknown man like all the others, this one had dark brown hair, a long face with a cleft chin, a big toothy grin, and an arm stretched around her. A bottle of something, too. Schnapps? Whatever, she was flushed, and, yes, Mother had found much love here. When she was lonely or depressed, she abandoned our little underground bar and came here, hoping for a raid, hoping for a warm embrace. Oh, yes, this wasn't her favorite bunker for its thick, thick concrete ceiling, but for the groping love like she'd found in old Berlin.

I pushed through the crowd, shoved the butt of some old dowager. She was there, talking, smiling to the soldier. My mother with those big eyes, eyes that were either enormous pools of happiness or sorrow. And the long dark blonde hair, the wide cheeks, the beautiful teeth, the narrow chin.

"Mama!"

I fell into her, drank in her syrupy breath that smelled so thickly of schnapps. I fell between my mother and the anonymous soldier who was due to be killed at the front when his leave was finished in just a few days. I fell into her skirt. And I was crying. It seemed like years since I had

seen her. I had forgotten how pretty she looked. How dark
she painted her eyes. And I had forgotten her voice. Yes, I
hadn't been able to remember it. But now it was back. All
back . . . yet I was so sad.

"I'm so scared!" I sobbed.

"Willi? Scared? You can't be scared." She leaned over
and kissed the anonymous soldier one last time before he
was forever carried away with the surge of people. "Now
just stop it. I need you. There's a delivery to be made . . ."

I looked up at her. Forget the coffee or booze or whatever
it was little innocent me was supposed to take to whomever. Forget my scrambling about the bombed city, so tiny
as to be unsuspicious and unnoticed. We weren't going to
make it. I had the deepest premonition. The surest feeling.
No, something terrible was going to happen. Yes, it would
wipe us away, carry us to the brink of death, then beyond.

I blurted the truth: "Mama, I'm afraid you're going to be
killed!"

"*Mein Gott*! What are you saying?" As if she were looking into the future, her eyes were unmoving, ghostly, and
I knew right then and there that she, too, feared her life
would soon end. She seemed to accept this, though, even
welcome it, and for a moment she was quiet. Then she
shook her head and said, "Oh, Willi, stop! You're always
carrying on so dramatically. I'm here. I'm fine," she said,
pushing me away. "Whatever has gotten into you, child?"
She glared at me, adding, "Me, killed? How could you even
think such a thing?"

"But Mama!"

As if I had lost her years and years ago, I wouldn't let her
go. If we parted now, we'd part forever. I cried. I didn't
know I could cry so hard, and as she tried to separate us, I
lunged into the folds of my mother's luscious body. I felt
her glorious, silky hair string across my face.

I knew without a shadow of a doubt that I was right. Oh,

yes. I was a small boy who saw it all. I had seen what my mother was involved in, I knew perfectly well the dangers that licked at her being. She shouldn't have started operating on the black market, but she had, dealing in brandy and schnapps and cigarettes and coffee from Denmark. Yes, it was a highly profitable underground network run by the darkest of people. And soon she would make a mistake, and for her betrayal she was going to be killed. Oh, Lord, I couldn't let go of her. Couldn't pull away. They would kill her. Absolutely. But why did I know this? Why, me, little Willi, who knew nothing else of the world except burned-out, bombed-out, flattened and crushed Berlin?

"No!" I shrieked. "No, I won't let them get you!"

"Willi, you're being absolutely ridiculous." As she tried to pull herself free of my clutches, she muttered, "You're so silly. No one's coming after me."

But they were. I didn't know who specifically, though somehow it was connected to Loremarie—the countess who had lost all of her estate in Silesia—as well as to that pilot and the Jew and the one-legged man. I felt a stab of pain. The Gastapo. Yes, they were after Mother, wanting her, desiring her.

I couldn't take it, and I started twisting and kicking, beating on her, my very own mother. A hand descended from somewhere else and pressed firmly on my shoulder.

Then a very distant voice called out: *"Willi . . . Willi . . . there's something you need to tell her."*

What? Oh, yes, there was something burning a hole in my heart. Something I needed to say but had never been able to.

"Mama . . . Mama . . ." I began.

"What is it? What's the matter now?" my mother demanded, looking at me angrily.

I looked up into her big dark eyes, smelled her sweet breath. I loved her, and I had to tell her that.

"I . . . I . . ."

Her body started to quiver, to shake. "Why, Willi, you look as desperate as a soldier!"

I needed to tell her how much I cared for her, but . . . but she was laughing. Her head fell back and a huge shriek of amusement burst out and echoed through the Zoo Bunker. Laughter? Why? She grabbed at her bottle, took a huge swig of schnapps, but nearly spit it all out because something was so funny and—

"No!" I screamed.

No, don't laugh at me! Don't make me go away! Don't! Don't! I threw my hands over my ears, pushed away and rolled off her lap and onto the floor. I heard her laugh and wanted to forget her and that high-pitched cackle.

"*Willi . . . Will . . .*"

Oh, God, what did I do? I screamed: "What?!"

Then there was more chanting and more counting and seconds later I opened my eyes and I was on my hands and knees staring at a fuzzy blue floor. Oh, God, where was I? Chicago. Yes. America. I had rolled out of my mother's lap and fallen into the Midwest. I sobbed more, buried my face in my hands. Deep within the rings of my life I felt my mother laughing, felt her still jiggling with amusement. And right then and there I knew precisely why a part of me had always wanted just one of those bombs to drop directly on her head. Yes. Before I saw that bullet-eye hole in her head, hadn't I always wondered if I'd cry if she died?

Chapter

6

After Alecia spent some fifteen minutes calming and essentially debriefing me, I stumbled from her office, incredulous but quite certain I'd seen and heard someone I'd thought lost forever. Yes, I had drunk in my mother's beautiful looks, been hypnotized by her song, collapsed in her lap . . . and felt her jarring ridicule. My mother, I now remembered, had had a favorite, and it hadn't been me.

I rode the elevator down, turned right on Madison, again right, and wandered down Wabash, the sunny warm day embracing me. I heard the rattle of a train overhead, stared up into the bright sky as the El charged madly by. How, I wondered, could this be? How was it that I was now here? No, this shouldn't be Chicago but Berlin. I should be seeing brown, bombed-out apartment houses and *feldgrau*—dingy field gray—trucks and soldiers, as well as wounded and maimed refugees. Uniform, uniform, uniform. Dear Lord, there weren't even any defeatist traitors hanging from the lampposts.

When Alecia had pulled me back from the Zoo Bunker,

I was in a state of shock, blown away as if there had just been an air raid. And like a bomb victim, I had to be pulled from the ruins of some deep, dark cellar. I had to be comforted, touched, talked to, reassured. I'd just been in wartime Berlin, and even though I'd emerged fully from the trance, Alecia still had to talk me into present day reality. It was the concept of 1975, me age forty, that I was having difficulty accepting.

Alecia said it was such a powerful experience for me because not only did I return as young Willi to Berlin, but I also carried with me insights of the future. I was part Willi and part Will. Past and future rolled into one. At that I was silent. Hadn't I really known, not just in the trance but in the past as well, that my mother was in mortal danger? Absolutely. I didn't know if what I had experienced on Alecia's La-Z-Boy was one hundred percent true, but I did know without a doubt that the essence of that regression was absolutely accurate. Back in the past my mother had found any number of soldiers with long arms and loose lips and she had often sung of Berlin. And I had even told my mother that I was afraid for her life, and when I had wanted to be close to her, she had laughed. Most horribly, I distinctly remembered having thought that I would welcome her end.

I now knew the key people involved in my mother's final day—the countess, the man with one leg, the pilot, Anton, as well as some eel from the Gestapo. And I had caught a glimmer of how deeply my mother was involved in the black market. Still, however, I hadn't lifted the darkness enshrouding that mysterious face and exposed the true identity of my mother's murderer. But I had to. For my own sanity, perhaps even safety, I needed to learn the truth of her death.

Alecia, though, was on a schedule and I had burned up all of her lunch hour. Quite distraught, I begged for more time, and she, recognizing my urgency, agreed that we needed to continue with all this as soon as possible. She suggested six that very same evening; she'd be done with clients at five, take a dinner break, then return. Appreciative of her offer, I left. I was to wander the Loop and return for an extended age regression, one that could last well into the evening.

I stopped at Kroch's, tried to browse the paperbacks, but couldn't focus. I came out, turned right and headed for Marshall Field's. I just wanted to be lost, and what better place?

On the next block, a crane was busy bashing apart a building, reducing it to ruin and rubble as if one of those Berlin bombs had just done its duty. I continued down Wabash and thought about my stolen file, and the ensuing general paranoia caused me to glance over my shoulder. I'd assumed I'd be safe down here, that the numbers of people would protect me from anyone or anything. And at first I saw nothing to fear. But then I noticed a figure lurking by a store window. An old man, he nevertheless looked formidable, and he twisted away from me, attempted to keep his face unseen. I walked another twenty or so feet, glanced back again. At this, the stranger slipped into a doorway. Shit, was someone following me?

I started across Wabash, sidled up to one of the El posts, clothed myself in the shadows of the overhead tracks. He reappeared on the sidewalk, and I saw him, not too tall, gray haired, and wearing a black patch over one eye. As he hurried in my direction, I started off. Had he been the man behind the wheel of the big blue car? I would be stupid to think otherwise.

I moved rapidly, still heading toward Field's. Forgetting about Berlin, Alecia, my mother, I skirted around clumps of slow walkers, looked back. The stranger was crossing the street, tracing my path, staring after me. He wore a long raincoat, and I wondered why. It was so warm, so humid. What could he have hidden in the folds of material. A gun? A knife? Was I crazy or did he mean me harm, would he attack me right here in the middle of millions of people? I thought about that Bulgarian who'd been killed in London by a deadly poison on the tip of an umbrella. Yes, there were lots of ways to eliminate someone in the rush of a city's core.

My pace doubled now. I had to lose this guy, had to get away, disappear into Chicago until it was time to return to Alecia's and *Deutschland*. I glanced back. This thug was probably a senior citizen, but he was surprisingly agile and now completely open in his pursuit. I tried to get a clear view of his face, but couldn't. The patch over one eye was large, and he kept his head hung.

I cut left, broke into a trot toward State Street. My head beaded with sweat. Where was a policeman? Where could I seek help? Should I circle back to Alecia's office? Yes, perhaps.

I ducked past two little ladies, looked back. My pursuer had just come around the corner, and now seeing me fleeing, he pushed himself into a slow run. Oh, shit, I thought. I shoved past a clump of teenagers. The old man after me was determined, and I looked for a place to charge into, to hide. Nothing. Coming to State, I tore to the right.

The subway. I saw one of the glass entries and bounded toward it. I checked behind once again, saw no sign of my pursuer, and leapt down the steps two at a time. I could board a train, ride it to the end of the line and back, then head to Alecia's again. Yes, I thought, digging in my pocket for change.

In no time at all, I was down on a dingy platform, sweaty and heaving. But safe. Hugging a column, I turned from side to side, scanning the waiting crowd. There was no sign of the mysterious man, no menacing figure circulating

among the strangers. Whoever he was, I realized, I'd lost
him. I began to relax. The grimy, gray station held many
secrets, I was sure, and now, I hoped, I was one of them as
well. Still, I kept my attention sharp, my eyes darting. I
could easily imagine him reaching State Street, not spotting me, then heading down here.

The subway stop began to fill to capacity, a steady stream
of blacks and whites filing down. Soon there was such a
crowd that I wasn't able to see more than twenty or thirty
feet. Where, I wondered, was the damn train? Couldn't my
pursuer now be lurking in the crowd, just waiting to attack?

I heard it. The distant growl of machinery charging
through the tube. I stepped from behind the column.
Hurry. Quick. I glanced down the tunnel, saw it warm with
light. Escape was on the way. I surveyed the mass of people
again. No sign of the stranger.

At last the train burst from the tunnel, charged into the
station. I, along with all the others, seethed forward. I took
two steps, prepared to stop myself a safe distance from the
edge. But then suddenly I felt something behind me. Something, no someone, that continued to push me forward.

"'Hey!" I cried, trying to brake myself.

Two boney hands grabbed me, continued plowing me
forward. I understood. It was him. My pursuer. I glanced to
the right, saw the tigerlike eyes of the screaming train. Oh,
Christ, I thought, he means to push me off the platform.

I heard a woman cry, "Watch out!"

I tried to twist myself, attempted to dash to the side. But
the grip from behind was so sharp and determined. He put
all of his body into it, and I felt myself hurled to the very
edge of the concrete. One foot was hanging over the edge,
and I looked down, saw tracks and water and torn candy
wrappers. To the right I saw the front of the racing train,
saw steel wheels that would roll over me, crush me. And
snapping blue electricity.

"No!"

With all my weight, I twisted to the side, leaned back against my assailant. I jabbed my elbow back as hard as I could, felt it burrow into hot clothing and soft flesh. A deep groan burst from his mouth, and that gave me courage, determination. I turned, pushed harder, but sensed myself tumbling, going down on my knees. That's okay, I thought. A huddled body would be harder to push onto the tracks. Angry now, I dropped to the concrete, saw hundreds of legs. His, too. I reached out, grabbed him by the cuff. Just as quickly, his other foot came kicking upward, sinking painfully into my shoulder. My grip loosened, he jerked away. I tried to lunge after him, but he dashed to the side, behind a woman with big, thick legs, then started taking off through the crowd.

"Stop him!" I shouted from below the mass.

I scrambled up as the train screeched to a final stop. In the crowd of people only the back of him was visible. Thin gray hair, a dark coat. I started after him, then heard the doors hiss open behind me. Get away, I thought. Get out of this dingy place. And so I turned, let the crowd press me onto the train, let the train carry me away.

Chapter

7

At six sharp I was back at Alecia's clinic, knocking on the door. The receptionist and, it seemed, nearly everyone else was gone. Moments later, Alecia herself came to the outer door. Despite what I'm sure had been a long day, she greeted me with her customary grin and motioned me in with a long stroke of her arm. We spoke of the weather as she led me back to her office, then closed the door. Settling back in that recliner, I told her about the incident on the subway platform, recounted it as calmly as I could. She forgot about the heat and was completely still.

"So then what?" she asked, dumbfounded.

"I rode the train to O'Hare and spent the afternoon at a coffee shop out there."

She bit her bottom lip, and her eyes lowered and scanned the empty air for a reasonable explanation. None came.

"Alecia," I said, about to reveal what had started growing in me out at the airport, "I have a new fear."

"What is it?"

"What if someone's realized that I'm trying to piece together my life in Berlin?"

"What do you mean?"

Afraid of a process I might have launched, I sat forward, and said, "You know those letters I wrote to Europe asking about my family? Well, what if they alerted someone, who then followed me to your office, and stole my file. Then maybe, just maybe, that person did indeed learn something that sufficiently scared him."

"What are you saying, Will?"

"Someone might be trying to stop me before I can remember who murdered my mother."

Alecia looked as if she'd been hit. She'd dealt with all sorts of distraught people, I knew, but this I assumed was a first of its kind. She just sat there, brow crunched in confusion.

Finally, I asked, "Did you get something to eat?"

She nodded.

"What?"

Irritated at my asking, she responded, "A taco salad." She also knew my penchant for details. "And no, it wasn't very good. Too many olives and the taco bowl-thing was soggy."

"Oh, olives make me gag," I said as I twisted around. What was that noise in the hallway?

"Will," she said, "This worries me. I wonder if we shouldn't—"

"Sh," I ordered.

I heard it again. Footsteps. Quite soft ones.

"Is anyone else here?" I whispered, sitting up.

"What? No. Everyone's gone."

I held a finger to my lips. Alecia turned, looked toward the door, was silent. She tensed, caught her breath, and I wondered if we'd left the outer clinic door unlocked, thereby making ourselves pitifully easy targets. I realized that although I'd lost the stranger this afternoon, I hadn't checked for him lurking down on the street when I returned.

The stealthy steps continued, and then seemed to stop right outside Alecia's door. If the door opened, she'd be in immediate view, and so I motioned to her to come over to my side of the room. She did so, calmly, quietly. I came to my feet, and the two of us stood there, staring and wondering who was about to enter. My eyes focused on the silver knob; I watched it quiver, then twist. Alecia nervously touched me on the arm. At once I grabbed a nearby metal waste basket. It wasn't much, but it was something.

Abruptly a foot kicked the door wide open. We were behind it, mostly out of view, but I saw a heavy boot, dark pants. I raised the black metal can in my hands, readied myself to hurl it at our assailant. One more step and I'd bash him in the head.

All of a sudden, Alecia caught my arm, and yelled, "Will, no!"

The figure retreated at once into the hall. I continued on, charged out. A man in dark blue clothing jumped back, raised his hands in protection.

"I'm sorry, I'm sorry!" he shouted.

"Will!" said Alecia, rushing after me.

I wanted to grab the man, shake the truth from him, but I stopped, held myself in check.

"Will!" continued Alecia. "this is George, the janitor."

"Listen, I'm sorry," he began, "I didn't know anyone was still here."

I stared at his balding scalp, his wrinkled, frightened face. No. This wasn't the man after me. This guy was too small, too cowardly.

"Sorry, George," said Alecia, lifting the waste basket out of my hands and handing it to him.

I took a deep sigh, and added, "Yeah, we . . . we were just in the middle of some primal therapy."

"Oh."

George accepted the trash and quickly went on his way, muttering how we wouldn't see him again tonight. I turned to Alecia, shrugged.

"I guess I'm a little uptight."

"Don't worry. Come on, let's get back to work." She called after the janitor, saying, "George, just make sure the front door's locked when you leave, okay?"

"Yeah, you bet," he snapped.

Rather sheepishly, I returned to her office and dropped myself again in the recliner. I was eager to move on, and I pulled the side lever and moved into lift-off position.

"Let's get on with it," I said, desiring to block everything out. "Just get me on the next trance out of here."

"I was wondering if we shouldn't call the police."

"And tell them what?" I had this horrible vision of Alecia and me, the shrink and her nut case, at the police station. "You think they'll do something if I tell them I'm afraid for my life because of something I learned while doing a hypnotically induced age regression?"

She groaned, "You're right."

"I know I am. I spent an hour thinking about just that out at the airport."

"Then first things first. Let's see what else we can find out." Settling herself in, she was unable to hide a slight smile. "Hey, you have quick reactions."

"I feel like a fool."

"Don't. George needed a little shaking up. Besides, you were simply taking care of yourself. Don't worry. Now calm down." She took a deep breath. "Relax. Just relax."

I rolled my eyes up, counted to three. And listened to her count and begin the you're-getting-lighter routine. My body continued to pulse and seethe, however, and all the time, I wanted Alecia closer. Fuck professional distance. I wanted her to take my hand and squeeze it and tell me everything would be okay, I wasn't a geek, and that perhaps she admired me. Even just a little bit.

"Four. That's good, Will. You're doing great. Breathe in, breathe out. Five."

"No," I muttered. "Go back to three again, would you? I'm kind of stuck at two. This is taking a while."

"That's okay. It'll come. Three . . ."

Concentrating, I keyed into her chanted words, her rhythmic breathing, and finally I could sense the pounding of my heart soften and slow. At last I felt the hardness of my muscles ebb, the tension dissipate, evaporate. I thought it would never come, but minutes later I sensed that vacuum again. I took a deep breath, a door opened and I floated right through, sucked into that wonderful, tranquil world.

"Oh, this is nice, this is what I needed," I said, full of relief.

Alecia asked, *"Are you there already?"*

"Oh, yeah."

Surprise. *"Good."*

Oh. What tranquility. But how fleeting that could be. A good trance was also the perfect truth serum. No, not serum. Rather, it always gave me the strength and the confidence to go directly to the fundamental issue and say exactly what I'd wanted to all along. Yes, hypnosis made me honest to my soul.

"We need to talk," I said, unable to restrain myself.

"I'm right here. I'm listening," came the voice from outside.

"I'm being consumed by guilt."

"Yes, Will, and that is a heavy burden for you. You have to remember, though, that when your mother was killed you were only a little boy—a little boy caught in the middle of a world war."

Well, not really. I'd been vastly older than my years. War does that to children.

"Yeah, but I was supposed to watch out for my mother and younger brother. I was the 'little soldier' of the house."

"Will, you grew up during a very difficult period and experienced something quite terrible. You felt so responsible for so many things, but no one is as powerful as you thought you were. You need to look at the limits of—"

"Alecia, I just can't live with myself not knowing—or rather, not remembering—who killed my mother. And that's not the only reason—for my own safety I have to find out who killed her. Now more than ever I have to look that dark face in the eyes and see who did it."

Yes, this constituted the little hamsters that had been gnawing at my mind all these years. Unless I discovered what really happened back there in late February 1945, I would never find peace. The war would continue festering within me until it or this mystery man killed me.

"I can't go on not knowing." I took a deep breath. "I have to find out who killed my mother and then tell someone so justice can be done. That's the only way I can lay her to rest, finally and forever, thirty years later. Then I'll deal with whoever is after me."

"I'm proud of you, Will," said Alecia. *"I admire your courage."*

"Charmed, I'm sure," I quipped. "So I have to go back again. I accept that." My ultimate nightmare—the black face of my mother's murderer—began to bubble up in my mind. Shit. All that was evil was represented in those smoldering eyes, in that hot breath. "I'm . . . I'm just afraid. I mean, it was a miracle I wasn't murdered along with my mother."

"Will, you have to remember two things. First, you survived that night and the war and nothing will ever change that. Do you understand?"

Yes, teacher. "I guess so."

"I mean that. It's something you're going to have to learn to accept: you can't change what happened."

But I didn't want to believe that.

"Second, you will be returning to that time in a very special state of hypnosis. You will become little Willi again, but you will have new and valuable insights. You will be a child with the perceptions of an adult, and that will shed a great deal of understanding on everything." She added, *"And, Will, I'll be with you the entire time. Don't worry, I'll bring you out of the trance if there's any danger."*

I took a deep breath, readied myself for launching. "Okay, I'm ready."

"Are you sure?"

"Yes. There's only one thing, oh Wise One." I took a deep breath as I lay in my suspended animation. "I don't want to do any of this in and out shit. It's too hard. I just want to return to Berlin and not come back until . . . until . . ."

"That's fine, Will. I have no more appointments. Nothing the rest of this evening. No one will disturb us. And I'm quite sure George won't be back."

"You had this all planned out, didn't you?"

"Well, several variations, anyway." Her voice more soothing than ever, she said, *"Don't worry. Everything's going to be fine. We'll get through this. I'll be your guide and you can go back and discover all that you need to."*

"Sure," I responded from a stupor of a trance. She didn't, however, know the all of it. That was my fear. "But . . ."

"Don't worry, you'll wake up if there's any real danger." She went silent for what seemed like a year. *"Now, Will, you're already in a good trance. You know how to proceed to the next step."* Air hissed delicately over her lips. *"That's it. Breathe in. Breathe out. Relax. Deep, deep relaxation that carries you dee—"*

"Uh-uh."

"I mean higher and higher with a wonderful sense of lightness."

I pictured myself in a fluffy white cloud above the earth. Higher. Higher. I had to seek the ultimate vantage point to experience it all, see it all. Smiling, I sensed myself growing younger, saw myself ascending. Cool gusts of wind rushed around my prone body. I looked at myself. A boy's body, lean and leggy. I touched my knees. So knobby!

"God, I'm so little! I mean, I'm kind of tall for a ten-year old, but I'm just so much smaller as Willi."

Willi, the scrounger of Berlin, his mother's conniving messenger. Willi, invincible, determined. And goofy. I laughed, and felt myself rising like some magical plane through the stunning white clouds and into the next universe. I did a loop like a fighter, breezed up and around, let the wind rush over my face. I couldn't stop giggling. This was fun.

Enough. I had to go back. Back. There was work to do. A terrible place to visit. A painful truth to learn. And the light began to fade, to grow dark . . .

"Well," I began, my man-boy voice thinner and higher, "all this took place at the beginning of the end of the war. It was the . . . the last week of February 1945, just a few days before the full moon, the night she was killed. The moon was so huge that night . . . but I'm getting ahead of myself. I should tell you about the Russians—they'd smashed through Poland, killing everything in their paths, and had already taken large chunks of Germany. And the Americans were already on German soil to the west. It was just a question of who would reach Berlin first." My body shook, was rocked by a distant rumbling. "Yes, everyone knew the end was only weeks away. Do you hear the bombs and the ack-ack of the flak guns?"

"Just follow that feeling, Willi. Follow it like a string and it will lead you to the truth you are seeking."

I sensed the next level. The next vacuum. Ripping, tearing, sucking me back . . . back . . . back.

"Oh, God!" I cried.

My beautiful trip was suddenly shattered by an explosion. As if I'd been shot down, I was falling from the sky, tumbling through the heavens and into a nightmare of a city and a time. I came crashing to the earth and into a dark cellar. I screamed out again because a bomb had just fallen on a building across the street, blowing the block to pieces.

And then there was an enormous explosion, this one directly overhead, and I hollered, "Ah!"

Chapter

8

I heard nothing, however, not even the crude noise that ruptured from my own lungs, not even the cries of terror from the other kids and their parents huddled around me. I looked up the cellar stairs, saw the door come hurling inward, blasted from its hinges as if effortlessly kicked in by some terrible giant. The next instant the wooden ceiling dissolved into splinters and exploded with dust. I looked over, saw Frau Schulenberg and a stranger in a long wool coat lunge for shelter beneath the staircase, saw my friend Klaus dive with his father to the floor. *Mein Gott,* we were all going to die!

"Go on, Willi, it's okay. I'm right here. Just let your mind tell the story that will reveal the truth."

A beam came crashing down toward me. All at once I realized that my mother would never know if I died here. I'd been out scrounging a ruined store, filling my pockets with treasure, then stopped at this building because Klaus was ten, too, and Konrad was just a little younger and . . . and I had to live! I dove to the side, threw myself beneath the stairs, covered my head, and the first, second, third and fourth floors came dumping down on us. Nearby yet another bomb exploded and we were assaulted by the blast's enormous pressure, then robbed of air by its absolute vacuum. Roar. Dust. Mortar. More bombs. Pressure-Suction. The air was so hot I couldn't breath. Fire! My hand pushed through a collage of rubble, rocks and boards that scraped at my body, tried to pull me into a grave.

"No!" I cried, never wanting my mother so much.

"That's right, Willi, there's something in Berlin you must learn. And you won't stop until you discover it."

I fought back. I would not be slowly roasted in the ruins of the apartment house where the Schulenberg kids resided. I must escape! But those screams! Those tight, high-pitched, animallike screams. What were Klaus and Konrad and their two spoiled little sisters doing back here? After the Hamburg firebombing that had killed tens of thousands, all my friends— all the *Mütter und Kinder*—were evacuated; the Schulenbergs had fled to the east, to their Uncle Otto's. Oh, but the Russians. The Russians were coming, and Klaus told me how they'd been evacuated a second time, returned here like rejected freight. Arrived just this afternoon because his mother wanted nothing more than to be back in Berlin, wanted nothing more than to be back home . . .

Something squirmed next to me, someone yelled, "Give me your hand!"

I grabbed the big stiff appendages of a man's hand, squeezed, felt a desperate, terrified flex in response. Then somehow I was being tugged toward the staircase. Yes, there were stairs all buried in brick. I hung on to the hand that belonged to whom I didn't know, was pulled upward. Yes, up, scraping against bricks and nails and boards and death. We had to get up and out. Away from this crushing mass of destruction, this suffocating heat.

This huge manly figure and I gathered frantic speed as if we were under water and we'd run out of air and our lungs were empty bags. We pushed and shoved, pulled and dug through pulverized mortar. The heat became more intense. We were nearing the street. The man heaved aside a board. Yes, escape! From the dark clouds of dust and into the fires around us. The stranger clambered over the bricks, tumbled. I popped out right after him, fell. He caught me. We collapsed on the ruins and I clutched this unknown person, wallowed in his big safe arms. We were alive. Our building wasn't ablaze. Just the rest of the street, just every other street, just the entire district of Schöneberg. And the bombs were still falling, still raining down on us, exploding with deafening pitch. Eight bombs to a cradle. Bomb, bomb, bomb, bomb, bomb, bomb, bomb, bomb. A pause. A momentary pause until the next batch was dumped, laying the *Bombenteppich*, the carpet of death, over us. PressureSuction. PressureSuction. In the distance I heard the flak guns chattering away. ACK-ACK! ACK-ACK! ACK-ACK!

I pushed away from the stranger, glanced at his wide face now smudged with dirt, his fair hair now black with grime. I tensed, wondered why he seemed familiar. He clutched me by the arm. Looking into his eyes, I could tell he wanted to say something. But I was all right, everything still attached, and I turned and gazed across the street. Wild tongues of flame licked out of windows, crackled in the night. Stunned Berliners, driven like rats from their destroyed homes, wandered aimlessly, mumbling, pleading, collapsing in death. I'd been so close so many times to death. It was all around me, right at my feet, every day. But never had I come so near to being really swallowed.

Behind me I heard a voice curdle with terror. Klaus' mother—the one who used to make that wonderful torte with Belgian chocolate—was all blackened and bloodied and crawling on her hands and knees like some monster.

"Otto? Otto?" she screamed. "My babies! My husband!"

The wind stormed right out of me. Not Klaus. Not Konrad. And those two bratty sisters? I cringed. They were all trapped in the cellar! I glanced up, saw an undamaged piano perched on a narrow ledge; that was their apartment and not long ago I'd played some horrid little song on that thing. The bombs faded in the distance, and I was flushed with a horrified realization. Yes, somehow I had known this tragedy would happen.

But perhaps there was still time. Both the strange man and I scrambled over and started pulling a huge chunk of beige stone all carved with flowers. Desperately digging, we then gingerly removed boards for fear that more rubble would collapse into the cellar. Heaving aside brick after brick, Frau Schulenberg was crazed. Her maternal radar pulled her down, and she dug like a dog, desperately pawing until she finally reached a voice, a hand. In seconds, a little dust-gray girl emerged, eyes glazed, arm and head oozing blackish fluid. Frau Schulenberg put her aside. One safe, three to go. Then came a voice. A deep pitiful voice. Crying. In minutes the heavy figure of Herr Schulenberg emerged, a round man, moustached, speechless, a dirty potato just dug from the earth. He reached out with one hand. We pulled—Frau Schulenberg, the stranger, and I. Attached to his other hand was a little girl, the real whiney one, her red hair gone black. They clambered out, collapsed on the ruins as if they were the softest of featherbeds. But his wife didn't stop.

"Klaus? Klaus? Konrad? Konrad?" She screamed, "Klaus, Konrad, answer me!"

But there was no answer. And I knew. I knew what Frau Schulenberg feared, what she would mourn for years to come: not only the deaths of her two boys, but the loss of their bodies.

Horrified, I rose. If only I'd thought earlier, faster. I might
have . . . if only.

*"Willi, remember that even though you've returned with
perceptions far beyond this time and place, you can't
change what happened."*

Frau Schulenberg shot me with a scream: "Dig, you little
bastard! My children are down there! Dig!"

I had known but at the same time hadn't realized it. And
now it was too late. I stared at her, at the stranger who was
digging so hard, and shook my head and started off. I
touched my bulging pockets. At least my secret prize hadn't
been lost. I needed to go back to our little bunker bar buried
beneath all this horror. There I could pretend as if Klaus
and Konrad had never come back to Berlin. There I could
listen to Dieter on the piano, drink in my mother's song.
Everything would be all right.

I hadn't gone more than a few meters when I stopped
and touched my forehead. Blood. Thick and gritty, brackish
like old motor oil. The blast had stunned me and I was
slightly confused. But I was essentially unhurt.

A thick acrid cloud of smoke swirled up and around,
filling my lungs with coarse soot and charred pieces of
Berlin. I gagged, caught my throat, rushed on. Away. I had
to move on, had to find my way home. But where was I?
The raid had rearranged the neighborhood, removed buildings and store fronts, lampposts and cars.

I heard a shriek of a scream behind me and turned. A
burning man emerged from a *Hinterhof*—a courtyard of
small buildings built inside a city block—and dashed by
me. His clothing and body were on fire and the tar of an
incendiary bomb was stuck all over him. First the explosive
bombs fell, cracking open the homes and exposing dry
wood and forcing people from their cellars. Then the incendiaries. Little stick ones. Bigger ones. Filled with blobs
of gummy coal tar. Gasoline-soaked rags. Whatever the

Brits had used this time. And this poor bastard had been splattered, and now he ran and ran and ran, the sticky flames clinging to him like sugary syrup. A fleeing torch. He streaked for his life down the street, stripping his clothes off with each step.

I found part of his blue shirt on the ground, picked it up, smelled it. No gas. No black spots. I waded it up and dashed to a burst water main, soaked the rag in the wonderful water. I drenched it like I'd learned and clamped the cool fresh dripping piece of cloth over my mouth. I looked upward. The planes—undoubtedly British because it was night—were blowing away like gray, metal clouds, leaving behind a bloodied sky. Torched Berlin had flown up and was still raining down on me. Ash. Glowing ash, falling everywhere like a hellish blizzard. How beautiful. Berlin was a total bonfire. Red it burned. Yellow it oozed. Orange it pulsed. What were Hitler's words? Oh, yes. *GEBT MIR FÜNF JAHRE UND IHR WERDET DEUTSCHLAND NICHT WIEDERERKENNEN!* Give me five years and you will not recognize Germany again . . .

As I passed a windowless building, a phone began to ring. I saw a woman with a candle clamber through a room; no electricity, no gas, no water. But somehow still phones. The woman picked up the receiver, and cried with joy: *"Liebling!"* So a child or father had survived. This time.

Bruised and dazed, I came to a crossroad. Ahead of me, the charcoal remains of a bus lay turned over, dented like one of my little brother's toys. Like all the other wandering lost souls, I clambered on, making my way over smoldering piles of bakeries, food shops, bodies. On the very highest pile I stopped, the wet rag to my mouth. Off to my right, the sky above the central district glowed a greenish red. More phosphorous bombs. It looked as if the entire area round Unter den Linden had been doused with them. One of the monstrous firestorms was brewing over there, that one looking particularly fearsome. It would grow in intensity, of course, as it gobbled up every single molecule of oxygen, then charge on with gale winds in search of more. Suck. Suck. It would suck the oxygen from the lungs of the people hiding in the shelters. Tomorrow, I guessed, cellars full of suffocated people would be found, tipped over as if they'd merely gone to sleep. Forever.

My head began to pound. I didn't know where to go, how to get home. My breathing came quick and short. I'd always been able to worm my way through the ruins of Berlin, past Gestapo, past SS. I'd always been able to play war as it rained bombs. Until now. For the first time I was lost.

"Look around, Willi. Trust your senses, your intuition. Go on . . ."

I turned around. The man who had pulled me from ruins of the Schulenberg's building was standing there, his hands in the pockets of his long dark topcoat. His face was streaked with dirt, and in the light of burning Berlin, I could tell that he was staring at me. No. More than that. He was following me.

I took off. I was running as fast as I could. Over bricks and boards. Past a burning car, a tram that lay twisted on its side, and an abandoned military truck. Stumbling people all around me. I looked back at him, saw him charging after me.

"Halt!" he cried.

Had he seen me before the raid, looting the remains of that grocery, hunting as if for gold? Or had he seen me earlier trading my mother's cigarettes? It was better, I knew, not to find out. People like him only meant trouble. So I just had to get away, melt like rubber into the pavement. Disappear. I ran over the skeleton of another car, over other shattered pieces of Berlin. I turned down a street, crunched over glass. Was there a single unbroken window anywhere in Germany?

I slowed, looked back. The mysterious stranger was gone. I'd lost him. So who was he? What kind of official?

In the orange glow of the burning city, I turned right, right, right, until I saw him again, a big desperate figure heaving and sweating, less than thirty meters away. More frightened than ever, I spun and took off. But my legs weren't as long as his. I couldn't keep my distance, so I ducked around a corner, grabbed a board, pressed myself against a wall. He was just seconds behind me, his steps drawing quickly closer, and then he rushed around the corner and I swung out the board. Caught him right in the gut, I did, and he spit out every bit of air and collapsed on the cobblestone. I raised the board overhead, desperate as I was clever, and stared down at this odd man.

Lying on the ground, a single word blurted from his lips: "Willi . . ."

He was bingo-right, of course, and that sent a wave of fear over my young face. I stood motionless. Who was he? What did he want with me?

"You're Willi," he gasped

Not sure whether to smack him again or run, I stared at him through clenched eyes.

"*So?*" I responded, my thick Berlin accent making it sound like "*zo.*"

"I just wanted to tell you, Willi, that you have a hole in your pocket and the sugar's falling to the ground."

My eyes dropped open, I grabbed at my pocket, felt the hole and the trickle of sugar. Quickly, I wadded up my coat, tried to stop the leak. So he had spied me earlier.

Obviously pleased that he'd stunned me, the stranger continued, saying, "Your little brother—what's his name, Erich? Well, he likes it, doesn't he when you bring him sugar?" He smirked. "But at the rate it's spilling there won't be much left by the time you make it home."

"'Our food coupons were registered at that store," I

barked. "I was just taking what was ours—what would've been rationed to us!"

"Sure," he laughed, still on the ground. "You think you're so tough. I bet you've used that line a hundred times."

I put both hands back on the board, lifted it high. There was something strange about the way he spoke. Even the way he looked.

"Who are you?"

He rolled on his back, looked . . . confused. And tired. Extremely tired.

"Tell me who you are!" I said, threatening this grown man with the board as if it were a saber.

He closed his eyes, just lay there. I don't know why he was so sure I wouldn't just whack him. I could, I was sure, strike him good and hard on the head, knock him into oblivion.

"I'm a friend. My name's Joe."

I understood, of course, and relaxed my grip on the board. There were a lot of different types at our place, always had been. Although that didn't make him dangerous, at least for now, it did make him even more questionable.

"You know my mother, don't you?"

As if he were lost in memories, his head went slowly up and down. "But I haven't seen her for a long, long time. Years."

He stared up at me and our eyes locked. All of a sudden I realized he was more scared than me. His was a matter-of-life-and-death kind of fright, and I knew I could do him far more harm than he could me.

"You're in trouble, aren't you?" I demanded with my new-found sense of superiority.

He nodded.

"So what did you do?" What was it? Smuggling? Desertion?

He flinched, then feigned coolness. "I need to see your

mother. I went to that apartment building looking for her."

My brow rose. The Schulenberg's building? Even though she still knew many of the people there, my mother hadn't lived in that house for years. Not since before the war, not since before I was born and her grandfather, Opa Wilhelm, was still alive. Of course, I thought. I get it.

"You're not German, are you?"

He shifted on the ground, sat up, shrugged, and leaned against a wall.

"That obvious, huh?"

"A foreigner! That's what you are. I knew it right away."

"Bullshit," he responded. "A lucky guess, that's all."

"No, it wasn't!" I shouted. "You look German I guess, but your accent's kind of funny. So what are you then? Austrian? Or . . . or Dutch? You haven't been here since before the war, have you?"

Glancing up at me, he hesitated, then simply said, "I'm American."

I gasped and jumped back, raised the board. This guy was the enemy! I had to call the police, I had to find some soldiers! I had to—

Suddenly a time bomb ripped the neighborhood. My heart made a fist, and suddenly I was tackled and pulled to the ground. This Joe from America grabbed me and threw himself over me as the earth heaved with a belch. PressureSuction. I heard distant screams, and little pieces of brick and mortar and glass showered down. But I was okay because this guy was my umbrella, and when I opened my eyes, his face was only inches from me. American?

He rolled off, and I pulled back. He didn't look so terrible, so mean. As a matter of fact, he didn't look so much different from any of us. So what was he? A spy?

"Mister," I ventured, "how did you get here? How did you cross the lines? Did you parachute in or—"

"Listen, I need to speak to . . ."

"*Meine Mutter?*" I asked in Berlin dialect.

He said, "Can you take me to her, Willi?"

Of course I could. But should I? Was it safe? What would she say? What would she do?

A brass doorknob was just sitting on the ground, and I picked it up, rubbed its pock-mark dents. Tomorrow morning I could go out, see what shops and houses had been hit in tonight's bombing. Maybe I'd find something incredible. Once I discovered a gold ring, which I later traded for two packs of cigarettes.

I said, "I don't think they'll ever find Klaus and Konrad."

"I don't think so either."

I shrugged. "I didn't like them that much anyway."

Living through the war was a continual process of building walls. Something horrible happened and you put up a barrier to block out whatever you didn't want to believe.

I looked at Joe. "And if I leave you the SS will probably find you and kill you."

"That's right."

String him up from a lamppost, they would. So what should I do? I stood. After all, he'd pulled me from the cellar, probably saved my life.

"*So*, Mister," I said, "it's not very far."

He pushed himself up, his movements now slow and pained. No sooner was he on his feet than he began to sway. I hurried to his side, steadied him. He was trembling.

"Are you sick?"

He shook his head, but I didn't believe him.

He asked, "Tell me, does she still sing?"

"*Na klar, jeden Tag.*" For sure, every day.

He smiled and we started off. I went slow because this Joe seemed no longer big and brave, but weak. And he talked as we went, told me how he hadn't seen her for eleven years. I understood, of course. It was the sad, dreamy way he told me that made me certain he was just another of my mother's lovers. Another in a long string that led all the way back before the war, back before my time.

Around us the air began to whip as if with fear. The fires in the area were growing and groaning, hungry for oxygen. Which way? How? Where to burn next, what block, building, corpse? In the distance roared a sound like a herd of locomotives.

"Willi, what's that noise? Tanks?" he asked.

"No," I responded, quickening my step as if fleeing an impending rain shower. "That's a firestorm."

Chapter

9

He started asking me questions, lots of them, and I told him how my father had not been killed by the Bolsheviks but by a pothole in Poland that had caught his motorcycle and flipped it atop him. Ever since it had been just me and Erich and my mother. Dieter, too, because he'd come back a couple of years ago. And even though we all lived together, I explained, Dieter wasn't a new father to me because he really wasn't involved with my mother. They were just good friends. Mine, too, for Dieter was my *Nennonkel*, my uncle by friendship.

"I met him before the war," said Joe. "He owns that little hotel."

Well, that was the very *Pension* where I was born and where we'd lived, I explained, until all eighteen rooms were destroyed, gobbled up by flames in one of the first bombings of Berlin in 1941. That was while Deiter was off at war and before he lost his leg. Mother had been taking care of the place, running it and not doing a very good job. Then came the raid, which gutted the building. And then my mother had this wonderful idea. She moved what little remained of the *Kneipe*, the tavern that had been on the ground floor, into the cellar behind the *Pension*. Surprisingly secure against the bombs, the underground space had once been a storage spot for beer and was more like a cave because it was down so deep, tucked under a thick layer of bedrock. Ever since that's how we had lived. Down there like trolls. In our very own bunker bar filled with song and booze and a vast number of Mother's acquaintances who just happened to be the looser, more questionable folk of Berlin. Dieter was back now, of course, bitter about his leg that had been blasted to bits, but relieved at least that it hadn't been his arm. He could still play the piano. Sometimes the accordion, too.

A siren began to rise in ominous pitch as I led Joe down yet another block of roofless, windowless, skeletonlike buildings. Joe tensed, stumbled, looked up at the fingers of light that picked over the night clouds. In the distance flak guns started to chatter.

"That's just the Brits checking the damage," I said.

"Oh."

I was right, of course. The ack-ack of the flak guns stopped as soon as the high-flying reconnaissance planes had disappeared, and then the all-clear siren whirled its high-toned blessing.

We came around a corner, and there up on the left was what remained of the *Pension*, its interior long ago burned away, its five-story facade only partially standing. All the windows were gone, as were the floors, the roof, all the furniture.

Joe froze as if he'd just bumped into someone from his past. Looking at him, I saw that his eyes were fixed on a single curving balcony that clung to what had been the big top floor room. Mother had hated the room that had stood up there, refusing to go in it, as if somehow the chamber were haunted.

"You were here before, Mister?"

He nodded, reached out for my shoulder for support.

I asked, "Are you all right?"

"I . . . I think so."

Whatever Joe's story was, something had gone terribly wrong. That much was clear. I knew, too, that my mother was one of the few people in all of Nazi Germany who could now help him, if indeed, she so chose. She was fickle at best. With her connections, her acquaintances, though, she'd be able to shelter Joe, the enemy, perhaps even get him some sort of documentation. Anton could do that. And that might be good for us. Maybe my mother would help him now because he'd be able to help us then, later. That is, if we lost, if there really wasn't a secret weapon to deliver us.

With each step I bore more and more of Joe's weight. And only with my help did we make it down the narrow path cleared in the middle of the bombed street, past the charred walls, over rubble of brick, stone, iron, around and right into the remains of the inn's original *Kneipe*. Joe cried out at the sight. Shocked, I was sure. It had been an okay bar, dark brown and smoky and covered with hundreds of beer steins and lots of antlers, too. But all that was long burned away. Now all that was left was an empty cavity of brick and clumps of metal.

"Dear God," he said as we passed through.

I led him out the back and into a little courtyard of ruins. We came to a big wooden door, available to only those who could pay my mother's price, and I sort of leaned Joe against the wall. I braced myself and pulled, for it was a heavy door that could be locked and braced against the bombs. Sealed tight like a cork. And now when I popped it open, Mama's voice rushed out like steamy champagne. Joe, who was fading each moment, perked up. So he wasn't lying. He really had once known my mother, been intoxicated by her and her song. He like so many others.

I pulled Joe through as my mother's voice curled upward and beckoned us with one of her favorites. *"J'ai du Rythme."* She and Dieter loved what Goebbels called Americano nigger kike jungle music. They loved jazz and swing, the forbidden glories of Gershwin, Armstrong, Miller, and every other American composer. It was all *entartete Musik,* of course, the stuff that just wasn't all German and pure, and I don't know how they got away with it, all the wild stuff. Dieter loved to play it "hot"; he could get so carried away with *"Flat Foot Floogie mit ein Floy Floy"* that Erich and I would scream with laughter. And Mother sometimes even sang in English, which was very *verboten.*

We twisted our way down and down over the stone steps, and the deeper we went, the clearer became her voice. The melody charged along, scooped, slithered, twisted and wrapped. My mother could bathe minds, seduce souls. She did it every night, creating an atmosphere that wasn't very warlike and certainly not very Nazi. While Berlin got its daily lashings, Mother and Dieter were down here with schnapps and a crowd and a one hundred proof tune.

Behind me, Joe stumbled on the stairs, scraped along the gritty stone walls. I caught him, helped him down the last of the curving steps and into the rear of a long grottolike place, a low arched ceiling hovering above. My eyes swelled to suck light from a few scattered kerosene lanterns as well as fat drippy candles perched on a round oak chandelier. The tables, thick and crude and bolstered by benches, were filled by drunken men and buxom, laughing women not drinking *Fusel*—rotgut booze—but good, quality stuff of which Mother had a mysterious and seemingly endless supply.

Quickly I looked around, surmised that my little brother was in the makeshift kitchen behind the piano and that he was still the only one who knew I'd been gone. Promises of treats always kept him in confidence. I'd snuck out after my mother's second schnapps. All the ones after that ensured that she wouldn't wonder about me.

"Did she drink often, Willi?"

It was the same scene almost every night. Mother and her lyrics, Dieter at the piano, the two of them laughing and touching, occasionally smooching mid-song. Beer, schnapps, brandy, precious cognac, too, and a roomful of people trying to escape misery. It was kind of fun, I suppose. At ten I was my own boss.

I turned to where all the chairs, all the noses were pointed. To the woman up front who leaned against a tall stool as if it were a virile Luftwaffe major. To the woman who crooned a Gershwin tune next to the cranky old piano on which a cranky one-legged man was playing. To the woman who parted her lips and breathed out in song all that these people wanted yet knew was now gone.

Joe clutched my shoulder again. He was swaying, not with the music but struggling to keep his balance.

"You need to sit, Mister," I said.

But he wouldn't move. He kept staring at my mother, her face full and sensuous as she sang. I watched as she brushed back her thick, dark blonde hair, then made a fist. She pinched shut her large painted eyes as her Lucky Strike voice, harsh and full of burned life, belted out of that exceedingly wide mouth. Her voice rolled along, beat with a happiness that seemed totally out of place, and then she finally opened those eyes.

At first I couldn't tell if she saw us standing there in the back. Then, however, the voice of my mother, the underground seductress, skipped like a gramophone needle. All at once her song lost its bounce and charm, fell to earth. I could see her grab at Joe with her eyes. The audience flinched, turned, expecting perhaps the Gestapo. I froze, expecting her unpredictable wrath.

She simply stopped singing.

Mid-sentence she cut herself off, slid away from her stool. Dieter lost a few beats in confusion, reached out and touched her on the waist, then continued playing as my mother lunged across the room. All at once I feared I shouldn't have brought this American here.

Joe started to fall. I caught him, struggled to hold him. He was on the edge of passing out. I glanced at my mother, saw her feet stutter, her hands reach out and desperately cling to the back of a chair. Oddly, her eyes were moist as she tried to ascertain the truth. Joe tried to call out, but only managed a few garbled words.

"It can't be!" said Eva, my mother, afraid to move any closer. "No, this is impossible!"

Joe mumbled: "I know I . . . I promised never to come back but . . . but I had no choice!"

He was crying, tears filling those big blue Yankee eyes, rolling down his cheeks. The Mister American infiltrator spy capitalist was now crumbling in my arms.

Mother came rushing at him, grabbed him from me, hugged him, and cried "Oh, *mein Gott!*"

Joe's eyes burst like an exploding dam, and I stepped back as the two of them clutched at one another, sobbing their disbelief and joy. Dieter stopped playing and everyone turned, stared. Who what where oh, well, they sighed, this is war, this is war, and that is someone who has returned from the dead.

Then finally Joe stepped over the edge. He teetered back and forth, his head fell, and in a moment my mother was struggling to hold him up.

"He's fainted!" shouted my mother. "Quick, Willi, this is Joe, my cousin. Help me lie him down!"

Chapter

10

I sat for hours by Joe's bed, a cot in the back room. My mother came and went, quite concerned, testing the warmth of his forehead with her palm. Joe didn't stir at all, however, and it seemed that he'd disappeared into a very deep sleep, his breathing regular and smooth. Finally, sometime well after midnight, Mother disappeared, and I curled up in a blanket and slumped over on the floor.

But my rest was not comforting. In my dreams it was dark, very dark, and I felt as if I'd traveled much too far from home. I wanted to go back, but I couldn't. Not yet. I had to wait for the end of this dream, which I felt certain was about to melt into a nightmare.

Then out of nowhere I heard an angellike voice beckon to me: *"It's all right, Willi. Just go on. You have the strength to push on, to make it to the truth."*

I opened my eyes, and realized that I was still in the little room. There was no angel and there was no evening sky. Overhead a naked bulb hung dead at the end of a long shriveled wire. The ceiling was rough and rugged, carved from stone. Deep stone. Yes, I was deep in our private bunker. I heard water being squeezed into a bowl or something, and without moving I looked over. In the glow of a spirit lamp, I saw my mother, perched on a three-legged stool, reach over to the cot and place a damp rag on Joe's forehead.

"*Hallo*," she whispered to him.

I watched my mother sponge Joe's face, and I realized again how afraid I was for her. Looking at her made me think of a beautiful night sky filled with a big white orb. What, I wondered, was happening?

"You have perceptions beyond this time and place, Willi. Go on, explain what you're seeing."

Huddled beneath my blanket, I feigned sleep and didn't move. Like a camera, I watched my mother and her cousin. I took it all in, recorded it.

"I thought we might lose you," she said to Joe, her large mouth stretched into a broad yet passionless smile.

"Eva," he gasped, not moving his large figure on the cot.

She removed the wet rag, then lifted a slender cracked glass to his lips.

"Brandy?"

It bit Joe in the throat, shot through his nose, squeezed his face. He coughed, choked. She lifted the glass from his mouth to hers and took a long, appreciative drink. Eyes closed, tongue sucking. Spying her from the floor, I knew she loved brandy more than schnapps. Better yet: cognac. Victorious Hennessy cognac from defeated France.

"What," he begged, "happened?"

Mother calmly set the glass down, lifted the rag, massaged out the water, placed the cloth again on his forehead.

As if she were addressing a patient in a hospital, my mother said, "You had a fever and you've been asleep since last night."

"You're . . . you're all right?"

"Ich bin wie ich bin." I am how I am.

Studying my mother as she sat alongside Joe, I couldn't help but see a haze of awkwardness hover over the two of them. Joe was our American cousin, of course. Mama had talked of him sometimes warmly, sometimes bitterly, but never at length. And gone now was my mother's eager joy at seeing him last night. They'd been close before the war, that much I'd figured out, but something had happened, driven them apart, and it wasn't related to Roosevelt or Hitler. No, it had to do with a night of excess long before the war.

Joe said, "My plane was shot down." He lifted his head, hastened to add, "They ordered me to fly some reconnaissance missions over the city. You know, to estimate the damage. But we were hit by artillery and . . ."

Curled in my blanket, I listened in amazement as Joe recounted in detail how his plane had been yanked out of the skies by flak from our feared 8.8 anti-aircraft guns, and how his craft had brushed treetops, then skidded and cracked up in a field. He spoke of flames and blood and stumbling into a ruined farmhouse and listening in horror as the other two surviving Americans were captured and gunned to death.

Then he took my mother's hand. I craned my neck to see. Yes, he was caressing it. My brow wrinkled. They were cousins, weren't they?

"It was somewhere near Potsdam," he said. "I hid there for days."

"Poor thing," replied my mother, withdrawing her hand.

"There was a trunk of clothes in the cellar. I changed into these," he said, weakly tugging at his dark shirt. "Then I buried my uniform and started for Berlin." His voice fell away. "I went to Opa Wilhelm's looking for you. There was a raid. Some little boys were killed."

Ja, my friend Klaus and his little brother Konrad. Gone.

Or rather, simply buried on the spot. And now it made sense why Joe had gone to that building in particular. My mother had lived there with her Opa Wilhelm after her own father had been killed in the First War and her mother taken by the grippe epidemic of 1918. That's who'd raised my mother, her *Grossvater*, my *Urgrossvater*, whom everyone except my mother spoke so lovingly of. And Joe, the grandson born in Berlin, then raised in America after his fortune-seeking parents had emigrated to Chicago, had visited them just as Hitler's eagle was ascending. I figured that must have been back in 1933 or 1934.

Eva touched his forehead briefly. "*Ja*, I think your fever's gone."

Joe reached out, caught her hand, pulled it close to his chest. He held it, I saw, just like any of the number of soldiers who'd lusted after my mother.

Using the endearing form of my mother's name, he said, "Evchen—"

I smashed my eyes shut just as my mother spun in my direction. Convinced that I still slept, she lowered her voice and snapped at him. I heard it all, though. I always had, always would.

"Seeing you last night, Joe, was like an opium rush, quick and short-lived. I've forgotten. Please don't remind me."

I clutched myself in feigned rest, grappled. What had happened? I carefully, slowly opened my eyes, bobbed back to the surface. My mother was taking a long, slow slug of brandy.

"It's a miracle you made it out of your plane, you weren't caught and . . . and you found us here," she said, then forced a laugh. "I've been saving a bottle of the best—and I mean the best—French champagne, and—"

"Eva," said Joe, softly, "I've . . . I've been so worried about you."

I suppose it was amazing that my mother, Erich, and I

were still alive, that we hadn't been lost under the bombs. Then again, I didn't think we'd die. Everyone else did. Not us. So many of Mama's friends were gone, her friends from before when she sang in the real cabarets. Most of that group, I'd heard whispered, had been slapped with yellow stars or pink triangles and hauled off years ago.

Mother poured him more brandy. "Here, this is good for you. It's French as well and it's simply—"

"Am I safe here?"

"Liebchen," roared my mother, "no one's safe in Berlin!"

"Of course." His voice faint, he said, "Thank God for Willi. If he hadn't been in that cellar, if the Schulenbergs hadn't asked him about you, then I don't know what I would've done."

Mother's face melted.

"Why?"

He'd mentioned my name. Joe talked about me, and that upset my mother. I lay there, knowing but not knowing, a sick feeling swelling my stomach.

Quickly, Mother downed the drink she'd poured for Joe, thereby drowning away any more of his questions. I studied her as the honey-colored liquid slithered out of the glass, into her mouth, into her body. I watched as a warm red glow enveloped her. Grown men loved her for her beauty and her voice. But why did I, her son?

"Food!" she proclaimed like a Russian tsarina as she set down the glass. "That's what you need, Joe!"

Mother spun on the stool, yelled at me. "Willi! Willi, wake up!"

I bolted upright, faked a stretch or two. She didn't suspect that I'd overheard, let alone that I was beginning to understand. Then again, Mother never realized how much I truly saw.

"Go get your big cousin some food. Something hot," she ordered.

I was up and running for bread or cheese or something. "Morjen, Mister," I called as I darted past.

He lifted an arm and waved. I grinned. I hadn't yet grasped it all, but I was happy he was here. Relieved. He wouldn't come and go like all the others. He was family. And we needed someone like him. I could do a lot but not everything simply because I was small.

"No, Willi, that's not why. You couldn't do everything because you were just a boy. You might have been tall for your age, you might have seen a great deal, but you were still only ten."

That's why I thought I was going to like Joe. He towered over me, reminded me that adults had more power. Once he was rested and fed, I was sure he would assume some kind of control, perhaps even come up with a plan. Or at least so I hoped. We needed to escape Berlin.

I dashed through the main room with its low ceiling and haphazard collection of glowing lanterns and candles. There was a handful of people already here, which meant there'd already been a raid this morning. Dieter, chewing on a cigarette, was up front on the piano, playing Django's "Nuages." My eyes darted from him to his very elaborate Hohner accordian to a plate on a chair. Potatoes. Fried potatoes cooked on a spirit stove fed with eau de cologne. Brown and glistening with rich goose drippings that we'd been rationing out like caviar. Dieter hadn't taken more than a bite or two.

Like a mongoose, I snuck up behind him and snatched the tin plate. I was out of there before he could cuff me on the head; all he could do then was scream. He'd never been able to catch me on his crutches.

"Willi, *du kleines Schwein!*" Willi, you little pig, he shouted.

But Dieter didn't even lift his fingers from the keyboard, and I tore back to the little room, weaving through the giggles of our patrons who'd witnessed the robbery. I could get away with so much.

Just outside the room, I stopped and patched the holes where Dieter had eaten, mushing the potatoes around so that it looked like a full plate. Then I licked the fork, clasped it nicely in my other hand. I glanced around for Erich—I assumed he'd been bedded down in our makeshift kitchen—then proceeded like a waiter at the Adlon Hotel bearing the finest *Schnitzel*.

Joe's rough-bearded face warmed with a smile as I entered. I would, I guessed, look something quite like him when I grew up.

With a big grin, I said, "You didn't scare me at all yesterday, Mister."

"Hah!" responded Joe, propping himself up on his elbow. "You were scared to death."

"*Nee!*" I responded in my best Berlinese.

My mother's eyes darted quickly from him to me to him to me. She grabbed the tin plate from me and rammed one of her fingers into the mound of potatoes. Frowning, she jabbed her finger in again. And again.

"Willi, these are cold," she said, glaring at me. "You were supposed to get him something hot."

Standing there clutching the fork, I said, "But—"

"How can I serve a sick man cold potatoes? Honestly, Willi, you don't think all the time. Do you know that?" she said, her voice rough with disgust. "Sometimes you're smart, and sometimes you're just plain stupid. Now go—"

It all happened in a matter of castrating moments. My face puffed, puckered. I became a kid again.

Joe reached out and grabbed the plate. "These are fine, I'm sure."

"No, Willi has got to learn to do things right. He just can't go running around scrounging up things on the black market. The war's no excuse. He has to learn to obey."

As if I'd been slapped, I bit my lip.

"Give me an insight beyond your ten-year-old self, Willi. What's really happening here?"

What was she, the woman whose stardom had been squelched by the Nazis, doing talking about obedience? Horseshit. She wasn't mad at me. She was mad at Joe.

He broke in, saying, "But I'm starved! I haven't eaten in two days!"

As if he were one with the Mongol Hordes, Joe sunk his fingers into the gluttonous mass and started scooping.

"Well, for God's sake, Willi," snapped my mother, "give him the fork!"

"Oh, yeah."

I handed it to him, and he rolled on his side. Putting the plate on the bed, he lowered his head and stabbed the luscious chunks that were soft with fat, sweet with tenderness. He went crazy, spearing, barely chewing, practically inhaling the greasy, perfumed tubers. Joe looked up once, saw me smiling at him, grinned back, delighted at the potatoes from heaven.

"What about your brother, Erich?"

Behind me came a light dragging noise. Scrape. Pause. I turned, knowing that noise would forever remind me of him. A very short figure entered. A boy, resembling me but different (thinner face, narrower nose) because Mother had done a *Fern-Trauung*—a marriage by wireless— marrying Erich's claimed-to-be father while he was alive but encircled at Stalingrad. A perfect boy with the glow of an angel, soft and pure, simple and clean. He gazed at me, then Joe, with faint blue eyes that shimmered in the dim light. He wasn't even five, yet already he was a child that could be studied and painted, but never copied. Perfect skin, button nose, full cheeks of youth. And already a soul that was wise and gentle.

"This is Joe," I said to my half-brother.

In his right hand he carried an enamel mug that smoked with hot coffee. In his left he clutched a tiny crutch, a wooden support he could not walk without.

Joe quickly wiped his mouth and, his voice hushed with sadness, said, "Hello, Erich."

"*Hallo*, Mister Cousin."

Voice not from earth. Face too perfect. I glanced down and saw the brace that was always part of him. Metal brace, softened with deep brown leather. It hobbled his shrunken leg, gave him support. Held him. The perfect Aryan child. The classic case of polio.

"I brought you some coffee," he said, his voice far too soft for this time and place. "Real coffee."

"No *muckefuck* for you," I added. No ersatz crud. "It's from Belgium." Mother had sent me down to the rail yards to trade for that just last week.

Eva chided, "And look at how steaming hot it is, Willi. Just look."

"*Vielen Dank.*" Thanks very much, Joe said, unable to take his eyes off the little one.

Good step, drag, good step, drag. His movements rough and uneven, Erich struggled toward Joe, delivered the black, black coffee without spilling a single drop. He handed it to him, and I was overwhelmed with . . . with . . .

"*With what?*"

Sadness. My brother, who was younger than the war, should be gone. To a farm, to the mountains. I could manage here, but he should be anywhere but in ravaged Berlin.

"This is *mein kleine* Erich." My little Erich, said Mother, kissing him on the head.

"Oh, *Mutti!*" Oh, Mommy, he replied, brushing her away.

"*You loved him, too. Why don't you show him?*"

I said, "This is *mein kleines Affchen!*" My little monkey.

"What? I'll show you, you *grosser, grosser Affe.*" You big, big ape.

Erich's eyes sparked to life. Suddenly he was no longer the holy child as his eyes shot up, his mouth opened, and his arm punched into my stomach.

"*Auch!*" I laughed, stumbling backward.

Erich dropped his crutch, dove into me with a string of giggles. I let him pin me against the wall, let him drive punch after punch into my gut.

"Oh, stop Erich!" I begged with a grin.

"You're going to get it this time, Willi!"

I brought my arms up, felt my body jiggle with laughter and a little pain because he did land a couple that kind of hurt.

I shouted, "*Nee, nee,* stop!"

But he only beat on me harder. And then the single bulb hanging from that wire burst with life. Electricity! Raid over. Bombers gone, everyone fine, all good. Berlin survived! The laughter snowballed from the other room, and I heard people shouting for beer, begging for schnapps. My heel caught in the blanket I'd been curled up in, and I tumbled back, pulling my little brother down on top of me.

"Willi, stop it!" flared my mother. "You're going to hurt Erich. Now take him and get out of here! Go fetch beer for our customers!"

Something struck me. Even as I was quieting Erich, handing him his crutch, leading him into the main room, I knew we were being sent out for quite another reason. My mother glared at me, then poured herself more brandy. She intended to tell Joe something. And it was obvious she didn't want me to hear.

"*But you need to hear it, don't you?*"

I'd already suspected it, of course. Deep inside, I'd felt the truth. It would have been better if I hadn't, though.

Better yet if I hadn't snuck back and listened outside the closed door because I never did learn it for a fact. It was just something I've assumed ever since.

"Keep following that, Willi."

I took Erich to the kitchen behind the piano, then crossed through the wild bar and Dieter's music, and snuck back to the little room. I glanced around, but no one noticed as I huddled next to the closed door, bent down, and listened to my mother blast Joe with tears.

"Why did you have to keep pushing? Why?"

"Eva, I'm sorry. I . . . I know once should have been enough, but—"

"But it wasn't, was it? *Mein Gott,* and then you just ran away!" Finally, she spat, "I've hated you ever since!"

Standing outside, I found it difficult to breath. An outline of a story flashed before me, a decadent outline set in the thirties. Dying nightlife. A young singer whose career was halted by the rising power of Hitler. A singer too wild for the times as well as her naive American cousin. And schnapps, lots of it. But just what had happened that one night my mother and her cousin had tumbled so deeply into Berlin's drunken spell?

Mother sobbed, "Opa Wilhelm threw you on the first train, then he dumped me here at this *Pension.* He barely spoke to me again!" With venomous words, she hissed, "I've never left this God-damned place or what remains of it. All these years I've never left because of you!"

I understood and wanted to die right there outside the door. Wasn't my mother really saying she'd never left because of me? Wasn't she really saying she hated me, that it was my fault she'd ended up at this dump instead of on the stage or the screen as the next Marlene? Of course she was because there'd never been a romance with a Wehrmacht captain. That man who was killed by a pothole in Poland was just someone my mother had married in desperation.

And she was telling Joe all this because he was my father.

A huge thing came flying at me. It was Dieter, catapulting himself at me on his crutches. I cowered, bent over, tried to shield myself from the expected blow to the head. Instead, he flew right past, blasted open the closed door.

"Get him out of here!" he said, aiming a crutch at Joe. "There are two Gestapo men up on the street, and they're on their way down here. They've been asking about an American pilot—I told you you were crazy to keep him here!"

"Oh, *Scheissdreck*!" Shit, said Mother. "I didn't mention this to anyone, did you?"

He stared at Joe, simply saying, "*Nee.*"

The next instant the little room exploded with confusion as Mother swigged away the last of her brandy. Dieter twirled around and hurled himself out, then I hurried in. Rushed in and just stood there, staring at Joe, who was now sitting on the edge of the cot. And suddenly I was in his arms. Mister Joe, my American relative, held me and rocked me and squeezed me and kissed the top of my head. So I was right. I could feel it in his tight arms that seemed to want to squeeze me into him. And I hugged back, clung to this man as if I were resurrecting an abandoned wish.

Claws sunk into my shoulder, pulled me back, ripped me out of Joe's embrace.

"Stop it!" ordered my mother. "Joe, you've got to get out of here right now! Willi, take him through the tunnel, show him where to wait." She straightened her dress. "I'll go out and stall them."

I didn't care that the Gestapo was stalking us. I wanted to ask her. I needed to know. But when I looked up into her eyes, her searing glare cauterized my question, sealed it in place. Never, but never was this subject to surface.

She lifted her finger at Joe, dropping her words into a threat. "Not a word of this!"

She stormed out just as Erich, who was as equally well trained as I, scurried in, dragging his bad leg. Wordless, he closed the door behind him, then grabbed the coffee cup out of Joe's hands and lunged for the bed. He took the plate, smeared his lips with the last of the potatoes and goose drippings, next pulled the blanket over him. A smile on his mouth, he looked up. This, his little face said, is a child's room. The child is a little sick. This room is not to be disturbed by anyone, not even the Gestapo.

Erich looked at me, and frowned. "Go, Willi!"

I jumped. Hurrying to the rear of the room, I remembered that wishes and hopes didn't exist in Berlin. I put my shoulder against a heavy wooden dresser, but it barely budged. I looked at Joe. He's just someone, I thought, who fell from the moon.

"Help me, Mister!" I said to Joe.

The chest was supposed to be hard to move because it covered a window of opportunity: a hole. We nudged the dresser back, then dropped behind it and crawled through the opening, Joe disappearing first into the black circle. As I followed, I called out to my little brother.

"Don't be afraid!"

"I won't you *grosser, grosser Affe!*"

Then Joe and I grabbed two handles that Dieter had bolted onto the back of the chest. Yanking and pulling, we dragged it back over the opening. Only a bit of light seeped through the cracks.

Joe's ghostly shape said, "Willi—"

"*Sh!*"

I jabbed a fat candle into his hands, then scratched a match to life, sparked the air, lit his wick. Like a big old lost priest, Joe came to life before me. Me, the littlest boss, brought my finger to my lips. We have to be very quiet, I gestured. And as much as I wanted to reach out and embrace him, I didn't, not out of fear of the truth, but fear of being wrong. I wanted Joe to be my father. I wanted that very, very much.

Clothes. Furs. Bottles. The spoils of early victories were stashed all around us. Against one crude wall were stacked a dozen or so oil paintings. Against another two crates of potatoes. And then three cases of red wine. Two of brandy. Four of schnapps. An entire crate of eau de cologne, enough to scent the entire Schöneberg district, enough to fuel our spirit stove for months. And crystal and china and marmalade and coffee beans. Cigarettes, too, of course. Cartons and cartons of Lucky Strikes and Camels.

"Shit," laughed Joe in a whisper, "this is the A&P of Berlin."

That was right. The black market's supermarket. No ersatz anything here. Using the booze that she'd stockpiled, Mother had been trading and dealing for years, hamstering all the time. The Queen Hamster, and I her dutiful knight who traveled far and wide to carry out her wishes.

I took a candle, lit it, then started out, Joe following close behind. We passed through another chamber, this one smaller and filled with several valises stuffed with furs and silver, then down a passage. I knew just where to turn, where to head. When to duck.

"Ow!" cried Joe, clutching his forehead.

"Oh," I said, trying not to laugh, "I forgot to tell you to bend over."

He looked at me, took advantage of the moment to offer, "Willi, I'm . . . I'm very happy that we've met."

I was speechless.

"No you aren't."

"Me, too."

My ears pricked up, focused on the passage behind us. I'd heard voices, but no one was coming. No one had found the hole. We were safe. Right now.

"Come on," I whispered, a big grin on my face because I couldn't contain my happiness.

I traipsed along, and in a faint voice sang, "No butter with our eats, Our pants have no seats, Not even paper in the loo, Yet Führer—we follow you!"

Joe was amused, amazed, impressed. He was all that I know because I was again his little saviour, leading him to safety. Doing things he could not. That made me proud of myself, made me certain that he liked me. Yes, I thought. He'd hugged me so tightly.

Bearing our candles, we emerged into a big tunnel, a sewer, filled with a rich, thick smell that made nausea tickle the back of my throat. Wetness seeped through my leather shoes. I looked down, held the candle low. I saw not water—not even murky brown water—but something rich and dark and red. My stomach turned. Joe and I were standing nearly ankle deep in blood. Instantly I pictured a building collapsing on a cellar full of folk and pressing the juice of life out of them. Human cider, I thought, as the two of us bolted across the little stream and rushed to the far wall. I gasped for breath, heard Joe gag, cough, nearly vomit.

I reached up and over, grabbed him by the arm, smelled biley coffee and greasy potatoes on his breath. Pulling him along, I directed Joe along a dry strip until we came to a ladder that led up and up. At the top I saw a gray patch of light. I dropped my candle to the ground, clambered hand over fist, bloody shoe over bloody shoe, up toward fresh air. Behind me, Joe began to climb, though slower, more weakly. Up above a building had caved in, and soon the ladder ended and we were stumbling over brick and rock and brick, through another hole, into a burned-out cellar, past a charred body and up the remnants of a staircase. I twisted my feet in the blasted, grimy dirt and watched as the dust caked onto my red-wet shoes.

Once I found my bearings, I darted through the ruins, went right up to a wall. I plastered my eye to a crack. We were across the street and down a ways. But there they were, standing in front of our ruined *Pension*. Two men. No, three, the third in a long leather coat with his back to us.

In a whisper, I said, "Look, that's them!"

Joe came up behind me, peered through another crack. "Who?"

"The Gestapo. I bet you it was those two big guys who went down to the bar. They've come poking around before." I added, "A lady who used to come down to our bar all the time disappeared last week. She got drunk and was complaining about the war and saying how we were going to lose. Everyone thinks these two hauled her away."

The two tall guys. One with brown hair and a moustache, the other bald and brutally strong. Both in dark jackets. Both in dark wool pants. So the goons had searched the bar. They had come on a tip, again found nothing but some Berliners drinking their way through the war's last gasp. And one tin plate of fried potatoes. A plate too big for the little boy who held it.

Then the third man, the obvious boss, turned around, exposing a face that was long and narrow with a tapered nose and slitty eyes and pinkish skin. And tall leather boots that matched the sheen of his leather coat. I'd seen him in our bar, hated the way his eyes never left my mother.

"Jesus Christ," muttered Joe in English.

I glanced at Joe, then the man out there. "You know him?"

"I . . . I . . ." Joe was silent for too long. "No. Nothing. He . . . he just looks like someone I met before the war."

Adults and their secrets, I thought, as this third man started barking orders, a fusillade of syllables pounding out of his mouth like flak: ack-ack, ack-ack. The two tall ones stood stern, determined. The muscular one nodded, ran his hand over his smooth scalp, and then he and the other tall guy took off, running down the street. The eely one, their boss, lit a cigarette and sucked a deep drag. A man of big power, I knew, and hated him.

I nudged Joe, the tip of my elbow poking him in the hip. I gave him the all-clear smile, and we plowed onward through a building, a hole, a shattered skeleton of twisted steel. We were like worms crawling through a skeleton, in and out and up and around and through a mass of mayhem that was randomly rearranged by every bombing. I knew the way, of course. After every raid I went out to see what new pile, tunnel, crater had been created. This was my playground, with colorized photos of Uncle Otto and Aunt Frieda still hanging on that remnant of a wall over there, and that twisted bed up ahead. I was a great explorer, and this was my realm.

We passed into an alley, and I found myself in a warm spotlight of sunshine. Stopping, I looked up. Brilliant blue winter sky. Chilled and clear like Mother's schnapps. No clouds. Führer weather again. And as I admired the cloudless heavens, I wondered what the night would bring. A clear midnight-blue sky adorned by a full white moon? The thought of it made me shiver. But why? Why was this vision again soaking my mind, leaving a bad taste, filling me with dread?

As we hurried along, Joe grabbed me by the sleeve, and I looked up and into the face of the man I was sure had created me. Is this indeed, I wondered, what I will look like?

He said, "Willi, you have to leave Berlin."

"What?"

"There's going to be a major raid. The worst of any."

He proceeded to tell me that on the night of the next full moon there would be an air attack that would make Hamburg and Cologne look like a carnival. A joint British-American raid to end all raids and maybe even the war. All this he'd learned before he'd left his base in England.

"When you go back you have to tell your mother to start packing."

I shrugged, glanced away. "We're going to lose the war, aren't we?"

"Yes," he said with the utmost certainty.

"But what about the secret weapon? There's supposed to be a secret weapon that'll turn back the Red Army and—"

"Willi, Cologne has almost fallen and the Americans are preparing for a breakthrough. Dear Lord, the Russians are about to cross the Oder—the frontal attack on Berlin could begin any day now. They're on their way. There's nothing that's going to stop them. Nothing. And they'll destroy what's left of Berlin as they take it." With a frown he pleaded, "Willi, you and your mother and brother have to leave. Right away. Berlin is about to be flattened. You have to leave, go to the west. Go to a village that'll be taken by the Americans."

"I've told Mama that lots of times," I said, quite proud of myself. "I don't know why she won't go—she's so afraid of the Bolsheviks."

I'd asked and begged, even invoked images of big red Ivans stomping all over her. But nothing worked. Mother was determined to stay in Berlin.

"Yes, you'd warned her."

I shrugged, started on. "Come on, we're almost there."

But I should do more, I thought as I walked. Perhaps I should kidnap Erich and the two of us should escape.

"You can only do so much, Willi. A boy can't do it all."

Maybe Joe could help. He was right. A smothering gag of death was about to be tossed over our little bunker bar. And after that the battle for Berlin would begin, which even I knew would be the bloodiest battle yet. So maybe the two of us could convince Mother to leave. If there really was a godly order to the world, then perhaps that's why Joe had been shot down over Berlin. His mission: to rescue Mother and Erich and me, his bastard son.

My mind was tripping over itself, trying to formulate our westward journey, when I stopped in my tracks. Up there on that wall was a tiny ledge. On that ledge clung an upright piano. We'd nearly reached our destination because this shell of a place was the remains of Opa Wilhelm's apartment house. I looked down into the mound of bricks and boards beneath my feet. Klaus and Konrad were right down there.

Suddenly I froze, nearly paralyzed. Something terrible was about to take place. In a matter of moments there would be gruesome death.

"Don't worry, Willi. It's not the night of the full moon yet and your mother is not here. You'll survive whatever is about to happen."

Even though there was a terrible sense lurking about this place, I forced myself on. I led Joe around and through some ruins just behind the building, on toward another. We trudged around a corner of rubble, and finally reached the remains of a collapsed three-story building that had belonged to a friend of my mother's. A man who'd owned a clothing store and who'd been killed at sea several years earlier. It was in the obscure and hidden cellar of this building that Mother kept a rucksack of supplies. Our secret place, known only to Dieter, Mother, Erich and me. Should we be forced to flee either the Gestapo or the bombs, this is where we were to rendezvous.

Reaching the entrance, I rolled back a sheet of metal, pushed it aside as if I were spinning through the revolving door at the Romanische Cafe. I took a step in, entered this dark little hole, and immediately smelled something. Sensed something. Burning tobacco. The real, genuine stuff. Pure not coarse. My eyes searched, could see no glow of ash. I tensed, froze. Joe came in right after me.

"Joe," I said, "we're not alone."

"What?"

The darkness laughed. It chuckled with deviousness, first low and then high. Something scratched, once, twice, and then a match sparked and lit a lamp. First I noticed a stick of tobacco, squished on the floor, its scent of death still hanging in the air. Then I raised my head only to see two large men, one with a moustache and the other quite strong, standing before Joe and me. And aiming terribly black pistols directly at us.

Joe settled his hand on my collar, pulled me closer. These two goons had come straight here from the bar. They'd been waiting, smoking away their time.

"Your papers!" demanded the moustached one.

Chapter

11

My mind clinked along, struggled to find an escape. Joe and I stood there, the pistols aimed at us, and each second that ticked by seemed like an hour.

Finally, I blurted: "My father and I don't have any papers."

I regretted it as soon as I said it of course. The father part. My veins burned with embarrassment. But how else was I supposed to make them think that Joe was German?

I looked up at Joe, whose entire being was fixed on me in shock. This was as close as we would ever come to speaking about our connection, and it had taken the threat of guns to push us this close. If only we could have shoved those Gestapo jerks out of there just so we could talk father-to-son.

Trying to dig my way out, my mouth began flapping full speed: "We were bombed out last night. This . . . this land mine came down and blew everything apart. A really big, huge one. And then there was a fire in the cellar and we just barely made it out." I choked. "Papa's . . . Papa's uniform was all burned and everything. He's in the Luftwaffe, you see, and his uniform was in pieces. So I found him these coat and pants, and now we have to get bombed-out certificates and he has to return to Templehof."

"You're pretty smart, aren't you? You can really think and act quickly. It takes a lot of guts to stand up to those guts, doesn't it?"

"*Ja, ja, ja,*" I muttered, taking sudden pride in my resourcefulness, "our house was totally demolished. Someone gave me these clothes."

Staring at me as if those guys didn't even exist, as if time would forever be suspended, Joe said, "Thank God my little boy is alive."

The Gestapo men grinned. A clever response. The response of a *Steppke*, a street urchin, their amused expressions said, and a spy, who spoke German well enough and who looked both blond and blue. But not clever enough. After all, if Joe was German, then what was he, a perfectly healthy forty-year-old man, doing wandering around without an insignia, badge, or even a gun? Bombs or no bombs, they said, Joe should have something that identified his military association. *Totaler Krieg,* Total War, Goebbels had decried already two years ago—total mobilization, total effort to save the *Vaterland!*

They descended upon Joe and me, pushing us with the nozzles of their guns, prodding us along like cattle. Since they didn't shoot Joe on the spot, it was quite apparent they intended to drag us down to Gestapo headquarters at Prinz Albrechtstrasse where rubber hoses, little knives, whips, and electrical wires awaited. I'd heard all about that in bits and whispers in and around stories about what was happening to the *Juden.*

A cold metal barrel jabbed into my ribs. *"Auch!"* I blurted.

"Hands up, you little piece of shit!" shouted the bald, muscular one. "Out!"

My hands shot to the skies, and within a few short steps we emerged from the hovel, Joe just ahead of me with his hands clasped behind his head. So they would torture this downed pilot spying about Berlin. What about me? Would they ask me a few questions, then dispose of me with a bullet in the back of my head for helping Joe, the enemy? And what about Erich and Mother? Would they go after them? Would all of us perish simply because blood was thicker than water?

In the distance I heard sirens. Slow rising wails predicting the horror that would soon fall from the heavens. These two thugs were shoving us out, guns at our backs, and Berlin was about to get it again. And I thought, why hadn't Mother taken us far away? Why hadn't she fled to some mountain village?

I tripped, stumbled to my knees. The grunty, muscular one charged up, grabbed me by the neck, kicked me and yanked me to my feet. I cried out, wishing this guy would end up chopped meat in a sausage factory.

"Willi!" shouted Joe, turning around.

The other thug pistol-whipped Joe in the side of the head, and even I heard the crack of metal against skull. As he sank, Joe looked at me, desperate and afraid. For me, I think. He was afraid for me, and I saw Joe struggle against unconsciousness that loomed all around him. And as I watched my . . . my father tumble down and down, I saw his fingers encircle a brick. An Angel of Death, I thought. Just as quickly, Joe bolted up, fired the brick through the air right over me. With perfect aim it struck the bald, muscular one in the side of the head. Catching him off guard, the brick dug into the man's temple. Blood spurting from his wound, he grabbed at his head and collapsed.

I jumped aside and Joe lunged at the moustached one, hurled a fist at him.

"Run, Willi!" shouted Joe.

I couldn't move, not even as the Gestapo man fired point-blank at Joe. The gun exploded, and a bullet whizzed past Joe, past me. Next, the earth hiccuped, rolled. I stumbled. Everything was falling. What . . . what was this?

Another ear-splitting blast. But not from a gun. No, from above. It was a bomb. Bombs. Lots of them shitting down on us! A glorious God-given air raid! I briefly glanced up and saw hundreds of little silver triangles. It was a raid in broad daylight, with Tom and Bill, Mike, Steve, Dick, Paul and Bob all tucking us Germans in with their explosives. As if I were standing out in a spring rain shower, I looked up and grinned.

"Run!" screamed Joe again.

Somehow he'd gathered Superman strength, and was battling the brown-haired one, raw fist after fist. Then Joe landed one square and hard on the agent's cheek. And the guy stumbled back and crumbled to the ground.

Above I heard a bomb whistling and then nothing. Silence. Dreaded silence, and I thought, You're all right as long as you can hear them.

"Get down, Joe!" I cried, dropping and covering my head and opening my mouth.

Some twenty meters away a huge metal thing plunged out of the sky and screeched, burrowed into the earth. But nothing more happened. Trembling, I glanced at it, a big cigar poking in the ruins. A dud? No, a delayed action explosive.

I was up, ready to bolt. "It's a time bomb!" I cried, grabbing Joe by the arm. "Come on!"

At once we were flying over the destruction of Berlin, escaping as fast as we could. Behind us the moustached one had wakened and was now aiming, firing. Bullets whistled like missiles, twanged off concrete, fortunately missing both of us. I stole a look back. The bald man was on his feet, brushing aside blood. And then clambering to his feet, weaving, next racing after us with the other man.

Joe and I ducked behind a wall. A bullet banged like a mad pinball around us. I spotted a hole, and Joe and I squirmed through and emerged in someone's house. Roof above long gone. Family long killed. Ahead I saw blasted couch, pieces of chair: living room. Charging on, we came to remnants of a table: dining room. Pieces of tile: bathroom. Twisted iron frame: bedroom. And then a huge opening: the disintegrated rear of the building.

Zzzzz-t! Bzzzz-t! Firing at us, the two Gestapo men were now not far behind. Joe clasped my hand, charged on, clawing over stone, over pots and pans, over a stove. He ducked, led the way into a courtyard that looked like an imitation of the moon. I spun around. Ahead of us a wall towered blankly to the sky. To the right a pile of carnage too high to climb. To the left, huge hunks of this blasted neighborhood sealed an alley.

"Over there!" ordered Joe.

We hurled ourselves over debris, hunkered down and hid behind a block of stone. I gasped, held the air, tried to quiet my surging lungs. And smiled. Looking at Joe, I grinned, and he lifted a finger to his lips. This was a deadly game. Yes, but . . .

I heard them. The two of them were running through that living room, that bedroom. Past soup pot, past dresser. They emerged in our tomb. This was it, they knew. The final kill. We were in here somewhere. Whether or not they had orders to bring Joe and me in for questioning no longer mattered. We had resisted; they would delight in our kill.

I don't know why, but I wasn't too worried. Joe held my hand. And I looked up and saw another wave of silvery triangles, smudges of black flak bursting around them.

Drop a handful of bombs right here, I thought. Nail these two thugs!

A scream answered my prayers. Another whistling scream from the heavens that started high high high and was plunging toward us with each second, pitch tighter and tighter. No, many whistles. An entire chorus. Then nothing. Silence. That was a full cradle of American bombs, I understood. Eight big ones that started landing—curling, cascading toward us like a tidal wave. Yes, I prayed. Let there be divine justice.

Joe wrapped himself over me and pressed us beneath a beam and to the earth. With my fatherly shield over me, I opened my mouth and screamed as the world exploded. PressureSuction. The all-too-close blast scoured my ears, the shock waves rattled my insides. My heart quivered. It was all so loud I didn't know if I made any noise. I only felt the earth heave, then heard rock and pebble raining down. Finally I did in fact hear myself screaming as wood and stone and shard and pebble continued to pelt down on us. But mostly on Joe.

One of those pots came clattering down, and an instant later it was disturbingly quiet. The wave of bombers had flown on, dumped the rest of their load in the next district.

Through the cloud of gray dust I heard a cry. A baby cry. Brushing aside debris, Joe lifted himself off me. I struggled to raise my head and climb to my feet. Looking over the beam, I saw that our tomb had been cracked wide in one corner and was now entirely different. And empty. The big, bald Gestapo guy had vanished, having apparently been rearranged into something altogether different that was most certainly no longer human and definitely no longer alive.

I gazed around, my eyes following my ears following the whimper. There, off to the side. The other agent, the one with the brown hair and moustache. What remained of him had been hurled to the side and wedged against a wall. He blubbered and looked at me, his blackened face begging for mercy. His right arm was gone, as was most of his left and fresh red blood was pumping out of the severed limbs and flowing over dangling white cords of ligament.

I clambered past Joe and into the opening, where I searched the new rubble that had been blasted from the old rubble. I knew what this Gestapo guy wanted: a bullet in the head. Instant death instead of this grotesque leak of life. But neither his black pistol nor, for that matter, his right arm that had held the gun, was anywhere to be seen. I realized I could bash him with another brick, but . . .

We looked one another right in our grimy faces, right in our eyes, his all full of tears. I felt glad, and with that realized he and the muscular one who had been blown to bits had succeeded in killing a part of me.

"Willi," called Joe from behind.

I stared at that sobbing, bloody stump of a man, then turned, and left him crying like a mouse caught but not killed in a trap, like a mouse that cries under the sink for hour after hour until insanity and a dry heart pushes it over the edge.

I walked up to Joe, and he took my hand in his. While distant bombs continued to smash Berlin, we moved on, leaving the crying brute to trickle to death. Yet while I felt safe with Joe and glad to be alive, I was very disturbed because I couldn't help but wonder who wanted both of us, Joe and me, captured and executed. Simply, I needed to know who had told the Gestapo that one downed American pilot lurking about Berlin had taken shelter at our bunker bar. More importantly, well, of all the stupid holes in Berlin, how had those thugs known precisely where to wait for us? Why were they so cigarette-sure that I would take Joe to the one with that metal flap for a door? And I wondered who had done the blabbing, for as far as I could figure it, aside from Erich and me, there were only two people in Berlin who knew of our secret hovel: Dieter and my very own mother.

Chapter

12

So who in this world of enemies had betrayed Joe and me to the Gestapo? Not who of the millions, but literally which of the two? I shuddered. Did I dare to find out? Did I really want to know the answer? What if it was Dieter, the man who'd been the closest to an uncle I'd ever had? He could want Joe dead, couldn't he? After all, Dieter's elderly parents had roasted under the Allied bombing of Hamburg, and the Allies had blown his leg to bits as well. But what about me? Was Dieter willing to sacrifice me just to get Joe?

So what would I, could I, do if it had been Dieter who'd finked on us? I was afraid. I'd recently waded through blood, and back there I'd witnessed something black and cold and bottomless. From all this I'd drawn sort of a horrific power, one, I knew, that I would never be rid of. I'd been forever infected. To solve problems around here you had to kill people. Was this how I would have to deal with Dieter?

Or Mother? What if she'd turned Joe in, wanting any

memory of him erased? What if that memory included me? Could that possibly be? I trembled. If it were so, what would I be forced to do?

As we came down a street that had just swallowed a few bombs, Joe asked, "How far?"

"Not very."

"Are you all right?"

"*Ja . . .*" I lied, entirely preoccupied with worry and what needed to be accomplished. "How's your head?"

"Attached."

We passed around a corner and onto Hohenstaufen-strasse. This was the northern part of the Schöneberg district and the remains of our little inn were between this street and Grunewaldstrasse, not far from a little park with a museum. It used to be such a nice neighborhood. Five-story buildings, square balconies with old ladies and pots of geraniums, millions of kids. But now . . .

My nose twitched as something rancid curled into my nostrils. Just then Joe stopped in front of a recently collapsed, smoldering building. Tacked to the remains of the entry was a battered sign that read: "Help, we're buried alive. Please dig us out!"

Joe said, "There're people down there, we have to get them out."

I sniffed the air again, smelled fat, all black and drippy, imagined it splattering on hot embers. And I knew those people down there had partially predicted their fate by placing that sign. They were indeed buried. But from the tangled mess of charred wood, from the rank smoke, I could tell a lot was cooking down there. Probably had been roasting since yesterday's firebombing.

"*Nee*, it's too late."

Wordless, Joe shuffled after me as we clambered over a sign that read *Parfums and Blumen*, turned down another of the endless streets lined with despair. Heard screams in the distance. Laughing. We passed a little girl smaller than me. She was crying and carrying a rucksack on her back, hurrying on. Was it her mother, father, or brother who'd just been killed? Were all of them now gone?

Minutes later the skeleton of our *Pension* loomed before us. I'd been thinking of murder, of what I would do to our own would-be murderer, and I realized Joe shouldn't go back down to the bunker bar. Not now. Not yet. It wasn't safe. If Dieter had turned him in, he could just as easily call the Gestapo again. If Mother was responsible, well . . .

"You'd better not come with me," I said, and then offered the last of my reasons. "You know, in case that other agent, the one in the leather coat, is still around."

The pinkish-skinned one, I meant. And that was a very real chance, for he could be down in the bar drinking a beer, caressing Mama with his eyes.

Joe said, "You're probably right. But what about you?"

Using my favorite English word, I said, "Okay, I'll be okay."

"You were great back there, kid. With those Gestapo guys."

He hugged me, but what could I say? Thanks, Papa. Gee, Papa, I got it all from you. Gosh, I just know how to get around. Or: I survive.

Instead, I looked at the ground, at Joe's feet. Why did I feel so ashamed? Why were the truth and I so secretively linked? I shook my head. I was right, wasn't I? Joe was more to me than a cousin, wasn't he? There had been an evening when booze and turmoil and Mother and Joe had all rushed together and conceived me, hadn't there?

I muttered, "I'll be back in a couple of minutes."

Joe slunk into the entry of a demolished building, and I hurried down the street, trying not to think of my beginnings, but instead a plan. As I neared the *Pension* I heard voices and slowed. Laughter. Was there an entire troop of soldiers here now? Did I even dare to return to my own home?

I slithered along the outside wall of our hotel and peered into the remains of the original *Kneipe*. Through a shattered window I saw her, wearing her light brown wool coat and that hat of hers, an oblong thing of wool rimmed with chestnut brown fur. I stared at her, my mother, and saw her fawning on the arm of some swarthy man with dark hair and dark eyes and sporting a fedora and long topcoat. Perfectly still, I watched as Mother lost her balance, clung to this man, giggled and whispered something to him that he instantly liked. Yes, there'd been a raid and obviously more booze and song. None too steady, Mother led him through the ruins of the *Kneipe* and up toward the front of the building. I'd never seen this man. Who was he, why was Mother pouring herself over him so? Was he also Gestapo, a partner perhaps of that slender man with the pink face?

The man stopped, unbuttoned his coat and reached in. He glanced from side to side, up and down, and no one but me saw the wad of money he pulled out and started peeling. *Ein, zwei* . . . It was, I thought, strange money. All the same size, all the same color. Where does such small green money come from? I nearly gasped. America. Those weren't Reichsmarks, but American dollars. And Mother was quickly accepting them, opening her coat and using them to plump her breasts.

That done, the swarthy one buttoned his coat, then seized my mother and pressed his mouth to hers in a long, lustful encounter that was whorish and disgusting. It went on so long that I cast my eyes down. And when they parted, a long windy sigh gushed from my mother's lips. Finally, the man darted off.

"*Auf Wiedersehen!*" laughed my mother.

The man trotted onto the street, glanced directly at me,

hesitated for just a moment, then turned in the other direction and hurried on. Disgusted, I rushed into our building. Mother, clutching her wool coat around her, was leaning against a wall, her painted eyes fully shut. I studied her thick red lips, those brightly varnished nails, and I thought, this is too much. There is a war. There are people dying, roasting all around.

The anger growled from my throat in a nervous cough. Mother's eyes fluttered awake, gazed down at me, blinked slowly.

"Willichen."

She raised her arm, hand dangling. I, of course, went to her, ready to attack but forcing myself to halt just out of arm's reach. A cloud of her sweet, flowery perfume enveloped me.

"Who was that man?" I demanded.

She lazily grinned at me, her son. "Just a friend of ours."

I breathed in her perfume and from her lips I detected a thick scent of over-ripe, intoxicated apples. *Apfelschnapps.* I would forever be disgusted by it and brandy because they would always remind me of my mother's daily stupor.

"You're drunk."

She laughed. "I keep telling you, Willi," she said, swaying slightly, "that I'm trying to enjoy the war because the peace is going to be horrible."

"What did that man want?"

She giggled, dropping down on me as if I were a luscious piece of fruit. "There are certain things that little boys shouldn't know."

Like where mothers get booze when there's none to be had. Somehow it just managed to appear. Once a week or so, like magic, a truck would pull up and glum Danish or French laborers would leave us with a case of this or that. Even a few bottles of the priceless Hennessy cognac. I knew where to get cigarettes and chocolate and coffee—

Mother often sent me down to the railyards to trade bottles of brandy for them—but her source of beer and schnapps and even vermouth was her most precious and most guarded secret. It was, she often laughed, her only trade secret.

She wrapped her arms around me, squeezed me into her waist, nestling me against her and nearly extinguishing my anger. Mother, I thought, just hold me, tell me everything will be all right. Keep me small so that you may always watch over me.

Rubbing my neck, kissing me on the top of my head, she said, "There was a raid, but you're fine. *Mein kleiner Soldat*, I don't ever have to worry about you, do I?"

Yes, she did. She did! Crushed in my mother's embrace, I wanted to start beating on her, begging her to worry, just even a little. Just sometimes.

"Is she ever sexually inappropriate with you, Willi?"

Disgusted, I shoved myself back. Mother was like this with everyone, she was a master at using her affections to manipulate the world. By stroking your back, cooing in your ear, growing angry, then giggly, she could change borders more effectively than any soldier. And nearly always get what she wanted. Her secret weapon. Though she never took it beyond this stage with me, I'd seen her push much further and ensnare countless men.

I brought my anger to a boil again, forced myself to keep hot-tempered.

"Mama, those two guys from the Gestapo—the one's who've been at the bar before—they knew just where to wait for Joe and me. We went to our secret place, and they were already there, just waiting for us!"

Her schnapps eyes snapped open. "What?"

"They were there—with guns! And they fired at us and they tried to kill us!"

She trembled, paled with fear. Her body tried to fight off

the truth. But couldn't. I stared up at her and realized what it meant. She knew. A part of her knew.

As meanly as I could, I accused her, saying, "It was you who turned Joe in, wasn't it?"

Drunken, appleish gasp. Cloud of disgusting perfume. Hand pulled back ready to bat my face. A swing . . . And I caught my mother's wrist and squeezed. I wasn't so young, so little. Not any more. And I could, I sensed, just snap that bone, break it like a dried branch.

"*Himmelkreuzdonnerwetter!*" she cursed, twisting free. "You little bastard, I didn't tell anyone!"

But I saw a flicker in her eyes. There was more. Of course there was. I wanted to strike her, to knock her down. To hit her for every man she'd caressed under the table, for every stranger she'd met under the sheets.

"Then how did they know?"

Switching course, she screamed, "*Mein Gott,* you've no idea what I've been through!"

Of course I did. I did because she'd pulled me through the deepest of the muck. That's why I hated her so. Oh, yes. I'd seen it all, often better than she because she always had brandy or schnapps to blind her while I had nothing.

I yelled, "Joe says we should leave Berlin as soon as possible. I think so, too."

"What?" she gasped. "You're just a child, a boy, you don't know what's best. I'm your mother and you'll do as I say!"

"But Joe says—"

"You think you know everything? Do you remember two years ago when they took Erich from us and put him in that home for the handicapped? Then they started to evacuate it, planned to take all the crippled children up to some castle in the mountains. Nice and healthy. And do you know what goes on up there? Well, do you?"

My eyes fell to the ground. "*Nee.*"

"Of course you don't. But I did. The papers have been filled for years with excessive obituaries. Of course Erich wouldn't have come back." She stared at me, eyes viperish. "So I rescued him. He has a bad leg, that's all. I won't tell you how, but I paid dearly for him. And he's here and hasn't been out of my sight since."

"Mama . . ."

Her voice rising, screeching, she added, "And do you know they wanted to take you last year?"

"What?"

"That's right, they wanted to take you to dig trenches in Alsace. But even though you're big for your age, you're just a child. A child. I couldn't let you go, and besides I needed your help here with Erich and everything. And so I paid for you too, Willi."

"What does this tell you?"

Perhaps I didn't know everything. Perhaps I was just a boy. I wanted to cry, to melt back into my childhood. And I felt guilty for never having realized that my mother had done something for me, for never having believed that she loved me.

"I pay—over and over and over again—to keep that bar of ours," she screeched on. "It should have been closed as superfluous to the war effort, but because of my so-called payments, it's viewed not as a bar, but a safe bunker for Berliners. And so it stays open and so we eat." She shook her head in disgust. "You naive little boy. We can't possibly leave. I have connections here, contacts. Do you understand? Do you? I can get anything we need, anything we want. I know how to keep us alive here in Berlin!"

Her face was streaked with black tears. She was right. I knew nothing. Understood nothing. I reached out, begged for her arms around me again.

"Mama . . ."

"Nee!"

Repulsed, she jerked away from me and buried her face in her hands and sobbed and sobbed. Disgusted with myself, I stood there, a boy-island stranded off the coast of his mother. My fingers crept over my own face and hid it, blackening the very sight of me.

Leather slid over bits of rock. I looked through my fingers. Joe. He was standing in what had been the doorway to the *Kneipe*. I was on my feet, running at him, hurling myself into his strong embrace. He wrapped a single arm around me, only one arm because Mother rushed to him, too, and he held her against him and against me. Then I felt fingers stroking my head, combing my hair, and I was happy. I clung to her hand as it curled around my neck, and I hung on to Joe. Never had I felt so secure.

"Remember this, Willi. Remember how warm and loving this feels, for this family portrait will be your anchor forever and ever."

I cried, wishing only that Joe and Mother could lift us all out of Berlin, could take us far away. Then something broke it all.

"Hey!" cried a small voice.

Behind us, leaning on his little crutch, stood Erich, having snuck out of the bar. He was never supposed to leave without Mother or me, but obviously he'd grown tired of waiting.

"What about the zoo, Mutti? You promised!"

She hurried to him, grabbed him and buttoned up his little wool coat.

"Of course, my *Mäuschen!*" My little mouse, she said, bundling him.

"Willi, too?" he asked.

I nodded and smiled, went over, and said, "I'm sorry, Mama."

Without looking at me, she quite soberly said, "War makes us all crazy."

Joe said, "Eva, did Willi tell you? There were two guys waiting for us."

She nodded. "It's not good. None of it."

What was she still holding back? There was something. I knew it. Was it connected to the black market and her source of liquor? Perhaps to the man with all those American dollars?

"Mama," I ventured, "Joe needs papers. If they stop him and he doesn't have anything they'll shoot him as a deserter."

Mother nodded and agreed. "Come on," she said, her voice dry. "Willi's right, Joe. You can't go wandering around without identification. We have to get you at least a ration card. I promised Erich the zoo—he hasn't been out in days—but this we'll do first."

She grasped Erich by one hand, and we all started out into the street. And there I stopped. High in the sky, against the day's chilly blue sky, hung a pale white moon. I shaded my eyes against the sunlight, stared up at the bizarre thing hanging there. Tonight it would be a big bomber's moon, but not quite the full one that Joe had talked about. Not yet. It still had a bit of a bite chomped out of it. In a day or two, though, Joe's raid would take place. Was that enough time to talk my mother out of Berlin? Would that ever be possible?

Joe reached down and scooped up Erich and plopped him down on his shoulders. I rushed after them all, jumped up and tweeked Erich on the butt. He shrieked a laugh, swatted at me. I leapt up again, this time striking the metal hardness of his leather-covered brace.

"Eva," asked Joe, "where are we going?"

"To get you papers, of course."

Mother said it as if it were as easy as picking up the evening paper. Then again, she could chip coffee beans from bricks, squeeze schnapps from bombs.

"But—"

"It's not too far. Up near the Tiergarten. We'll drop you off and then wait for you at the zoo."

"Drop me off?" said Joe, unable to hide his puzzlement. "Where?"

"At Loremarie's," I chimed.

Erich whispered, "She's a countess and she has a special secret."

Chapter

13

She was a real Brünnhilde. Big, plump, pointed breasts that had always amazed me. Beautiful large face with high cheek bones that dominated, overshadowed green eyes— eyes that seemed buried with distrust. Complexion: Alpine rosy. Lots of dairy. White teeth. Good white teeth. Good skull, and the great facial proportions I'd been taught when I'd last attended school—small mouth, narrow nose. Motherly broad pelvis. A prime example of an Aryan *Fräulein* from toe to top and hip to hip. Just missing the dirndl.

Whenever I saw her I thought of pure German blood, ancient blood, and the Kaiser and Wagner and Prussian estates. Sometimes I feared her. In fact, I was sure she would attack Joe, the enemy, and when Mother led us up to the remains of the once stately house not far from the Tiergarten—a house that had no windows, only holes; no stucco, only blast-beveled brick—when Mother, Erich-on-Joe's-back, and I crossed the shattered walk, then continued between two burned columns, and through a rectangular hole, into the shell, to the left, around where

120

the upper three floors lay now compressed in the salon, and back to the small room. When Mother walked in and we found Loremarie eating a hard roll and pale ersatz eggs that had been cooked on a little burner until they'd curdled into rubbery bits, Mother blurted out:

"*Hallo,* this is my *amerikanischer* cousin."

Well, that's when I nearly lost it. For a handful of seconds, I watched as Loremarie studied Joe, ran those deep greens of hers over him like an x-ray, and I thought: This is it. Over. *Kaput.* She's going to turn all of us in. No, first she's going to shoot him, then us.

But then Erich wiggled down, dropped to the floor, and threw himself fearlessly at this real countess named Loremarie—actually Tante Lore to Erich and me for she was a *Nenntante,* an aunt of affection—and she burst out laughing and giggling. And that's when I was sure once and for all that the good side in her had won. When I saw her face light with life, her lips pucker with love for my little brother, I charged her, too, for obviously she had won the battle against evil many, many years ago. I threw myself at her, clutched her big waist, and she kissed Erich and me, poked at us mercilessly until we both cried out in a chorus of giggles.

Then she turned to Joe and in perfect English said: "Where the hell you been all my life?" She sloughed off Erich and me, steamed right over to him, smooched him on the cheek and bellowed, "Welcome to beautiful Berlin."

"*Danke,* it's a pleasure to meet you," the stunned Joe managed to stammer in German.

She roared. She threw her plump hand to her mouth as great balls of laughter shot out like cannon balls. "A Berlin accent! A pure Berlin accent!"

Joe looked at Mother for help. Is this lady, his eyes said, for real? Can I trust her?

Mother nodded, proudly said, "His parents were Berliners, you know, and he grew up speaking German at home."

"Really?"

"Really," Joe added.

She quizzed: "Say *d-a-s*."

Joe said it the only way I knew how to pronounce it, nice and hard: "*Dat.*"

"Say *w-a-s!*"

"*Wat.*"

"I-c-h!"

"Ick."

She screamed a laugh. "*Wunderbar*—a Berlin accent! I can't believe it. There's something a little odd about it—a tinge foreign perhaps—but that's it! Thick and coarse. Amazing!"

Smothering arms, hefty embrace. Erich and I watched as Loremarie nearly squeezed the air out of Joe. Obviously he'd passed the acid test.

Mother settled into a chair. "He has no papers. Can you help us?"

Silence. She studied him, bit her lower lip. Her hand on his chin, twist: right profile. Twist of the chin again: left profile. She was pensive. Joe was obviously worried. Finally, her smile.

"*Ja, ja ja.*"

"How soon?" asked Mother.

"No problem. He won't have any trouble doing one for a German face like that."

No, I thought. Loremarie's special secret wouldn't have any trouble with Joe. I'd seen what he could do. Even I knew this would be a snap.

I looked around. There was the little wooden table Loremarie had been seated at eating her ersatz eggs, a ratty couch with a blanket that doubled as a bed, a cracked mirror on a pale blue wall. A dresser. No, none of this furniture belonged in here. What belonged in this expansive room with its elegant molding and white burst of plaster in the middle of the high ceiling was a huge plane of wood. A dinner table. Yes, this had been the dining room of a fancy city home. Aristocrats from all across the continent, she'd told me any number of times, had dined here. Aristos from Germany, Russia, Hungary, Czechoslovakia, Poland.

An instant of old Berlin shot through my head. Civilized, cultivated, orderly Berlin, the one that had been recounted to me like a beautiful fable. The artistic mecca of Europe where all were accepted, tolerated. I looked at the dusty floor, saw an oriental carpet and a little packed suitcase and a thermos flask. And now this is where Loremarie lived and was ever-ready for the next raid. *Ja, ja, ja,* as she would say, her little empire had been reduced to these few square meters.

Mother plunked herself down at the rough wooden table and pulled out her sterling silver flask that was always filled with Hennessy cognac. I stared: Do you have to? Loremarie stared: Now?

"Well, just don't stand there, Willi," Mother barked. "Get us some glasses."

With a sit, sit, sit, Loremarie instead banished Erich and me to a wobbly settee, pulled a chair for Joe, then bustled over to a little wooden cabinet. Over her shoulder, she asked a double-loaded question.

"No one else coming?"

"What?" asked Mother.

Bluntly: "No one followed you?"

Mother's face flushed, fell. Followed? Us?

From the sidelines, I blurted, *"Nee,"* for my eyeballs had lingered behind us several times.

Joe said, "I didn't see anyone either."

"Gut."

Loremarie put exactly four biscuits on a plate, handed

the dish to me. All at once Erich was slathering over me like an eager puppy, hands poking, voice whining.

"Don't wet your pants!" I ordered.

He snatched two of the precious things, one in each hand, and immediately started stuffing his face. I rolled my eyes. He was dropping more crumbs on his trousers than he was cramming into his mouth. I was sure I'd never been such a slob.

As I defended the last biscuit—my second one—from a brotherly raid, I ate my first slowly and adultlike, not enjoying it, I realized, nearly as much as I would have otherwise. Then again, they were weak, watery war biscuits. And as I chewed, I watched Loremarie take out a cracked glass, a china cup with little roses on it, and another china cup with little chips flaked from its rim. She handed the nicest one to Joe. Our guest, I thought. Our hero?

"Sorry," said Loremarie. "We used to have a lot of nice things."

She looked upward. Not to God. Not to the Heavens. To the triangles in the sky. Yes, she used to have a lot of nice things before the bombs fell. All this she said with her eyes, a little shrug.

"Sorry about this place," she also said. She started laughing and shaking like a big bowl of gelatin. "It used to have windows!"

"So what? This city used to have fantastic cabarets and wonderful jazz." Mother poured them cognac and proposed a toast: "To a speedy end!"

Loremarie giggled, glanced through her holey house to make sure no one was peeping in, listening in, ready to shoot us all for defeatism. She then leaned forward with a *Flüsterwitz*, a whispered joke, which calloused Berliners had always excelled at. She even motioned at Erich and me, eager for us boys to hear as well.

"You see," she began, glancing at Joe, wanting his approval, "there were three good fairies right there at Hitler's birth. The first decreed that every German be intelligent, the second wished that every German be honest, and the third that every German should be a National Socialist. Then came along this bad fairy who said every German could possess only two of these three things. Hence we have intelligent Nazis who are not honest, honest Nazis who are not intelligent, and honest, intelligent Germans," she blurted, banging her chest with a pointed finger, "who aren't Nazis!"

The humor primed their throats for cognac and the cognac primed their laughter. Erich and I followed suit, chuckled with crumbs on our lips, laughed loudly to make sure they heard us, to make sure they understood we understood. Beneath us, the settee wiggled, and Erich crammed one of his biscuits into his mouth, then snatched my last one from the plate. I swatted him, weaseled it back, careful lest Mother should see us struggling. Someone, she would scream, is going to get hurt!

"Eva, this is great cognac," Joe said, a warm glow coming over his face. "Where did you get it?"

"Oh, Evchen," quipped Loremarie, "can get anything. Anything. She knows how to get by, this one. And thank God."

"What's their relationship like?"

"I can't imagine a better friend," said Loremarie, her appreciation so strong that she sounded sad. "I truly don't know how we'd have made it this far without her."

Coy as the cabaret singer she'd always wanted to be, Mother poured herself more and said, "I have my contacts."

And her little people, I thought, to do her errands. I was Mama's little delivery boy. Go ahead, Joe, I thought. Ask her. Push. Learn it all. I wanted him to have the full picture of this wartime woman.

"What kind of contacts?" he asked naively.

Loremarie blurted, "Every kind! Eva knows everyone in Berlin."

"*Ja*, Tante Lore's right!" I chirped.

So many contacts that I couldn't keep track of them all. So many dealings that I was out and about every day.

Mother stared at Loremarie, face stern, then turned to me. Silence, you little brat, her eyes burned. I smiled. Forget it.

"Really?" said Joe, not at all surprised. "So what do you do with these contacts?"

Tension pulsed the air. Shot through. The black market was part of our gene pool. Blonde hair, blue eyes, and God-damn-it, I'm going to make it thought this shit. Yes, good for Mother. She was—with my nimble help—keeping us alive. But Joe had to know more. I wanted that because I saw a halo of darkness hovering over Mother's head. And I wanted him to dust it aside. I wanted him to protect her.

Chewing my biscuit, I casually cracked the stalemate. "First she was dealing with ration cards, then coffee and French perfume. But now it's cigarettes for drinks, isn't it, Mother?"

"Willi!" she snapped.

Erich, who was licking crumbs from his fingers, looked up and matter-of-factly said, "We sell beer for cigarettes."

"You boys be quiet! Both of you!" she ordered, then quickly took a gulp of cognac.

"Really, Eva," said Loremarie, "I think it's interesting for him." She turned to Joe, and added, "You see, whatever's hard to obtain is the new currency here in Berlin."

I looked from her to Joe to Mother to Joe. That's right. People rushed to our underground bar for safety, for drinks that calmed nerves, for Mama's song that calmed souls as the sky fell and Berlin shook, collapsed, burned. Yes, while all this was happening above, the adults were wooping it up below, living, laughing, drinking, all for the mere price of a few cigarettes. Sticks of tobacco that Mother would then have me trade for whatever was wanted or needed, whatever her contacts had or whatever was found down at the train yards. Caviar or eau de cologne, occasionally potatoes.

I sat forward. Press on, Joe, I thought, willed. There was more. The dangerous part.

"But no one knows where she gets beer and schnapps," I dared murmur.

Joe grinned, slyly asked, "So where do you get it, Eva? That has to be the tricky part."

Embarrassed by this dirty corner of her life, she was on her feet and storming me within an instant. I knew what was going to happen, and I jumped from the settee, the plate crashing to pieces at my feet. I was ready to dart away, but then I stood still. I hadn't backed down from the Gestapo today. I wouldn't from my own mother.

She grabbed my shoulder, pinched through my clothing, squeezed my skin. "I told you to be quiet!"

I bit my lip, felt my anger at her bubbling just below the surface. I'd always done her errands, but no more. Why should I when she wouldn't even take us out of Berlin? In defiance, I slowly raised my right hand and open palm in a salute to my very own little Hitler.

"*Sieg Heil!*"

She blanched, froze, just as I'd planned. "Oh!"

"Willi!" gasped Loremarie.

I did it again, just for the shock of it. "*Sieg Heil!*"

I expected to be slapped, but I didn't expect her fury. Suddenly my own mother was upon me, shaking me, screaming. Her frustrations came at me tanklike, rolling over me as she yelled and shoved me from side to side.

"Stop it!" she shouted.

Suddenly I started to crumble. Although my recently-recognized anger at my mother was real, my just-flexed strength was only pretend. I was trembling all over. Some-thing struggled to the surface. A stretched wail, a huge sob. A man-child's plea. Erich hopped off the seat, limped over, reached out for me.

"Don't!" Mother snapped at him. "Get away! He's got to learn to do as I say."

My weak defenses fell to the ground, and all my fears streaked forward, naked and shivering. Bomb, blast, fire had all taken a toll. And this was the real me: terrified to the inner core. Mother released me, and I stood there, crying out of anger at what had already been lost and what would never be.

Head shaking in disgust, Mother turned away. Turned back to her chair and her silver flask of cognac, took a deep, ribbony gulp. Mother glared at me, looked at Loremarie and Joe. It's not my fault, she shrugged. Really, it's not. What did I do?

I admitted defeat, took a weak step toward her. "Mama, Ma—"

"Quiet, Willi."

"But—"

"Quiet!"

I melted into sniffles.

"That's quite enough," continued my triumphant mother between swigs two and three.

With a long slide of my sleeve, I cleaned my nose and my eyes. I reined it all in, and I thought, Can't I be afraid just a bit?

"Now come here," commanded Mother.

Arms at my side, face drooping with shameful tears, I inched toward her. I went to her, and she reached out and I flinched. But then her hard fingers went through my hair. Once. Twice. No, I thought. More. Give me more!

"That's better," she said. "That's my little soldier. I can't have two babies to take care of, can I?"

I stood there, silent.

"Answer me! Can I?"

"*Nee.*"

"Of course, I can't," said Mother, patting me briefly on the back but keeping me at a distance. "There's just too much to do. We rely on you for so much. You have to be strong. We need a man in the house to protect us. And that's you, *mein kleiner Soldat.* Right?"

Peep: "*Ja.*"

"That's right. You have to take care of us. Now apologize to Loremarie and Joe for the scene you made."

Joe said, "That's not necessary."

Her neck stiffened as she cocked her head back. "This is none of your business."

"But—"

"Don't you start, too!"

Loremarie was up and bustling, soaking a cloth in a dish of water, rushing over and scrubbing my tear-soaked face. If only Adolf could be wiped away so easily. If only it weren't costing tens of millions of lives just take his.

"Take a good look at yourself, Willi. Step away and tell me what you notice?"

Everything seemed to freeze, caught in that particular moment. And while I found myself unable to move, an invisible part of me separated, floated upward and around like a ghost. I hovered behind myself, and as if my own head were a simple clock that had been opened, I could see in clearly, perfectly. And all the strange workings now made sense. I'd been forced into adulthood, I realized, but I wasn't mature. I was ahead of my time but I was still a kid. I had all the ammo but none of the means to handle it. Yes, I understood. My mother needed me and my brother needed me, and I was trying so hard to serve them. But I needed help, too. I was carrying a burden too great for my tender years. I just needed what we all did: an untorn place to grow.

"*Exactly.*"

It was that simple, and I could now see it all and had to communicate it all. Mother had to know. She was too overwhelmed with the war to see. So I had to tell her, because if she knew, she'd understand. And make everything right. I needed that.

Suddenly the scene resumed, snapped back into motion by Joe.

"Eva," he said, as if he'd heard all my thoughts, "he's only ten. He's only a boy. He's afraid. We're all afraid."

"That's right," she barked. "We're all afraid. So we all have to rise to the situation. We all have to be more, do more. Isn't that right, Willi?"

Why couldn't I say all that I felt? Why did I have the ability to see everything, feel everything, but lack virtually all of the means to express it? The dichotomy of youth. It was so tortuous. As if I were casting out a lifeline, I turned to Joe for help.

He said, "Give the kid a break. He's—"

"Enough!" pronounced Mother.

She stared at me, burned me with her eyes. Forced me to squelch my anger, confusion.

Loremarie again broke the war, suggesting, "We'd better get to work."

"What do you mean?" asked Joe.

Quite queenly lest we forget to whom we were all beholden, Mother said, "Your documents, Joe." She stood and held out her hand. "Come along, Erich. Let's go to the zoo while they do their business."

I was staring at the floor, mesmerized by the swirl of red and blue flowers of the oriental carpet. I was drifting away when I felt a little hand brush my own. I looked into my little brother's eyes, and I realized there was something this very tiny child understood about me that I would never understand. Something about the guilt I experienced for not taking up even more of the slack, the slack that curled at my feet, and sometimes tripped me. Oh, and how I admired the early dignity that Erich's handicap had led him to, a dignity that I could never claim. Already my life was soiled. Always I would be on a stage of war.

Mother was holding out a hand, and Erich smiled at me, then limped over to her. Mother fastened his coat, her own, then started out. On the edge of the hallway, Mother turned but did not look at me. Was it because she truly didn't care for me? Or couldn't she bear looking at her shame?

"Willi, be a dear," she said, "and bring Joe to the zoo in, say, an hour. We'll meet by the elephant pen. All right?"

"*Ja.*"

Mother and Erich left, plodding their way through the ruins of Loremarie's once fashionable house where actors and artists and aristos had vented and drank.

As soon as she was gone, Joe turned to Loremarie, and said, "She's changed."

Beautiful Brünnhilde motioned out to a hole, to a crater, to the moonlike city, and laughed, "So has Berlin." Then a hiss of frustrated air whistled over her lips, and she admitted, "You know, she's never been the *Kinder, Kirche, Küche* type. And that's why I've always loved my dear Evchen. She blazes the way for the rest of us. But you're right." Glancing at me, she hesitated, then added, "*Ja*, Eva's . . . Eva's different now."

I turned away from Loremarie, stepped into the hallway, looked up at the cascade of shattered boards and beams. Wiping my face, I thought how it really didn't matter whether or not Mother had changed. Not now. What mattered was getting out of here. Mother had said we needed to stay in Berlin because she knew how to stay alive in this place, but didn't she see, wasn't it obvious that Berlin was dying and that this great metropolis would take her and everything else with it to the grave?

I heard Loremarie and Joe whispering behind me. I didn't know what they were saying exactly, but I sensed pity, worry. I was a magnet. Or a big ear. At the same time, I didn't realize how tired I was. No matter what, though, this I had to do, push for. I spun back into the dining room.

"We have to leave the city," I blurted.

"Oh, Willichen, of course we do," said Loremarie, coming up to me and wrapping a hand around my head. "Everyone's nerves are shot. This is especially no place for children."

I gazed up at her. "Tante Lore, I don't want the Russians to get my mother!"

"Of course not." Loremarie looked at Joe. "The Reds are killing and raping everyone, you know. They're taking the most disgusting revenge for Stalingrad and Leningrad."

"I've heard rumors."

"It's true, Joe, it is," I said somewhat desperately. "Herr Lichter—he lives down the street—said they made his brother watch as ten Russians raped his wife."

"Willi!" gasped Loremarie.

"Herr Lichter told me himself! It was in Silesia. And then . . . then they nailed her to a barn door and made her watch as they cut open her husband."

"Oh!"

Joe said, "Loremarie, there's got to be a way to get out of Berlin. We have to go west and meet up with the Americans."

"*Ja, ja!*" I shouted. "We could leave tonight!"

Disturbed, Loremarie started bustling about. She gathered cups and glasses, straightened up dirt over debris that would undoubtedly be entirely shifted, dusted, destroyed after the next raid.

"We've . . . we've been working on something, you know," she said. "But it takes time. Travel is very difficult now—there are so many check points and the trains are barely running. And then there's the strafing." She stared at Joe. "Thousands of people have been killed by your low-flying planes, you know. I just hope it isn't too late."

Too late? No. No! It was never too late. My mother was just mixed up. Confused. She'd been under too much pressure. She'd been struggling so hard and for so long just to stay alive and feed herself and Erich and me and her soul, and this wasn't right. She shouldn't even be here, buried in Berlin. No, Mother's rightful place in the world was on a star, singing, enchanting. There was still time. The full moon wouldn't arrive for another day or so.

"We can make it!" I insisted.

"Perhaps." Loremarie's feet crunched over bits of carved ceiling plaster. "Well, let's get to work. We haven't much time."

"Much time for what?" asked Joe.

I replied, "For Anton to do his work."

Chapter

14

"Who's Anton?"

"A special friend," I said as we headed out of the room. After all, he was even closer than a *Nennonkel*, which was why Erich and I called him by his first name. Anton. Just Anton who made us things. "An artist."

Ahead of us I saw Loremarie glance back, her face blush red. He was her very good, very close friend.

"He'll do papers for you, Joe," I continued.

Loremarie said, "Actually, he's doing papers for all of us. Me, him, Eva, the boys. Dieter."

Dieter. My one-legged, would-be uncle. What should I do? Should I tell Joe that it might have been Dieter who'd directed the Gestapo to us? Then something else struck me. If he wanted Joe dead and perhaps me, what about Mother?

"What kind of papers?" asked Joe.

Ones that would lead us to Switzerland or at least as far as Yankee territory, she said. Of course we had to get out of here. With the Ivans nearing and the Führer about to go

134

into his final throes, Berlin would be sucked down in a whirlpool of blood.

Switzerland, I thought. Good. Out of here. Away. Now. I pictured Erich and me in that mountain-studded fairyland, Erich's cheeks out all bright and rosy. I tried to imagine a night without bombs.

We made our way back through the ruins, from the once fashionable dining room, down a broad hall that was littered with wood splinters and pebbles of glass. Our special friend, Anton, was no less than a troll. A troll who hid in the bowels of this house and who painted and drew with anything on anything. Still lifes and forged papers.

"So where's this Anton?" asked Joe.

"Just wait," I said. "It's the best hiding spot."

This had been a beautiful place, Loremarie told Joe as she crunched through her home, leading us across a soggy red carpet, over boards and debris. A glorious house, just a block from the Tiergarten. A city residence for an old family whose seat was a modest *Schloss*, castle, in Silesia that had been in the family for over four centuries. Now the castle was gone, or at least gobbled up by the Ivans, who had ground up her two brothers during the crushing defeat of Operation Zitadelle—our last big offensive in the east. Her mother had died before the war, and her father? She didn't know. They hadn't spoken in years. He was a staunch supporter of all the Hitlers, little and big, and he'd outfitted them with their favorite uniforms from his vast mills. In a way, she mused, she hoped he was dead so he wouldn't see what had happened to his beloved Vaterland, wouldn't become aware of her activities that had made it impossible for father and daughter to ever again speak. It would hurt him less to be killed than to spit fires of hatred at his only surviving child.

"Oh, but such times we had here before politics became more important than people." She let loose a big whipping-cream laugh. "So many people. They came every night and stayed all night. My parents entertained the continent."

With that Loremarie started disappearing down a steep narrow passage that was melting into stairs that were dripping into a cellar. Gray into black. Nowhere into nowhere. I clambered after her, knowing the way because I'd been down here a lot. Erich and I loved to visit Anton, and we could only see him in his hidden chamber.

"It's not much farther," she called back to Joe and me.

I hit a board, banging my shin. *Auch!* Black. Oh, it was black, and I half-slid, half-crawled down remnant stairs, heard dripping water. One soggy, slurpy step. Another. From the other side came a teeny little splash, then teeny desperate thrashing. Blech. A rat, I assumed, making its way through the underground seas of Berlin, where new waters emerged constantly from all the broken pipes. I took a step down. My socks and shoes were like sponges. It was water, wasn't it? Please let it be clear, please let it be murky if not clear. Just don't let it be beet red.

"Willi?"

"Joe?" I responded. Better yet: "Tante Lore?"

"Shh," hissed the darkness.

Tap-tap. Pause. *Tap-tap-tap.* Pause. *Tap-tap.* From behind something came movement, then creaking, groaning. LIGHT! A heavy door was thrown back and the flooded basement was flooded with brightness.

"Oh," I said, squinting. "*Hallo.*"

Joe and I were not too far apart, ankle deep in brownish—thank God, brownish—water, and Loremarie and Anton were up a foot on dry concrete. Anton the troll, thin, smiling, who had something special to do with papers and was hidden down here and might actually have the wherewithal to get us all to Swiss land.

"*Hallo,*" he echoed as he held out a hand, beckoned us into his underground chamber.

Loremarie explained Joe's presence, his family ties to Eva, and Anton nodded and nodded, his face blooming with a huge grin. Then Joe and I stepped up to dry land and into a studio. Yes. An artist's studio, full of easels, countless canvases painted countless times, brushes, oils, a table covered with official papers, a radio, a huge map. Turning around, I looked at Anton: dark hair and eyes, faint moustache set against the palest skin I'd ever seen. Face: long with a broad smile and a narrow chin. He was a U-boat. One of the chosen people who'd been forced with that menorah over there to submerge down into this submarine pen. Amazing. A sinker sunk, hidden beneath the surface of Berlin.

"How long you been down here?" Joe asked.

"Since September 1942."

He grinned. A smile as white as his skin though brighter. A happy face. He reached over and embraced Loremarie and they kissed and they grinned. Yes, in love. He was a U-boat and she was his lifeline and his everything else. And he was her everything else as well. Their aura flashed: We are to be married when all of this is over.

Anton hugged me and told me he had a new picture for Erich and me, a painting of the zoo. Then he turned on Joe, the-enemy-who-was-really-one-of-the-good-guys, and machine-gunned him with his own past.

"Before all this my family had a wonderful apartment on Holsteiner Ufer overlooking the Spree, just by the Moabiter Bridge."

"*Wie bitte?*" said Joe, unable to take it as fast as he was getting it.

"You know, the bridge with the bears on it. And my father had an art gallery just off the Hansaplatz on the other side of the Tiergarten. It was the best in Berlin, and he sent me to art school."

"Ah," said Joe sadly, as if he were forming an image of Anton's previous life.

Then, not quite ten years ago, he continued, they'd been forced to sell the gallery so it could be "Aryanized." Anton said it like they'd taken the place to the cleaners. Whatever. It had been lost, wasted, never returned. Anton painted on. They'd lost their large apartment overlooking the river. But Anton still painted. Then his parents and sister were rounded up, hauled away for resettlement in the east, while Anton was herded into a place here in Berlin. Anton the budding painter was caught by—*oi, yoi, yoi*—the Ministry of Propaganda and put to work.

"Jew faces," he said, smiling.

That's what they wanted and that's what he painted. Canvas after canvas, Jew face after Jew face, so he could stay alive, eat, sleep. Canvases that became posters that were plastered all over town screaming RECOGNIZE THE ENEMY! THIS IS THE ETERNAL JEW! STOP THE CONNIVING JEWS! Hundreds of paintings later, he went crazy, left a note that he was hurling himself into the Wannsee (also letting it be known that he couldn't swim), and escaped over a wall and ran and ran and walked and stumbled and came down with a terrible fever and bumped right into the big chest of Loremarie who had bought several pieces from Anton's father. HELP! he had begged of her. Help she had given.

"I've been buried here two and a half years," he laughed. "I only go out at night, and then only during the raids when all good Germans should be tucked in their shelters."

Loremarie beamed: "But we're going to make it! We're going to make it!

Anton laughed. "You, an American!" He waltzed his thin figure over to Joe and kissed his hand. "The war will be over in a matter of weeks."

"Let's hope so."

"Anton, what about the travel documents?" I asked. "Are they ready yet?"

"Almost, my little friend. Once I've finished carving the authorization stamp it will look perfectly legitimate. I'll be done soon."

Yes. Before the Russians. Before . . . I was suddenly nervous. I looked into Anton's face, a visage that had remained happy, smiling, full of hope down here without the sunshine. And I was afraid. The road to the end of the war was still to be built over the bodies of millions of yet-to-be-killed people. Which ones of us would be among those? If only I could see the future, anticipate it and save us all.

"Willi, there's nothing you can do to alter the course of fate."

"But first we have to get Joe some identification papers," said Loremarie. "We can't have him getting shot as a spy."

No, that wouldn't do. Not Joe.

"And," Anton said, "we have to bandage him up some— make him look wounded. Loremarie, you and Willi can do that. We can't have him getting strung up as a deserter."

No. That wouldn't do, either.

"Yeah, we can make him look real wounded," I said with a grin. Lots of blood and goop. "Come over here, Joe."

As if he were merely a mannequin, I shoved Joe past gray stone, cold, dismal walls, past a big dented tea pot, then plunked him down on a three-legged stool. I found myself staring at this man, who maybe was my father, while Loremarie fished for materials, Behind us in this hidden tomb, Anton the Painter a.k.a. Forger, studied Joe's face, then set to work.

"The best we could get you," he began, talking over his shoulder, "would be a *Kennkarte,* the national identity card. But that would take time. For now . . . for now . . . a baptism certificate—I'll make sure it's from a church that's been destroyed—a few ration cards, a priority card, a bombed-out certificate, and something from the *Volkssturm. Ja, ja,* that would be good. You can be some governmental so-and-so whose offices were bombed and then moved to the country. But you stayed on and you're not a soldier, but some organizer in the civilian army."

He rattled on as if he were a grocer checking a list. Sped up, spun around. Creativity in a hailstorm. He sorted through one stack of papers—had he printed all those?—found one, pulled it, inspected it, then started down another pile. He withdrew a pen as if it were a scalpel, mumbled something about how Joe would need a photograph for this and that card and that Eva could see to it tomorrow but today, today, well, at least this was a start. If he were stopped at least it wouldn't be as obvious as a yellow star.

I found myself noticing the tiny bed by one wall, the huge map of Berlin hanging on the other. The radio.

Joe saw what I was looking at, and asked, "Anton, do you listen to the radio much?"

"Of course he does," I volunteered. "Anton knows everything."

Anton laughed. "Well, little one, maybe not everything. But everyday I listen to our news, the BBC, and all the music I can."

"And the bombs," laughed Loremarie.

Anton, she explained, spent his time cheering on the Allied bombers, listening to military broadcasts for their positions, and pinpointing their attacks on the large wall map. Anything that fell on the Tiergarten was from the ghost of his father. Anything that fell on Alexanderplatz was a gift from his mother, for she had liked to shop there. And any destruction on the western part, well, that was from his sister, for she had loved the lakes and parks. Yes, he said. They were dead. He was sure of it. When he'd first heard of the gassings he knew, felt, smelled it. He was all that was left.

Loremarie nodded, pulled out a role of gauze, and said, "Willi, let's use this to do something nasty."

Joe groaned as Loremarie wrapped a white turban around and around his head, swooping it just over his left eye. Then she took out some eosin and artistically dabbed it all around.

"Do a big blob above his ear," I eagerly said. "You know, like he has a real disgusting shrapnel wound. And . . . and put some on his pants, too!"

"Gee, thanks kid," said Joe, peering out from under his disguise. "Am I going to be able to walk after this?"

"A cane!" I cried. "He needs a cane!"

"Oh, come on."

Loremarie said, "He's right, Joe. I've got one upstairs. You should take it and walk with a limp so that it looks like there's no way you could be at the front."

Loremarie and I stepped back and admired the eosin, which was drying a deep, convincing red.

"It looks like he's really been blasted," I said, pleased.

Anton looked over. *"Ja, das ist sehr gut."* Yes, that's very good.

"So Anton," began Joe, fiddling with the gauze, "if you're such a master falsifier, why can't you just write yourself a ticket out of here?"

Returning to his work, he laughed. "Go on, show him, Loremarie."

Loremarie scuttled over to a cabinet. She flung open its door, fiddled around, checked something, rejected it, then found two large pieces of paper. *Ja, ja, ja.* She laughed, drew them out. Two posters branded with the Star of David and a face that was hauntingly familiar. A face that was long and drawn, dark hair, dark beard. Even though the smile was absent and the beard added, this person was easily recognized.

"That's Anton," I said.

Joe nodded in surprise. "Of course it is."

"They told me to paint Jew faces," said Anton, still huddled over his table. "I lied and said I had no idea what a Jew looked like. They beat me. I told them I still didn't know whether a face looked Jewish or not. So they got smart and shoved the brushes at me: paint your face or die. What? Paint your face, they said. You have a typical Jew face. So I painted poor miserable me. Again and again. They liked it. I hated it. Hated myself for what I was doing, the lies my image was helping to spread across Europe. *Ja, ja,* every Jew face in every Nazi poster was based on . . ." He glanced over at us. "On my face. Right cheek. Straight on. Left profile. Growling, laughing. Cheating. Not only did I do posters, but I did caricatures of myself for the hardline Nazi paper, *Der Stürmer.*"

I'd seen my Anton, the man who'd fed Erich and me with color, plastered on buildings everywhere. The lines and curves, eyes and nose of this man, drawn and painted, stretched and ridiculed over and over, turned into posters hung all across the Reich, all across conquered Europe, printed in a newspaper that was distributed to every hate-loving fascist.

Loremarie beamed: "After our dear Adolf, my Anton is the most recognized man in the *Vaterland!*"

He laughed, somehow having forgiven himself, somehow having found the energy to move on. "If I were to stroll the Ku-damm people would stop and stare, then pounce on me. If I were to go for coffee at the Cafe Kranzler—that is, what remains of it—my table would be surrounded."

Yes. Surrounded by SS or Gestapo not asking for autographs, but offering a free cattle car ticket to the east. That's why he couldn't go out.

Anton shrugged. "And if the officials by chance didn't get me, the 'catchers' would."

Catchers, he explained, were the Jews who worked for the Gestapo. Jews who sank beneath Berlin and identified other U-boats and turned them in. Jews who paid for their lives with the lives of others. But that didn't surprise me. Everyone was desperate.

"I've thought about disguises, but even if people didn't recognize me as the Evil Jew they'd seen plastered everywhere, then they'd probably just notice a Jew in hiding. Because . . ." He smiled. "Because after all, this face is very Semitic. Even my own mother—may she rest in peace—said, 'Oi, Anton, yours is a *shayna Yiddusha punim.*' A beautiful Jewish face."

Loremarie poured us hot ersatz something-that-was-dark-and-bitter, and we watched Anton finish his work. All the while my mind churned. Couldn't we come up with a temporary disguise for Anton that would last long enough to get him out of Berlin? Perhaps a wounded soldier, his face all battered and shattered and bandaged? Yes, someone terribly hurt fleeing to the countryside.

Anton said: "We couldn't have survived without Eva. She can get anything on the black market, and she gets enough for us, too. Without her I'd be dead. *Ach.* What a wonder worker she is. Of course, I supply her with a bundle of forged ration cards and anything else she needs, but Eva sees that Loremarie and I eat better than any other Berliners!" He sighed. "Hopefully I'll be able to get her and Erich and our little Willi here out of town."

I sucked in gloomy air, glanced around at the little underground room, nodded and nodded as Loremarie went on about how all Germans weren't bad Germans. I watched Anton as he peeled a real hard-cooked egg and picked off every microscopic bit of shell, then rolled the baby-bottom smooth thing over an original stamp—picking up nicely the red ink—then gently rolled the egg over some papers. The result: counterfeit documents with an official stamp.

"It looks perfect," I said, looking over his arm.

"It is perfect," retorted Anton.

Something went *cuckoo-cuckoo*, and I looked over on the wall and saw rough stone and on that an incredibly elaborate wooden clock with a little tweet that chirped the hour. Something frivolous saved, remounted down in this artistic dungeon.

"Willi, you and Joe should be going," said Loremarie. "We don't want to keep your mother waiting."

Heaven forbid, I thought.

Looking at Joe pensively, she added, "I think I should come with you. If there's any problem, I can claim Joe is my husband."

With a twinkle in his eye, Anton said, "Be very, very careful with her, Mister. No funny stuff. I want her back, you know." He held out several cards and a folded piece of paper. "Here's a baptism certificate, some ration cards, and a couple of other things. Be sure to hang on to the bombed-out certificate—that's a good one."

"Thanks Anton," said Joe, accepting them. "Thanks very much."

"You bring great joy to me. The first American, which means the end is near. Thank God! You must come back and we can discuss the future of Germany. The Allies must nurture us after the war, you know. Nurture us with freedom and democracy, inspire us. Otherwise, Bolshevism will flood into the craters left from the war and fill people's minds."

Joe said, "They say it's going to take at least until the end of the century to rebuild Europe. The engineers say it will take forty or fifty years just to cart away all the rubble. So there's plenty to be done."

Yes, I thought, clutching my Joe by the arm, I was almost happy because the end was near. The Good Guys were on the way.

"Your stamp for Switzerland—when will it be ready?" Joe asked.

"In a couple of days. I need a special ink."

I yanked on Joe's arm. "But that's not soon enough!"

Joe glanced down at me, then up at Anton, and said, "Willi's right. If we're going to make it out of here, we don't have much time."

I knew tomorrow's forecast. I sensed it: clear skies. Sunny day and moon-dripped night. Perfect weather for that horribly perfect, all-destructive raid. Then suddenly in a rush of fear, I wondered why we should even bother running from here. We might be able to escape Berlin. We might be able to flee into the future and to a distant time and place, but I knew I'd never be free. I would always be running, always looking over my shoulder and back into my memory because someone or something would always be hunting me. I imagined myself a grown man, chased through a city with tall buildings, and dodging tank-sized cars and steel-wheeled trains. My heart churned. It was useless. There was no getting away. There never would be. No safe place. Ever.

"No, Willi, there will be. If you keep going toward the truth, you'll discover who's after you, and that knowledge will give you the strength to find peace as well as safety."

Snapping me back to here and now, Loremarie said, "Come on, we haven't any time to waste."

We didn't, of course, and without another word, Loremarie and I led Joe up and out of one of Berlin's secrets and toward another.

Chapter

15

Loremarie hunted out the cane for Joe, and we headed off, cutting through the Tiergarten district, past continual ruins and continual people trying to pretend it was a normal day. Past people pushing, pulling carts of every kind; carts that held precious belongings that they would try and push and pull into the countryside and away from the bombs. I glanced at destroyed buildings, saw chalk messages scribbled on the facades: "Hans, I'm alive and staying with Friedel! Love, Gretta." And: "Momma, where are you? Fritz." And: "I've taken the girls and we've gone to the country. We are all safe and healthy, Sigi." I smelled frying potatoes and onions, and spotted a woman cooking in the shadows of a blasted building that had no front or roof. The Red Army was so close yet life was going on.

Loremarie, Joe, and I came to Tauentzienstrasse, turned right, and up ahead I saw the battered figure of the Kaiser Wilhelm Gedächtniskirche, the memorial church. The towers somehow still remained, but the roof of the church was gone, consumed by fire. Loremarie, her ample figure bundled up in a singed gray fox coat—she'd been caught out in a firestorm—led us down a sidewalk, and then down a narrow trail carved between a row of boarded shops and a line of debris. Above hung a whole row of square balconies, or what remained of them. On the street: few cars. A dreadfully skinny horse pulling a wagon. A mother and two children, all carrying bundles. All fleeing from the east.

Joe nudged me, and keeping his voice low, asked "Willi, what's the central district like?"

"Really blasted. They bomb it almost every night."

"*Ja, ja, ja,*" added Loremarie. "Most of the governmental buildings have been destroyed. The museums and palaces as well."

Silent, we trudged on, past the Gloria-Palast, circled the island that the memorial church still struggled to occupy, looked toward the even-in-ruins-fashionable Ku-damm. Traipsed over streetcar tracks.

"My God," said Joe at the horror around us, "Eva brought me here before. It . . . it was so beautiful."

"Really?" I asked because I had so little memory of Berlin without ruins.

"Oh," said Loremarie, sadly, "it was so wonderful. The Tiergarten and the Brandenburg Gate and Unter den Linden."

How could I? This was my world, one vast exploding and crumbling one.

I whispered, "Hitler's in his bunker, Joe. He has this huge underground bunker and they say he never comes out anymore."

Suddenly Loremarie commanded: "Limp, Joe. Limp!"

Cane in hand, Joe twisted and bobbed as four large army trucks rumbled past, weary soldiers loaded in the back. Not one of them looked in our direction, however, even spite of Joe's weird gyrations.

Once they'd passed, I said, "Erich's going to have to give

you lessons. You're walking like you've got an acorn in your shoe."

But he didn't respond. Rather, his eyes were fixed far to the right, on a shattered pile of stones crumbling over the remains of two prone carved elephants.

"The Elephant Gate. Eva and I had our photograph taken there," he mumbled.

Glancing at that and the charred shell of the Aquarium, I shrugged, for now it was difficult to imagine it otherwise. Pressing on—we were to meet Mother and Erich on the other side of the zoo—we started down Hardenbergstrasse, the Bahnhof Zoo visible in the distance.

A woman passed, and her eyes stuck to Joe, searching, wondering what was wrong with this picture. An old man's brow puckered as he walked by.

I asked, "Do you think people think Joe's really wounded?"

"*Ja, ja, natürlich,* the blood on the head bandage is perfect," stated Loremarie as she steered us around a deep dish in the ground that a lone bomb had scooped out. "Believe me, I've gotten hundreds out of Berlin by making them look wounded."

Something hooted, and we all looked to our right and through a hollowed building, straining to see into the zoo and spot what God-forsaken creature had survived thus far.

Joe said, "Jesus, the zoo's been wiped out."

"It was bombed by an entire convoy of British planes," I said. "You should have seen the flames!"

"Oh," moaned Loremarie, "it was awful."

As we walked along, I recounted the night more than a year ago when the Brits had been off target, thought they were striking some industrial plant. One thousand incendiary bombs had hit the zoo, all within fifteen minutes. There was a huge, horrible firestorm, I told Joe. You could hear the shrieks of lions and elephants, tigers, monkeys, as they were roasted in their cages. A few were fortunate enough to escape through shattered walls, only to be later hunted down in the Tiergarten by a squadron of crack soldiers. That's when the Aquarium had been blown to bits.

"They say it rained snakes and alligators for a whole half hour," I concluded.

"*Ja, ja, ja.* Before there were three or four thousand animals," added Loremarie. "And now there are less than a hundred. I saw the remains of Pongo, the gorilla. He was caught in the heart of it, and all that was left was this shrunken black skeleton, you know, sort of burned and engraved onto a rock."

"Dear God."

"Mtoto, the rhinoceros, was blown to bits, too," I said. "But Knorke, the hippo, lived through the firestorm by just sitting in his tank of water."

We passed the remains of the Ufa-Palast, that once great movie house, and before us stood the Bahnhof Zoo, a long, low, modern train station with elegant steelwork and a wealth of sparkling glass long ago disintegrated. Turning, I spotted part of the towering Zoo Bunker, then peered to my right through the iron fence and saw the ruins of the elephant exhibit, a templelike structure of domes and towers and bright tiles that was still exotic even though it had been squashed like a sand castle. And around it: torn trees, twisted trees, splintered stumps. A ghost jungle. In my mind I could still hear the grotesque cries.

Something moved. Erich. He was alone and laughing, hanging onto a fence and holding out a handful of brown, wintry grass. Then a long dark trunk curled out. Next a war-broken tusk. Finally elephantine ears.

"That's Siam," I told Joe, recognizing my pachyderm friend.

Loremarie nearly stopped in her tracks. "*Ja,* but where's Eva?"

I shrugged and ran on. Officially, the zoo was closed, and had been closed since that fateful night of destruction, but I charged on, knowing where to breach the fence. Just as Erich and I had done often, I pushed aside a loose bar, wormed through, held it open for Joe and Loremarie who had to squeeze themselves through the tight opening.

"Hold your hand nice and flat!" I called to my brother as I hurried up to him.

"It is, it is!"

Just as I arrived, the elephant schnozzle groped about, landed on Erich's open hand, and hoovered up virtually all of the blades of grass. Erich laughed in delight, then carefully studied the clear slime left in his palm. Wiping his hand on his pants, he turned to me, his grin long and proud.

He saw Joe approaching, and pointed to his head. "Hey, what happened to you, Mister?"

I said, "He ran into a tank."

"What? *Nee*, Aunt Loremarie was playing with eosin again."

Horrified, Loremarie rushed forward, a finger to her lips, hissing a hush. *Kleiner* Erich. Just a boy, we all laughed. No, he hadn't blown it. Not this time. No one was around, no one had heard, no one would surmise, no one would report us. Sometimes Erich knew when to be quiet, sometimes not. So what. He was just a kid.

But Erich really was like me. We knew too much. We knew about the black market and fake papers and Anton and . . .

With her face puckered, Loremarie asked, "Erich, where's your mother?"

He shrugged.

"You mean, she left you alone?"

Not bothered at all, Erich nodded. "I'm supposed to wait right here. I'm not supposed to go anywhere. And if the zoo keeper comes, I'm supposed to tell him that Mutti has cigarettes for him." He grinned. "Mutti has cigarettes for him and the zoo keeper lets us come in and feed Siam."

A pang twisted my heart, and I turned away from Erich and Loremarie and Joe, and reached through the bars. Siam raised his trunk, and I stroked his bristly, charred hide. All of a sudden I pictured us in Africa, Siam and me. The sky was clear, the air warm. And all around us was this huge, wonderful jungle full of animals. I saw myself climbing atop Siam, then riding off and exploring the rivers and lakes and thick forests and . . .

"You have a good imagination, Willi, and someday you will make good use of it."

It was so clear in my mind. All around Siam and me there were monkeys swinging on vines. And parrots. Big bright parrots with yellow beaks and turquoise wings and red tails.

"Willi, there's something else you know, isn't there? What is it you're trying to avoid thinking?"

She'd been doing this to me all my life, even before Erich was born. She would leave me, park me in some cafe or here at the zoo, and rendezvous with a man. Always a man. But different ones. Sometime she'd even leave Erich and me at a restaurant and slip off. To a hotel. For an hour or two. Sometimes it was for love. Other times for deals.

I was trembling, shaking all over as if I had a horrible chill.

"Feel your pain. See where it takes you."

I felt sick because, although I didn't know who Mother was meeting, I knew where to find her.

"That's good. Stick with it."

I turned to Loremarie and Joe. "She's back outside. Down by the Zoo Bunker, I think." She met someone here at least once a week, and I was moving, hesitant at first, then quickly, clumsy step after step. "I'll . . . I'll go tell here we're here."

I broke away, bolted for the fence, squeezed through the

bars. No sooner was I on the sidewalk, than I heard a motor roar to a start. A car? I looked in the direction of the mono- lithic castle of concrete—the Zoo Bunker—and spotted a long black sedan, the kind that would belong to an English movie actor, parked near the ruined planetarium. And there she was. Climbing out of the back seat, straightening her coat and fur-trimmed hat. Mother. Mother? She was laugh- ing and smearing on fresh lipstick. More decadent lipstick in this time of collapse. A man's leather-gloved hand reached out after her. I saw the man's shiny dark leather jacket and I thought, Oh, *Scheisse*, that's not an English actor in the car. The engine was purring, the man was in the back. That meant, of course, there was a chauffeur. Whoever that man was he was important. Important enough to keep an able-bodied man for his personal service while everyone else from twelve to sixty had been called up to beat back the Red Horde. Car. Gas. A driver. Who was it? Who had that kind of power? Oh. Christ, Mother. What have you done? What are you doing? Why have you cursed me with fear that will always shadow me?

The hand reached out, direct and confident, and landed on and cupped and caressed my mother's left breast. My heart prickled as if it were being poked by shards of glass. But she laughed. Enjoyed it? Obviously, because she didn't swat away that lecherous leathered hand, but slowly took it and kissed it. Then the car—rear door still open—started off. The vehicle hit a bump, the open door flapped a fare- well, slammed shut.

Mother laughed that high girlish giggle she could turn on, and called, "*Auf Wiedersehen!*"

I knew it wasn't the same man I'd seen earlier, the dark swarthy one with the American dollars. So who was this? Who? She laughed, turned and saw me staring at her. Who, Mother?

She covered her hiccup of surprise well, looking shocked

for a brief second, then composed herself. She smacked her lips, dipped her head, then strode around a crater as if she were a model on a runway.

"Hello, *mein kleiner Soldat*," she chuckled as she neared me. "I was thinking of you, wishing you were here. And, well, there you are!"

This time I saw it coming, saw her turning on. No, I wasn't going to let her defuse me. Not now. Not ever again.

"Who was that?" I demanded.

"Someone who helps us."

"Well, what were you doing?"

"Just trying to keep us alive, Willichen. That's all."

She bent to kiss me, and a toxic cloud of brandy breath swooped over me. I gagged in disgust, and suddenly knew that I was going to live way past this. But not her. Not unless I did something.

Screwing up my courage, I pronounced: "Mother, we have to leave Berlin."

She scowled. "Have you been listening to Joe again? I don't know why he's—"

"He said there's going to be a raid, a huge one!"

"Oh, Willi." She put a hand to her head, tried both to catch her thoughts and keep her balance. "We'll go. Soon. I promise."

"But we have to leave right away!" I begged as she strolled past me. "Tonight."

"What?"

"Joe says the raid is going to be on the night of the full moon. That's tomorrow night, Mama! Tomorrow night! So if we don't leave this evening, then we have to go in the morning so we can get far enough away."

"Oh, Willi, that's impossible. I just can't close down the bar. I have so much to take care of. Besides, what does Joe know? War plans change every day!" She held out her hand. "In four or five days, maybe. But no sooner."

I refused her hand, stepped away from her. Somewhere in the distance I heard a wail, and I raised my voice over it.

"Mama, that's not soon enough!"

Her eyes cut into me, then she reached into her purse and pulled out her little silver flask. "We'll go when I'm ready!"

"Then I'm going to take Erich! We'll go into the country and wait for you but . . . but we're going to leave tonight!"

Her eyes screamed at me, and her voice climbed high. "You'll do no such thing! You'll do exactly as I—"

Her words were beaten out by a distant ack-ack, ack-ack! I saw puffs of black smoke blooming in the blue sky. I turned, looked down the fence. Loremarie was squeezing through the bars, a Berolina of a figure who popped out onto the street, stood statuesque, and screamed: "RAID!"

No, not another one, I thought, cursing our enemies, Eisenhower, Churchill and Bomber Harris. Hating them all exactly as Goebbels wanted. Just a few minutes peace. Just an afternoon in the park. Just give us that!

Somewhere in the direction of Grunewald I heard plops of destructive thunder. Bursts of it. One after the other. Here we were, all of us. Caught away from our little bunker. Away from the little bar where we could burrow in safety. This was bad. Extremely dangerous. We were all out. Exposed. I looked at Mother. She was staring at me, terrified. Then she tilted her head back to down her flask of cognac, took an entire mouthful as she scanned the sky.

I turned to Loremarie, all alone on the sidewalk, realized what that meant and screamed: "Where's Erich?" Charging at her full speed, I called in desperation: "Where's my brother?"

"I don't know! Erich had to pee and Joe took him into the bushes! I can't find them!"

I glanced behind me, saw Mother weave, stumble. "My baby! Where's my baby?"

Loremarie and I shoved our way back through the bars and into the zoo. Behind me I heard the flak guns atop the Zoo Bunker start to bite: ACK-ACK, ACK-ACK-ACK! Overhead I saw little triangles of silver. Hundreds and hundreds of them. Oh, God. Americans in their stupid glittery planes. Why hadn't the sirens sounded earlier? Why was there no real warning? We've got to find Erich, rush to safety! Got to slip into the nearby mountain of concrete, have to crawl into the Zoo Bunker!

We reached the elephant house. Split. I ran one way around it. Loremarie the other.

"Erich!" I cried.

Loremarie: "Joe!"

I heard a trumpeted cry. Siam was charging madly about his ruined pen. Trunk held high. Blaring. It was another storm of death and he was dashing around trying in vain to avoid it.

"ERICH!"

I scanned blasted cages, twisted bars. Roasted, leafless trees. They couldn't be far. They had to be here somewhere. Desperate, I followed the low fence that circled the elephant pen.

"JOE! ERICH!"

And then Loremarie: "Willi!"

My head spun. There, coming around the other side was Loremarie, holding Erich, clutching him on her hip, his straight-braced leg and all. Her face, however, was still desperate, terrified as she ran toward me.

"Joe thought he saw you back there!" she shouted. "I couldn't stop him—he ran off looking for you!"

I heard a distant grumbling. Bombs rolling toward us like a great wave. Joe would be blown to the heavens out here. He didn't know where to go, where to hide. But I did.

I charged past Loremarie. "I've got to find Joe!"

"Willi!" she screamed. "Willi, no!"

"Joe doesn't know how to get to the bunker!"

Over Loremarie's shoulder, the bobbing Erich called, "Willi!"

I raced on, down another path, sensing that I'd never be able to move fast enough. Beneath me the ground quivered as the carpet of bombs unrolled. Above me the planes surged. I glanced upward through shattered, splintered trees. Why? Why weren't those planes swooping toward the manufacturing districts in the north?

"Joe!"

There! Having abandoned his cane and any pretense of injury, he was racing along the edge of a death-filled pond.

"Willi!"

We ran at each other, around the pond and down a path. And then right into one another. Just as quickly, I clutched his hand and spun, desperate to escape this deathly park.

"Where're the others?" he asked.

"Up ahead!"

The first bombs were closing in on us. I could hear them, feel the earth quaking beneath us. The flak guns growled. We ran. Never in my life have my feet moved so swiftly, so desperately. Back around Siam's house—I cried out to my panicked friend—and on through some bushes, around some rubble. I squeezed Joe's hand, yanked him through the bent bars, emerged on the street. Oh, please. Please!

I saw them just past the burnt planetarium. Dear God, what was taking them so long? Why were Loremarie, my mother, and Erich moving so slowly? Then I knew. I saw Mother sway, stumble. God-damn her! As we ran, I watched her cover her ears, fall to the side, fold in on herself. No! You have to run! Loremarie set Erich down on the ground, reached out for Mother. Reached out—

An enormous blast shattered my vision, my hopes. A bomb fell into the gentle folds of the zoo, and the earth exploded. A clod of dirt hurtled toward my head, slammed into me. I tripped, skidded to my knees. Joe grabbed me, yanked me on.

"Willi!" he cried as the horror dumped down on us.

Somehow we were up and going again as a rain of dirt and tree deluged us. The sun was gone. I searched for Mother and Erich and Loremarie. Vanished. Had they made it to safety? Had they reached the bunker? Somehow Joe and I managed to get around the corner of the planetarium. We charged the enormous, four-towered Zoo Bunker. I looked up to the gods. More little triangles in the now death-gray sky. More and more and more and more. Was Joe wrong? Was this here and now the gargantuan raid he'd been predicting for tomorrow evening? ACK-ACK! ACK-ACK! The flak was non-stop. We dashed toward the bunker. Bomb after bomb rolled toward us, like a giant stomping onward and onward, crushing all in its path.

Zoo Bunker! Dear Zoo Bunker, I thought as we lunged toward it. The blasts were all around us, blowing everything to pieces. We ran past abandoned prams, dropped crutches. We've got to make it. But no. We rushed to the door, only feet from safety, Führer protection. Oh, Christ. The heavy steel door was solid, sealed. We banged on it, pounded for our lives.

LET US IN! LET US INNNNNNNNNNNNNNNN!

But even I couldn't hear our frantic begging over the racket of bombs and flak and, horrified, I realized the bunker was a can, sealed and packed. Filled. Unopenable. I turned, saw a little zoo building sitting there, then saw it explode into gray, powdery dust, rising into the dark sky with a whoosh. We had to get underneath something. I turned. Saw the arched columns that held the elevated tracks emerging from the Zoo Bahnhof. I pointed to it, and clutching Joe's hand, we ran. Safety. Perhaps safety over there. At least something to crawl under.

There was an explosion that I didn't even hear. The earth

belched and all at once Joe and I were flying, picked up like two leaves in a gust of wind. Magically, we were carried. I looked at my would-be father as we were carried along, wishing this were a ride of delight instead of a flight of death. I held his hand, feared that his arm would come off in my grasp. And then we were skidding along the ground, tumbling like two bowling balls.

Heat washed over me. I laid there, crumpled, my hands bent in, my legs under and around. Heat. Oh, God. I could barely breathe. Incendiaries. I pushed myself up. Joe was not far away, a mound of unmoving man. *Rzzt! Chzzzt!* Shrapnel started flying, zinging through the air, slicing through life. I looked at my hand. All was fine, all fingers still there, but even as I looked, something cut across, leaving a trail of blood.

Go. GO! I stumbled over, prodded Joe, poked him, pulled him back to life and to his feet. A bomb, okay. Just no burning goop from a phosphorous bomb spread all over me. Together the two of us stumbled through clouds of smoke, found a wagon, and collapsed beneath it. I tasted mealy dirt, was pelted by little bits of buildings. I lay next to Joe. Joe who was no longer moving. Who had a rivulet of blood trickling from his head.

In a lull of bombs I heard crying off to the right. A familiar voice now rising in her most perfect pitch ever.

"Mama!"

She was beneath a nearby lorry, her face black, clothing shredded. Next to her was a furry, gunnysack blob. An unmoving figure. Loremarie. Alive?

"Mama!" I screamed between bombs.

She turned to me, her face long and horrible, twisted as if it were made from half-melted rubber. She screamed something. Rose to her knees and crawled in my direction.

"Get down!" I yelled. "Stay there!"

Over and over and over she was calling something.

Screaming in deathly panic. I didn't understand. Couldn't hear. But then I realized she was calling a name.

In horror I whispered, "Erich?"

And with a horrible bob of her head, she nodded. I looked out toward the planetarium and the zoo and the bunker. Green flames were dancing, leaping everywhere, dripping off of trees and blasted walls, rolling and oozing down the street. The air was oven hot, just now beginning to twist and whirl. Oh, Christ, I thought. A firestorm. And *mein kleiner* Erich was somewhere out there.

Chapter

16

I think I fainted. It was so hot, the air so thin, that we all passed out. The flames gusted, blew heat in our faces, sucked precious oxygen from our lungs. And when I woke the planes had gone and the flak guns were quiet and all that could be heard was the gentle, fireplacelike crackling of nearby buildings. Burning. Everything. I felt something move, struggle next to me, and I rolled to the side. Joe. He pushed at the hot earth, sat upright, his face black and smudged and streaked. His hair totally gray with ash.

"Are you all right?" I asked.

He nodded, and in English said, "I'm okay."

Far away one of the delayed ones exploded. Then across the deathyard in front of me I sensed something, and saw the first of the lucky ones emerging from the Zoo Bunker. Nearby I heard a faint sobbing. I pushed myself to my hands and knees, crawled from beneath the wagon, crawled across the burnt grass, managed to make it to the lorry. I reached out, touched Mother.

"Mama . . ."

Hair twisted, knotted, face black. She was sobbing but not crying. Screaming but quiet. Begging something but wordless. Her eyes were crazed white balls. I scooched over, touched the motionless furry ball next to her.

"Tante Lore?"

Nothing.

I jabbed her. "Tante Lore!"

Nothing until a faint and exhausted: *"Ja, ja, ja . . ."*

She moved, rolled over. Her face was also black. But dripping from her left ear was the most beautifully colored blood I'd ever seen. All nice and brilliant and glistening.

I grabbed onto one of the lorry's wheels and pulled. Weak, stiff. I stood. Looked around. Erich? I stumbled forward, made it over to the wagon. I reached down with one hand, took Joe.

"My brother's missing," I gasped. "We have to find him."

Holding each other by the hand, Joe and I started toward the bunker. Nearby a woman started to scream as she bounced like a pinball among the wreckage.

She shrieked: "I can't see! I can't see! Where am I? I can't see!"

Part of her clothing had been burned away, exposing flesh that looked like a toasted blob of drippy cheese.

I ignored her, stumbled through the crowd that was now pouring from the shelter, my dry throat calling, "Erich . . . Erich . . ."

Joe broke away, pushed on ahead. I swerved, searched toward the planetarium. Maybe Erich had taken shelter there. Maybe he'd found something to protect himself with. I bit my lip. Erich who had so much trouble walking. Hampered by that brace. No, he couldn't have made it this far by himself. Why wasn't he in the countryside? Why? Oh. Please. I began to cry. Warm drops on my steaming face.

"Erich . . . Erich . . ."

I turned back, made my way around the edge of a smoldering car, nothing left of it but a smoking shell. Then suddenly I saw something odd and black stretched on the ground. Staring at the black lump that was all charred, I froze as if my own heart had been plucked out. That thing, I realized, was a figure, the remains of something caught in the very eye of the firestorm. But, God, no. Please no!

My hands turned to tight claws. My face flushed lobster red. I rushed forward, then stopped and studied this . . . this thing. It was a body shrunken from the intense heat, and now baked and charred into a crispy shape. And I was staring at a wing. No, an arm. Oh, Lord. Everything in my body wanted to rush out, be squeezed into the universe. At the other end I saw a piece of twisted metal. It was a frame. No, a brace with all its leather burned off and now gently melted, and I knew and I screamed to burst my lungs, to kill my heart, when I realized that I was staring at all that was left of my little brother.

"ERICH!"

Chapter

17

Now that I'd touched death, I felt it black and thick in my heart. Some odd haze descended over me, wrapped around and around, and after I'd screamed until my vocal cords nearly tore, I just stood there, not believing, not comprehending. I closed my eyes, sealed them with tears. This couldn't be . . .

"I'm sorry, Willi. I'm so very sorry."

I remembered Erich diving into me, calling me a big ape, punching and punching until it even hurt. Oh, Erich. Hit me again. Please!

Hands took me and pulled me aside, buried me deep in someone's coat. Fur. Yes. It was Loremarie. She pulled me into her as my mother collapsed on the ground and screamed to the heavens, shrieked for her little boy's return, cursed the world. But nothing happened. Barely anyone noticed or even heard. There was crying all around us. For others.

Joe slipped off his coat and wrapped up the remains of my little brother, and we started home, a shocked party of mourners traversing a city aflame. Death had been all around me before, lingering, nipping but never biting. Until now. And now I felt it everywhere, saw it everywhere. Crushed bodies. Headless ones. Burned figures. And crumbling buildings and blazing cars and smoking homes. Something terrible beyond my imagination had happened, and there was no fixing it. Ever.

Passing through the waves of smoke and cries that rolled continuously over us like a nightmarish fog, Joe led the way back to our bunker bar. Mother stumbled after him, hysterical, sobbing, lost in a drunken nightmare. And I walked numbly, like a zombi, pulled along by the ever-stoic Loremarie.

As we passed the Bahnhof Zoo, I heard a plea unlike any other. I looked through a cloud of smoke, saw a horse, it's hide singed and blackened. Over and over again it cried out, opened its wiggly lips and exposed huge teeth. Over and over again the creature tried to rise. But the old nag couldn't for it's rear legs had been grated to the bone by shrapnel.

I broke Loremarie's grasp of my hand and tore toward the horse. I couldn't stand that animal plea. I was going to get a board, do what I should have done to that Gestapo agent. Yes, I would get something big and long and hard and I would smash that horse, beat its head again and again, beat the misery right out of it.

"Willi!" shouted Loremarie, charging after me, seizing me by the shoulder.

"Let go!" I cried.

I had to get to that horse! I had to—

Right before me, the creature collapsed, caving in on itself like a deflated balloon. It crumbled onto the rubble-strewn street, quivered, and was still.

"It's all right now," said Loremarie, taking me firmly by the hand. "See, the horse is all quiet. It won't hurt anymore."

No, not anymore because it had escaped. Like Erich. Gone far away.

In the distance a building collapsed with a roar, shattering the peace after the raid. Of course, I thought, as Loremarie led me on after Joe and Mother. We're trapped. We will never escape. I looked up. Before it had been a perfect winter day, the sun low but sharp. Now, however, the sun was gone and the sky was swirling with sparks and snowy ash. Berlin, I realized, was an enormous coffin in which we were to be buried, nailed right up, for eternity. The Red Horde was gathering on the other side of the Oder River, just waiting to seal our death.

But there were, of course, no coffins in Berlin; the living were too busy trying to stave off death to worry about that. Nevertheless, late that afternoon Joe and I went looking. We saw a sardinelike stack of baked bodies pulled from a shelter and piled out in the open, but there was nothing to cover them with, let alone bury them in. And here and there lay corpses covered with sheets or blankets, and of course bodies dropped everywhere like discarded waste. But nothing, not so much as the simplest pine box, could be found, and I sniffed the dirty-sweet stench of fresh-killed flesh everywhere. The only buried bodies were the thousands mushed in the ruins of the bombed buildings. And I thought, if this war ever ends, if the bombers ever go away and never come back, so many of the dead will never be found. But an end? No, I couldn't imagine it.

I wanted to scrounge wood from that apartment building, salvage nails from that window, that door. A coffin. My Erich had to have a proper box. A real final home. I could hunt for the material, Joe could construct something, no matter how crude. But that might take days, Joe said, and besides, where would we find a hammer?

He shook his stubbly face. "And what about a saw?"

I couldn't argue much because I couldn't speak much, my throat raw from screaming. So in the end I gave up, and we did what all the other Berliners were doing. Stole cardboard. The windows of the city had all been shattered years ago and people had given up the reglazing which they had done early in the war. When success was only a matter of weeks away. But later, mostly after Stalingrad, sheets of cardboard were used instead of glass. It didn't crack, didn't shatter, and the corrugated kind could black out a window at night, yet be removed for fresh air during the day. Very practical then, and now too. Fairly plentiful and good for wrapping bodies. You didn't need a hammer or saw.

I led the way to a block that had been bomb-pounded over and over again yet never firebombed. We salvaged enough cardboard from just two windows of a smashed house; we didn't need much because Erich was so small. I found a board, too. Held it up to me. Erich was that tall, just a bit over my waist. That could hold him. We'd wrap the body in a sheet, place it on the wood for rigidity, then fold cardboard around it all and secure it with twine.

The next morning, with Erich my brother made into a package, we carried him to a cemetery just past Potsdamerstrasse, near Yorkstrasse and the heavily damaged railyards. Of course the graveyard looked like the moon, all pockmarked with craters, but Mother, her body bound in as much black as she could find, didn't want any old hole. She wanted a fresh one, so she led our little troop to a far corner, to the shadows of a wall. We had no burial permission. There was no one around to ask. Either the groundskeeper was dead already, or he was off digging trenches or being killed that very moment.

We did have a shovel, though, a big, solid one, just in case we ever needed to dig our way out of our underground *Kneipe*. Joe started, breaking through frozen earth, then carving a clean, deep hole—very deep—because in deathly peace we all wanted Erich to be as safe and as far away as possible from war. Over and over Joe jabbed the earth, and Mother and Loremarie stood and watched in silence.

Dieter was off to the side, fashioning a cross out of several pieces of wood. I sat next to him, dropping myself onto a fallen tombstone. I watched him twist and pull a piece of wire. Then I looked up. I was almost surprised to see that the sky had cleared of ash and soot and dust. As if a whole new front had blown in, the sky was clean and crisp now. No. There, toward the central district, great columns of smoke still bloomed into the sky. I stared up and up and up, and—

"That's good," said a coarse voice.

I glanced at Mother, then over at Joe. The hole was now almost as deep as he was tall. How long had he been digging?

"Oh, *ja*," agreed Loremarie. *"Das ist tief genug."* That's deep enough.

Joe heaved out a few more shovelfuls of soil, scraped the walls, packed the floor. Then he lifted out the shovel and extended his hands. Gently. This child would be put to rest gently.

"Pass him to me," Joe said.

Dieter hopped over on his one foot, and Loremarie groaned as she bent down to the bundle of cardboard. I sat there and watched as the two of them attempted to lift the makeshift casket. Then suddenly there was another voice, a strange, deep one.

"Here, let me help."

Loremarie looked up and gasped, "You shouldn't be here!"

My fingers clenched the tombstone. I spun around. Approaching us was a tall figure with very dark hair. And a face that was long and thin and extremely pale.

"When a ray of sunshine is buried, all must come to mourn," said Anton. "Don't worry, I was careful."

"Dear Lord," muttered Loremarie.

Then the two of them, Loremarie and Anton, bent down and lifted the remains of Erich and carried him to the edge of the grave. Mother stepped right up to the edge of the hole.

Flatly, she said, "Willi."

I understood that she, the mourning mother, wanted me at her side. But I said nothing.

"Willi, *komm her zu mir!*" Come to me!

She held out her hand. I was to be the dutiful son, stand by her and comfort her in her loss. But who was to comfort me?

"Damn you, Willi!" she screeched.

I pushed myself to my feet, walked slowly over the dirt, took my position at her side. Her hand did not reach out and hold mine, though. Rather, her tight fingers wrapped around my shoulder, held me in position. And I smelled cigarette smoke, thick and musty, in the folds of her coat. Brandy, too, all sweet and syrupy on her breath. Yesterday it was drink to ward off fear. Today it was drink to drown all that hurt.

"There's more, isn't there, Willi?"

I was numb. My face rested flat and glazed over, my arms hung heavy and still. The bombs that had killed my little brother yesterday were still bursting within me. I was the big brother. The little soldier of the house. I'd promised Erich I'd take care of him. I'd promised! I should have stolen him from Mother, ripped him away. The two of us should have run off to the mountains where we would have been safe. But I didn't do that, any of that. And now Erich was dead! He was dead because I didn't think soon enough, act quick enough!

"No, Willi, your brother is dead because he was killed in an air raid. The world is at war, and he's a victim and you're a victim, too. Just look at your hands and your arms

and your legs, too. Look at how small you are. Small be-
cause you're just a boy. A boy who could have done noth-
ing."

But—!

I felt something squeeze my shoe. I looked down. Joe
was touching my little foot, pressing his love into me and
staring right into my boyish face. I started to shake. He
knew I would have done anything, given anything to save
my brother!

Holding one end of the cardboard coffin, Anton knelt by
me, and said, "Will you help me!"

I wiped my eyes and nodded. This was the reality: Erich
was dead and there was no way I could change that. I
accepted a corner of the coffin, and Anton, Loremarie and
I lowered it down and into Joe's arms. Then sliding the
thing downward, Joe lowered the boxed remains onto the
dirt floor of the grave. Ashes to ashes. . .

Joe reached up, readied himself to be hoisted upward
and into the world of the living. On his knees, Anton
reached down.

Suddenly, Loremarie noticed something at the other end
of the cemetery, and snapped, "Stay down! There's a
Striefe!"

Starting to turn around, Mother said, *"Eine Streife—*
Kettenhunde?"

Mother was referring to the MP force of the Wehrmacht,
those troops who wore shiny metal breast plates and often
patrolled these railyards looking for deserters. Roaming in
groups of twos and threes, they were the one's who'd been
executing AWOL soldiers and stringing them up from
lampposts.

"Ja, but just stay still, Eva!" commanded Loremarie.
"Pretend as if all is normal."

My heart clenched and buckled tight. Dear God. We
hadn't yet returned to Anton's to get the rest of Joe's iden-

tification; the measly ration cards and what-not that Joe did have were only enough to get him killed as a treasonous German instead of an American spy. And Anton. I glanced at his white face, his squinting eyes. If he were caught he'd be executed on the spot. No, if he were caught, we'd all be shot.

"Deiter," said Loremarie, maintaining calm as she shifted closer to Eva, "get your crutches and come stand by me. And Willi, get up and stand next to your mother. I think we can block their view."

Dieter cursed and mumbled. Grunting, he grabbed at his crutches, pulled himself up, and catapulted himself over and around.

Flushed with anger, he said, "I won't be killed because of some American, particular this one!"

"Shut up or I'll kill you myself!" threatened Loremarie.

I bit my lip. So it was Dieter who had tipped off the Gestapo, brought them snooping about the bar. Of course it was. I could hear the hatred in his voice.

Loremarie continued, "Now, Anton, just help Joe up." Joe scrambled up the dirt walls and out of the grave, and she said to him, "Good. Now keep low and crawl backwards. That's it. The wall's only five or six meters behind you. There's a hole. Just crawl through it and get out of here. We'll be all right."

"I'll see you at the house tonight," said Anton.

"*Ja, ja, ja.*"

I stood rigid next to my mother, and watched as Joe and Anton pushed back over the cold earth, across the stubbly, dormant grass. They snaked around a gravestone, over a mound of dirt and a cherubic stone head. Next a wing. Someone's guardian angel, I thought, blasted to bits.

Keeping, low, beneath the height of the crosses, Anton made it to the wall first. He glanced at Loremarie, offered a hopeful smile, then crawled through the hole. Joe followed, his gut to the ground, his hands pawing over bricks. And then he was gone as well.

I looked up at my mother and, my voice hoarse, said, "He doesn't know the way back, does he?"

"He'll be all right."

But he might not be. And in an instant I broke away, swerved around the pit of death that held my Erich, dashed over a mound of fresh dirt, and reached the cemetery wall.

"Willi!" cried my mother.

I popped through the hole, emerged on the other side, and found myself standing in a rubble-strewn street. I looked to my right and saw Anton slipping into the shell of a nearby building. To the left I saw Joe cutting into an alley. I chased after him, eager to show him a safe way home and to ask him again about escaping from the city.

"Joe!" I called, my voice hushed.

But I already knew the answer. The full moon was tonight, and I had to accept that it was now too late to flee, had to accept that we were caught here in Berlin.

Chapter

18

I was sitting on a bench at one of our heavy wooden tables. The piano was only a few feet away, Dieter's accordion slumped over next to it. I remembered when I'd first brought Joe here, how crowded and lively it had been. Mother had been pulling a song from her body, her life. Now it was empty. Dark and quiet in our bunker bar. Joe was in the back room, lying down on the cot.

I had my head in my arms when they returned. I heard the door above, scraping as it was pulled open, and I looked up and gazed around. I'm still here, I thought. Still really here. But not for much longer. No. Not much longer at all.

I suppose it could have been the SS or the Gestapo or something else horribly official coming down the stairs, but I heard the steps and knew it wasn't. Slow steps, sliding down the curling stairs. That was Mother, walking on the front of her heeled shoes, the dark brown ones. And Lore-marie. And the odd noise—Dieter on his crutches. Glancing over, I saw all three emerge.

Mother gazed at me through a veil of tear-soaked eyes. I

was sure she was going to scold me, but then her face suddenly expanded in fear.

"*Mein Gott*, Joe wasn't caught, was he?"

"No, I'm right here," said Joe, emerging from the back room. "We made it back about a half-hour ago."

Loremarie glanced from me to Joe. "What about . . . ?"

"Anton'll be all right."

Dieter headed for the bar, saying, "That is, if he's smart and doesn't try to make it the rest of the way until dark. He was foolish to come out at all. How are we supposed to stay alive with the likes of him and an American wandering about?"

I saw Loremarie's mind clicking, wondering what she should do. Stay here a while longer, see what she could do for Eva? Or head back, see if Anton had returned? At all.

"What about the patrol?" asked Joe. "Did they bother you?"

"*Nee*," responded Loremarie. "Not really."

Mother took off her coat. "They. . .they filled the grave for us."

Oh, I thought, sitting at the table. So they weren't all bad. Never mind that they would have killed Joe and Anton.

Loremarie mumbled something about potatoes and water for coffee and getting something hot in us, and she slipped into the little kitchen area behind the piano. Meanwhile, Dieter went to the bar and poured two glasses of brandy, one for mother and one for himself.

"*And what about you, Willi?*"

I was just sitting there, staring at the floor. All of me felt numb, like I'd lost control of my body and I'd never be able to move again. No, I was stone. Cold, hard stone. And I was wondering if it was too early to look for my brother's ghost.

A big something descended next to me. "Willi?"

Joe. He put an arm around me, pulled me close to him.

"*What's he doing, Willi? Think. With the knowledge you*

have as an adult and with what you've learned in therapy, imagine what's going through Joe's mind."

As he wrapped himself around me, I suddenly heard his voice. No, not his voice. His mind. I could hear it, plainly, clearly, and Joe was thinking how he wished he could bring Erich back to life, how he wished he could get us all out of this hole and up to the mountains. But, I knew, Joe could do none of that, and that's when I sensed Joe thinking that it was his fault. That there was something he could have done, should have done.

Wait, no! It was *my* fault, not Joe's. It was my job to protect Erich, and . . . and . . .

"Willi, death is only simple for those who die."

And Erich was dead. So would his ghost return to haunt me, torment me for not saving him?

"No, but his death has already started to fester within you, and you need to clean that wound so that it can heal. Joe would like to help you, wouldn't he?"

Joe held me tight, he really did, and kissed me on the cheek. He didn't speak, but via some mystical loudspeaker I could hear his mind. He was thinking how sorry he was about Erich, how much I, Willi, loved Erich, and how much I would miss him forever and ever.

"Now let yourself do the grieving that you both want and need. You've waited a long time to express how much you feel for Erich and how sad you are about his death."

A cry popped out of me like a cork from a bottle of champagne. A bad bottle, for out of me came not bubbles of happiness, but an explosion of sorrow. I hung onto Joe and cried for my little brother. For all that wouldn't be. I snapped, and realized that even if I came to accept Erich's death, I was forever broken. Willi, the *steppke*, would never be again. I'd thought myself and all around me whom I loved invincible, but now I realized how at risk I and they truly were.

Out of nowhere came a sharp crash of glass smashing against stone. Then immediately another. And another. Joe and I jerked apart. Spinning, I saw my mother, a ball of fury, leaning against the bar and hurling glass after glass at the stone wall. Her face was covered by rivulets of tears, and her agony and pain and anger came screaming out in lioness cries. Only a few meters away, Dieter sipped his brandy and watched as if this were some great sport and Mother its master.

"Eva!" shouted Joe, jumping up.

Loremarie came rushing out of the kitchen area, only to duck as a glass skimmed her head.

"*Verdammt noch mal!*" Damn-it, Mother screamed.

She grabbed another glass, brought back her arm, and threw the tumbler through the air. It smacked like a crystal bomb against the wall. Then she reached for a bottle of Schultheiss beer. But Joe was quicker. He charged up behind her, grabbed the bottle from her hand. Spun her around.

"Let me go!" she cried, beating on him.

But Joe wouldn't. She beat on his shoulders, grabbed his hair. Then he caught her completely, his arms locking her arms at her side. As if she were being electrocuted, she opened her mouth and screamed, her pain long and high. Finally, she collapsed into Joe and began to sob deeply.

"*Mein Gott, mein Gott!*" she wailed. "Why *kleiner* Erich? Why my baby?"

I watched as Joe clutched her, hugged her, rocking back and forth. He took deep breaths, made hushing noises. Finally, all was quiet. Only the sound of potatoes frying in the back room.

Something tinkled, soft and melodically. The sound expanded, filled the bar and our ears. Dieter, I realized, was playing the piano. Some American jazz tune, very slow and drawn out. I think it was "Begin the Beguine," and I watched Mother and Joe begin to tilt and sway. She pressed right up to him, and I realized, yes, they were dancing. Joe's eyes drifted shut and he pulled her closely to him. Dancing. It made me happy to see them so close and finally in harmony. It lasted only a few short minutes, however. Almost looking frightened, Mother broke away from my hoped-for father, pushing herself back, twisting away.

"Eva . . ." called Joe, reaching out for her.

She shrugged him off with a scowl. Stepping over bits of glass, she went to the bar and poured herself something to warm a place that none of us could touch.

With Dieter still poking at the piano, Mother's body started to drift with the music. With a quick pitch of her wrist, she downed one glass of brandy, poured herself another, emptying the bottle. Then turned around, eyes closed, hips swaying to the languid tune. She sipped on her glass, raised a hand and marked the music in the air as Dieter hit key after key.

Then Dieter changed melodies and of course Mother followed, for this song had caught not only the *Vaterland*, but the whole world. With lyrics by a little Hamburg poet, it was the most German song my mother ever sang.

"*Bei der Kaserne, vor dem grossen Tor,*" chanted Mother, "*steht 'ne Laterne, und steht sie noch davor, da woll'n wir uns wiederseh'n, bei der Laterne woll'n wir steh'n, wie einst, Lili Marleen.*"

Forgetting about the war, about my little brother, I listened as Mother sang about a man waiting for Lili Marleen, a woman no one had ever known. And I thought how the world would never know my mother's voice, either. A voice that was more rich than Lale Andersen's—whose gramophone version of the same song was broadcast so frequently—but a voice so less valued, buried here in this bar. This was Mother's pain. She had something to sing, and besides us, no one would truly hear her.

Mid-song Mother took a sip of brandy, and it clouded her throat. She opened her mouth, but what emerged was out of pitch and painfully flat. Then of course, Erich began to drip back in. And the SS and the Russians and the bombs. All this seeped back into the world, and I felt myself plummeting. Mother had always been able to transport people with her song, but no longer. She reached for one more note and her voice cracked painfully.

"Oh, crap," she said, forcing a laugh.

Giggling, she waltzed behind the bar and swooped down like a drunken bird. Emerging with a fresh bottle of brandy, she twisted open the top and poured herself more. I started to step forward, wanting nothing more than to bash that drink out of her hand. I moved forward, but then Joe stuck out a hand. Halted me in place.

Approaching her, he said, "Eva, let's have some coffee."

"What? *Nee*. Sorry, I'm all out of cognac, but try some of this, Joe. It's my last bottle!"

"Don't you think you've had too much?"

She scowled at him, shook her head. "Aren't you the judgmental American."

"Eva . . ."

"I mean, really, look at you! Now come on, have a drink with me. Let's have some fun!"

She gulped down her glass, then started to refill it. Missed. Chuckled at the pancake puddle on the bar. Tried again. This time the brandy flowed into the glass, which she then lifted to Joe's face.

"Here, have some!"

"Eva, stop it!"

"Oh, Joe baby, you used to be fun!" She shrugged. "Well, sometimes."

Joe grabbed the bottle from her. She looked at him and giggled. Then she downed her glass and held it out, a puffy schoolgirl frown on her face.

"Can't I please have some more, *Liebchen*?"

Watching my mother, I caught my breath. Looked down at the floor. What was going to become of her? How would her story end? She would never, I sensed, recover from the war. Too much was broken and lost. This person would never be right again. I looked over at my own mother and couldn't see any future in those cloudy eyes. She'd fallen and she herself was making sure she'd never get up again.

"You've had enough," said Joe. "You need something to eat and a cup of coffee."

"*Nee*, I want more brandy!"

Joe backed away. "Eva . . ."

"Give me that bottle!"

She lunged at Joe, and he jabbed his hand out, smacked her in the chest and pushed her away. His face all tense, he clutched the booze, obviously not about to surrender it. That much and more was clear. I was on my feet, suddenly afraid for my mother.

"That's mine!" she said.

"You're drunk!" shouted Joe, flushed with anger.

"You're a piece of shit!"

I was shaking. Watching them, I realized something I'd never known.

"What are you sensing about their relationship Willi?"

Joe could hurt my mother. In fact, he wanted to hurt her. In his face I saw all this pain. Pain she'd caused him. I saw Joe's body turn rigid, and knew that he wanted to reach out, strike her with a hard fist, knock her down. There was a part of him that hated her. I didn't know exactly what had happened between the two of them before the war, but I was certain now that Joe had gotten all tangled up in my mother's melodic fantasies. To capture his attention, she'd probably plied him with her booze and song, ensnared him, and he wanted her. All of her. But that was too much, more than she could give, and he hated her for that. For pulling him so close that he could never get away, while at the same time forever rejecting him.

With deadly anger spitting out of his body, Joe said, "You bitch!"

Attempting to defuse the situation, I charged over and grabbed the bottle of brandy from Joe's hands. Just as quickly, I turned and hurled it with all my strength. Like the glasses my mother had broken, the bottle shot missile-like through the air and shattered on the stone.

"Willi!" screamed Mother.

I moved away, stepping backward as she rushed the wall and stared in disbelief at the dripping brandy. Then she turned to me, eyes boiling. I tensed as if about to be shot because I knew what she wanted to say.

"Stay with this. There's something you need to learn."

Of course she wanted to tell me how much she hated me, how much I'd ruined her life. And more than that, she wanted to tell me how it should have been me, me who was toasted instead of her precious Erich! I saw the words come right to the tip of her lips, but at the last moment she turned, fired on Joe instead.

"God knows why I just don't turn you in and let the authorities butcher you!" she said.

"So that's only how you feared she felt toward you. She didn't actually say—"

Laughter splattered our bunker. God, she was laughing and Erich had only been in the grave an hour or two. Coy amusement bubbling out of her, Mother sauntered over to the bar, and from behind lifted a small black phone.

"That was only my last bottle of brandy. Certainly not the last in Berlin." She fired a smile at me. A piercing, mean smile. "I know where I can get more. Even more cognac. And soon."

When she lifted the receiver to her ear, however, her smile melted. She tapped the button on the phone a couple of times. Nothing. Then again and again. A storm of anger swept across her face.

"*Scheisse!*" she shouted.

She hit the button several more times, but apparently was still unable to get a dial tone. Red with frustration, she swept the phone from the bar and it crashed on the floor. Mother glanced at it, then burst again into laughter.

"There, now it really won't work!" proclaimed Mother.

Watching from the kitchen doorway, a black frying pan of potatoes in her hand, Loremarie said, "Oh, Evchen."

"Guess I'll just have to go out and get some more!" She turned to me. "Willi! Willi, fetch me my coat."

I froze in a tight spasm. The last thing my mother needed, of course, was more booze. And the last thing I wanted was to go poking around looking for it.

"No," said Joe.

"Evchen . . . Evchen," began Loremarie, "why don't you just stay here for a while? Let's have something to eat. We'll go out later."

"What?"

"You shouldn't go out," said Joe, flatly.

"That's right." Loremarie held up the potatoes. "Food will be good for us all. It's been a terrible morning."

Mother shook her head, waved away Loremarie and her food.

"Don't be ridiculous. Willi, now fetch me my coat! Come on, we're going!"

I was too tired to fight, and I turned, saw her brown coat and fur trimmed hat lying on a stool.

Joe stopped me, saying, "No, Eva, I won't let you go."

"What?" She stared at him for a moment, then broke her disbelief with still more laughter. "Oh, Joe, you're so ridiculous."

"No."

She shook her head, started across the room. Almost like

a quick dance, Joe spun out in front of her and caught her
by the wrist.

"Eva—"

Just as quickly something dropped between them. A
round pole. No, a crutch. Dieter's bitter crutch drawn out
like a sword.

"Let her go," he demanded.

Balancing on one leg and one crutch, Dieter stood poised
to lunge, his stubbly beard rough and ugly. More than just
tolerating Mother and her antics, he'd always been extremely protective of her. She was, I knew, the only woman
in his life, and he took delight in kissing her and having her
kiss and flirt with him. But there was something else. He
needed her for some terrible reason that filled him with a
dark and deep fury.

"Dieter," said Joe, "she shouldn't go out. She doesn't
need more drink."

"It's none of your business. Now let her go."

*"Bring in your awareness, Willi. What else do you know
about Dieter?"*

There was a secret. I was supposed to forget, pretend I'd
never seen it. I was very little when it happened, and
Mother said we'd all be sent to prison if I ever mentioned it.
So I had to forget.

*"But years later it's all right to remember because you're
just trying to understand. Nothing will happen now. It's
safe for the truth to be clear."*

I was very young, only four or five. Dieter had been off in
the army, but then he came back on leave for a few days.
This was before the *Pension* burned down and before Dieter lost his leg. And I was looking for Mother all over the
inn. So I went upstairs. No mother on the second floor. No
mother on the third. I kept going up and up until I reached
the top floor, where I heard noises coming from the front
room, the big bedroom with the curving balcony. There

wasn't anyone staying there, so I thought Mother was cleaning. I tried the door but it was locked. I looked through the keyhole . . . and that's when I saw him. Dieter. He heard me at the door and he looked up. His face was all tense, as if the enemy had just surprised him. He was in bed with someone.

"With whom?"

I don't know. I couldn't really see the face.

"Think, Willi. Go back and picture yourself looking through that keyhole. What did she look like?"

She? She? Dieter wasn't in bed with a woman, he was in bed with another man! I saw them in that top floor room, the two of them under the sheets. Mother came rushing up the stairs only seconds later and pulled me away. I wasn't supposed to ever, ever talk about this, she said. If I did we'd all be punished. And that's when I understood. Somehow I put it all together. Ever since Mother's grandfather had thrown her out, Dieter had given her shelter. In return Mother gave him more than just someone to help run the *Pension*. She gave him his alibi. With Mother around to laugh and kiss and flirt with, no one ever questioned Dieter, no one ever made him wear a pink triangle. That something terrible pent up in Dieter was, of course, his sexuality. And now he was afraid Joe was going to ruin everything, throw their delicate world off balance, send it careening out of control.

Joe said, "Dieter, I—"

"I said, let go of her!"

Mother's mouth tightened into a flat smile, and she twisted her wrist free. Her sauntering body said: See? See?

"Eva, please. Just wait a minute, would you?" Joe turned back to Dieter. "Can't you tell I'm worried about her? Can't you see I'm only trying to help?"

"She had enough of your help before the war."

Stiffening yet more, Joe demanded, "What does that mean?"

"It means I'm only sorry the Gestapo didn't get you."

Joe lunged forward, his arms plowing into Dieter, hurling him back. Dieter lost his balance, skipped and tumbled against a column, where he caught himself. And I wondered, was it true? Was Joe really responsible for my mother's long, fiery plunge, which had yet to end?

"You fascist piece of shit," said Joe, marching toward him.

Dieter grinned. "She loathes you, you know. I mean, really loathes you."

I watched from the side as Joe went flying through the air, arms out, ready to grab Dieter by the neck and rip out his throat. Just as quickly, Dieter's crutch came swinging around. Caught Joe in the side. The wind batted out of him, Joe missed a step, but still managed to lunge out and seize Dieter by one arm. Brought him twisting down to the stone floor. Fists were brandished and swung, Joe striking Dieter squarely in the shoulder. Dieter, all the force of his body having risen to his arms, responded with a punch to Joe's jaw, knocking the American flat on the floor. I stepped from the side, ready to reach out, take sides. But which?

Joe snapped, "It was you, Dieter, wasn't it, who called the Gestapo here?"

Dieter lifted his fists and smiled and nodded. "I want you dead before you can hurt us."

Joe hurled himself up and off the floor. Threw himself and his anger at Dieter, tackling the one-legged man. They rolled across the floor, slamming into a bench and toppling it over.

All of a sudden some huge force barreled behind me. Screamed: "Stop it! Stop it!"

Loremarie plowed me aside, rushed toward them. That there was a war here, now, was far more than she could comprehend.

"I've always hated you!" shouted Dieter as he swung at Joe.

Loremarie grabbed him by the back of his shirt, and screamed, *"Nee!"*

Her great body dove downward, rammed them. She was far stronger than I would have thought, and she started wrestling them apart.

"Get out of the way!" shouted Joe at her.

"Stop it, stop it right now!"

Dieter: "I'll kill him!"

Loremarie dropped herself between them, but Joe kept trying to swing. Dieter shouted his anger—about his leg, his parents who'd been blasted and burned in Hamburg and—

"Eva! Willi!" shouted Loremarie, still trying to hold them apart. "Come here! Help me!"

I turned. Mother! Mother? She wasn't there, wasn't right behind me watching from the sidelines. Wasn't by the bar or sitting at a table, either. My heart thumped, then took off. Her coat and hat were missing. At once I raced over to the bottom of the stairwell. A ball of cool air came rolling down, washing me with its chill. My mother, I knew, had escaped, gone off in search of drink.

Chapter

19

Unnoticed, I abandoned the arguing mass of voices and fists, grabbed my own jacket, and bounded up those curling stairs. Shoving open the oak door at the top, I ran out, through the courtyard, through the ruins of the *Pension.* I squinted in the sun. Which way? She couldn't have gone more than a block or two. But which block?

I'd find her. I had to. I cut to the right. Ran over rubble. Sped down a path that some tidy neighbor had swept of debris from the last raid. Would sweep again and again until Germany was back on its feet. And then sweep more. I pushed through the chilly, late winter day. The sun was big and bold, like the moon would be tonight. Was there any hope left, any chance of getting out of Berlin? No. I had to accept that.

There were only a few people out. All women except for a few old men. Some soldiers. But no Mother in her wool coat and fur-trimmed hat. With Erich no longer slowing her, she was moving quickly. Or had I gone entirely in the wrong direction? I came to a corner. Turned around. Yes. I had to go back in the other—

Wait. There she was, weaving quickly through debris, one tipsy foot after the other. So she wasn't so fast. Not really. I started running forward, ready to call out to her, ready to try and bring her back, but then I slowed, reining myself to a stop. It struck me that Mother was stumbling toward the answer to a long-pressing question. Yes, I wanted to know, had to know, who was supplying her with alcohol. Was it the man with the swarthy aura and the fist full of American dollars? Or was it the man in the long car with the chauffeur and the flapping door? A surge of angry curiosity came rushing out of nowhere, flooding the street, pulling me, dragging me into the shadows. I wasn't going to call after her. Of course not. No, I'd tail my mother, follow her to this, the most secret piece of her life.

"And what will you learn, Willi?"

Something terrible. That was what lay at the other end of her trek.

"Be more specific."

I nearly tripped over it. I was about to learn what kept Mother here, why she felt she could survive nowhere but in a place that was dying. And that's what I really needed to know, too: why she'd never wanted to leave Berlin. To see that truth, to find something so hidden, I had to be sharp. An excellent observer. Then with that knowledge maybe we could get her to leave.

I shrank to the side of the street, drew myself behind a pile of brick, and played my mother out like a fish on a line. Give her space, I thought, let her roam, and she won't know she's already been snagged. I let her go another twenty paces, then started off, determined to discover where Mother was swimming in this sea of debris.

Up a street, around a corner. She moved on, her step more sober and confident with each moment. I didn't know where she was headed, of course, except that it was north. Again toward the Tiergarten district with its smashed expensive houses and flats and diplomatic missions. She shied away from the broad Potsdamerstrasse, actually headed more to the west, which relieved me because the main Gestapo headquarters were more to the east, not far from Potsdamerplatz. So that was good. That would mean, I hoped, that whomever she was involved with would more than likely be a government official or diplomat or perhaps someone rich and noble. Not the keepers of the horror.

I followed my mother through nothing but ruins, entire blocks that had been bombed and burned over and over again. Across a once grand avenue, a crowd of old men and young boys was overturning the shell of a streetcar; they then started filling it with bricks and other rubble. Somehow this and other haphazard barricades sprouting everywhere were supposed to stop the Russians, who had pushed and shoved and marauded all the way from Moscow, across the steppes, through Poland and into Germany.

Berlin was but a facade. That was all that was left. The interior of almost every building had been hollowed out, and all that was left were these grand though heavily damaged exteriors. Pockmarked, skeletal dowagers, that's what they were. Everywhere hung ornate balconies with no apartments behind them. Huge, arching windows that were glassless as well as meaningless because there were no roofs and there were no floors or homes on the inside. On and on. Four, five, and six-story buildings that clung precipitously to one another because there was nothing inside to support them.

So it was a mask, this whole place. And now I understood why Hitler hadn't already surrendered, why he hadn't called a truce before the final and worst damage was done to the heart of Germany. This was a pretend city. Pretend it still existed. Pretend there was a secret weapon. Pretend there was still a chance of victory.

Mother disappeared around a corner. I hurried to the edge of a building, peered around. She was picking her way down the middle of a narrow street, and I'd gone but a few feet when I heard the deep growl of an engine. Slowly making its way toward us, lumbering over this and that from last night's raid, rolled a huge *feldgrau* army truck. Mother clambered to the side and out of the way of the huge open vehicle that was blooming with helmets and rifles. Quickly I slipped into a narrow alley. I was her son and I was smart. Easily as clever as her. I wouldn't let myself be seen.

Down at the other end of the narrow passage, only some twenty meters away, lay a dead horse. At the rear of the creature stood an old man, hearty but easily in his eighties, entirely bald and wearing wire-rimmed spectacles and a fine dark suit. He looked like a retired professor or doctor, and he stood there, a large knife in his hand, staring at me. I nodded politely at him, he returned the greeting as if we were taking torte and coffee at some *Konditorei*, and then continued carving the hind quarters of the horse.

The rumbling of the truck began to fade, and I checked, found the truck had passed and my mother was moving on. Ever my mother's tail, I passed onto a larger street and into a stream of people. This was some main thoroughfare, wider and more clear of debris, and Mother continued up it, then turned at the first corner.

Sensing she was near the end of her journey, I darted in and out of the throng, slowed at the edge of the block, and observed her approaching a medium-sized building. Occupying one side of a small, open square, this place was very official and not at all friendly looking, all its windows filled in with sandbags. Battered, too. Huge divots had been chipped from its stone walls, and about half of it was tinged black from nearby fires. So, I realized, somehow this building had so far escaped the heavy bombing dropped on this area. And this was where Mother's keeper of the cognac worked. Yes, and this miracle man, her angel of the Reich who had safeguarded her for so long, most certainly was not the same man I'd seen passing Mother the American dollars. No, this guy was big, someone who dealt in blocks of gold, not in bundles of American dollars.

I watched as Mother mounted the building's wide staircase, as she knocked on its heavy door, as she disappeared inside. Suspecting it wouldn't be long for a single bottle, I made my way closer, over some recently charred boards, and into a demolished bakery. My nose twitched. Everything was deathly fresh. A fire, perhaps as recent as yesterday's bombings.

Stepping over the remains of a display case, I got a better view of the plaza and the dominating office or government or diplomatic or whatever it was building. Next to it I saw the shell of a long car, undoubtedly once shiny and elegant, but now torched and horrible. Tires melted. Paint fried away. Interior roasted. Of course I couldn't be sure, but as a ghost of its former self, it certainly resembled the one with the flapping door. The one at the zoo. Perhaps, quite possibly, that person and his driver had made it all the way back here before the car was caught in the fire. Then again, this could be another car altogether. There were hundreds like it littering Berlin.

I leaned against a wall and wished I had some of Loremarie's potatoes or coffee. Across the street I saw a tattered sign whose headline read: *Soldaten der Armee Wenck!* Then a big line at the bottom ordered: *Berlin kapituliert nie vor dem Bolschewismus!* So, I thought, Berlin wouldn't capitulate, particularly not to the Bolsheviks. But it wouldn't be saved, either. Joe was right. I knew it now. There was no secret anything. Nothing to save us. All of

Germany was about to be crushed, and Berlin, the heart of it all, would get it the worst. These years of bombing had only been the appetizer.

I heard steps, looked over to the building and saw two men in leather coats emerge. I started trembling, from the cold as much as the sight of the leather. Only the most powerful men in Berlin dressed like that. Mother, Mother, I thought, what place is this? And what are you doing in there, who are you seeing? My blood began to thin, race through my body as I imagined every hideous possibility.

My feet began to ache from the cold. Staring the entire time out a big hole that had once been a large window, I stomped on the rattly floor of the burned bakery. Finally, I saw the door of the mausoleumlike building crack, then open. All-smiles-Mother stepped out. I knew that face, that my-charm-wins-all look of victory, and in one hand I saw her clutching her flask surely refilled with cognac, and in the other the neck of a bottle. I didn't know if Mother thought herself beautiful, but she was a master at using what God-given attributes she had. She was a make-up artist, able to apply charm like cosmetics to achieve stunning results. And once again she had succeeded.

Mother spoke to someone still inside, reached in, pecked the unseen person on the cheek. No. Rather, she gave a full, lengthy kiss. And I turned away. I wondered what it was like to grow up in a place where you could sleep in a bed above ground, where the loudest noise you'd ever hear would be your very own alarm clock. I wondered what it was like in America. That's where I wanted to go. That's where I would go if the war ever ended. If I lived that long. America. It sounded like a dream. I tried to imagine myself in a time of peace, but could not.

I stayed hidden in the shell of the bakery, watched from the charcoal shadows as my mother slipped her flask into her coat pocket, then descended the stairs of that building, crossed the square and came closer and closer to me. So now I knew where her protector roosted, though I didn't know what he did. Unfortunately, it didn't even occur to me to wait, to simply follow Mother back to our bunker bar and corner her there. This secret she'd kept from me for years, and I had to know it all now, that very moment, despite the horrible consequences.

"*Hallo*, Mama," I called softly from the innards of the bakery.

I liked her reaction. Shot with disbelief, she turned in the street as if she'd heard an angel, then looked at me standing there as if I were the devil. Face bursting red, melting to white.

"Willi!" she gasped. Immediately she looked back at the building. "*Mein Gott!*"

At once it was apparent how dangerous situation this could be, and each second things became still more clear, for those big dark eyes of hers telegraphed an even deeper secret to me. It was so simple that it hadn't ever crossed my mind before—this was why our little bar had never been closed. My stomach tightening and shrinking, I stood reading the truth at last so clearly exposed on my mother's face. Liquor was never free, and now during the war it was even more expensive. And Mother had been paying its hefty price all along. I thought back to all those who frequented our little bunker bar, to those not of pure Nazi thought like that lady who'd spouted off and then disappeared just last week. For years now Mother had been offering plentiful drink and singing racy songs, creating an atmosphere of loose lips. So what had she learned? How many had she turned in? Of those, how many were left alive?

Clutching a brown boozy bottle under her arm, Mother stumbled toward me, through a hole, over bricks. Eyes seething, she came at me. Someone had caught her. And that someone was her own son. But would I tell Dieter, Loremarie, others? Even I didn't know.

"Come on, we've got to get out of here!"

"You're a *Spitzel*, aren't you?" A snitch. An information whore. I stood in shock. Me, just a kid, but knowing there was nothing worse. My very own mother. "He's Gestapo, isn't he?"

"Don't!"

Don't ask, she was saying. So that meant, of course, he was a man of power. So much power it was better not to know. Which in turn meant he was indeed one of the ruthless ones. With a snap of his finger he could liquidate Mother and me and Dieter and Loremarie and, of course, Joe.

"The bar hasn't been closed because of him, right?"

My very own horrible mother moved yet closer to me, saying, "*Ja,* of course, but . . . but don't you understand?" She shook her head, pulled at her hair. "*Scheisse*, at first he threatened to send me off to a labor camp, and then what would have happened to you and Erich? Later he was the one who saved both of you, too!"

"But . . ."

"I had no choice, Willi!" she pleaded. "He's kept us alive!"

Disgusted, I turned from her. I quickly tallied up everything, and Mother lost. I wanted her out of my life.

"Willi!"

I had to get away. Escape this crazy world. I didn't know how I'd do it, where I'd go. But I had to. I had to leave my own mother, my own city. Escape. Perhaps Joe would come with me. Perhaps Loremarie and Anton, too. Standing there in the remains of some strange bakery, it was odd how adult I felt.

"Mama, I want to leave Berlin."

Mother reached over and ran her hand through my hair. "You're right, Willi. We'll all go. I'll—"

"*Nee*!" I twisted away, wanted no part of her.

"But Willichen, you need the passes." She curled her voice, smoothed it nice and sweet. "I'm sure Anton's finished them and they look wonderful. We can get everything from Anton, and then leave!"

Spearing our argument was a dry snap of wood, a branch-like cracking as if we were in the woods and some unseen person had just revealed himself. Immediately, Mother and I fell silent, turned. Searched the bakery shop ruins for a spy. And there he was, quite confidently revealing himself as he stepped from the street and into the building. Altogether nicely dressed in a shiny leather coat and dark slacks, and holding a pistol in his gloved hand. I found myself staring at those leathery fingers gripping that gun. Yes, that was the hand I'd seen cupping my mother's breast outside the zoo.

Mother gasped, said, "Heinrich, I . . . I . . ."

And that was a man I'd seen before. My entire being jolted with shock.

"Passes?" he said. "Eva, my dear, you never said anything about wanting to leave me. And who's this Anton?"

Never could I forget him, this man with the narrow face and long nose and pale skin and hair. I couldn't forget him because he was an eel incarnate. This was the very man who had sent those two thugs down into the bar, searching for Joe. The one we'd later spied on the street and who Joe had seemed to recognize. The one who'd had a death squad waiting for Joe and me. My heart sputtered like a flak-hit bomber desperately trying not to crash. Did this mean that Deiter, who'd brought the Gestapo running, was in on Mother's *Spitzel* work as well?

"You've been keeping some secrets from me, haven't you, Evchen? You know how I feel about that. It's certainly not part of our agreement." He casually lifted the pistol, flaunted its barrel at her head. "Leaving? You wouldn't betray the *Vaterland*, would you, by running away at so crucial a moment?"

"Please, Heinrich, I can explain!"

"Oh, I should like that."

I was numb with disgust and hatred for my own mother. She'd abandoned Erich at the zoo to go embrace this man who'd nearly had Joe and me killed. Anger rushed through me, caused every part of me to burn and shake.

He spread a slime of a grin on that face. *"Hallo,* Willi. Your mother's talked all about you. You're quite the delivery boy, aren't you?

On impulse, he squeezed the trigger of his gun, and a bullet went whizzing past me and zinged against something metal. Mother screamed and dropped her precious bottle of brandy. Heinrich stood there, quite complacent, and I locked up my fear, called on all my strength to merely blink at the shot.

"Maybe there's something you'd like to tell me, Willi?" he said. "Such as, who else your dear mother's been seeing and where this Anton is obtaining transit passes?"

Mother was crying. Her eyes lifted, met mine, and I saw they were filled with tears of shame. As we teetered on the edge of disaster, her integrity stood naked in front of me, and she knew as well as I that it was slovenly and disgusting.

"Willi . . ." she begged.

Just then a second shot blasted, this bullet whizzing closer, just over my shoulder, before striking a heady board with a dull fleshy thud. I jumped aside and Heinrich focused on me. He smirked and I could see something dangerous and quite deadly in his aim: jealousy. He wanted my mother, wanted control of her. For much more than state security reasons, he was bent on learning everything about Anton.

Heinrich cuddled up to Mother, his arm slithering around her, massaging her back. Then he started kissing her, moaning venomous grunts in her ear. Mother's head dropped forward, she bit her lips. Tears streamed. Then his hand came up, and his fingers snaked through her hair, grabbed, and yanked back her head.

"Tell me about this Anton and his passes or I'll shoot your son!"

As his arm straightened toward me, the air rushed from my lungs. I couldn't move. He really would, I knew, kill me.

"Please, no!" sobbed my mother.

Heinrich laughed, this chortle high and slimy, and in that millisecond I saw Mother's arm come forward, then jab back into his stomach. Faster and harder than I could ever have imagined, my mother heaved herself into Heinrich. His foot catching in a crack, he lost his balance and began to fall. Desperate, he clawed out, clutched at Mother and brought her tumbling down with him. Just before they hit the floor, the gun fired in my direction. I dropped, heard the bullet zing past me.

"Run, Willi!" screamed Mama.

She belted him as hard as she could, tried to beat him down. I pushed myself up, started toward her. I realized that I couldn't abandon her because I was her *kleiner Soldat* and I had to help, protect! Any second a group of Heinrich's men would come storming over. My mother and I had to get away!

"Mama!"

"Run!" she screamed as she wrestled the eel around her.

Heinrich swung his gun out at me. I didn't want to go. But the pistol, he was waving it at me, taking aim!

I dove to the side just before he fired. Then I was on my hands and knees, scrambling my way out of the burned bakery. Bursting into the street. Charging away, rushing as fast and as far away as I could from my mother the informant and her Gestapo controller.

Chapter

20

I ran for blocks. I burst across one main street, then twisted into an alley, scrambled over a pile of rubble. My hands black with grime, I pulled aside a board, ducked into the darkness of a ruined building. It came above my heavy breathing, however. A huge whistle. Shouting. Then there was lots of tromping. Though I had no idea how many there were, it sounded like a squadron of soldiers. I heard them fan out. Comb this district, they had undoubtedly been told. Capture the boy! Drag his bloody body back here! And it struck me that I would forever be chased and hunted.

I moved on, slipped into an alley that was almost untouched. I looked up and down the narrow space. Brick walls. A pile of crates. No one. Only a sliver of light at the end. I passed what had to have been the last pane of glass in all of Germany. A little window. Sooty, but intact. I peered in. Saw a grandmotherly figure sipping tea and listening to the radio. Black. She wore a bulky black dress. Probably all her kindred had been wiped out. Husband, son, grandson. I stopped and stared at the kind face, admired her breadlike bun of hair coiled neatly on the back of her head. Here was her little untouched corner of the world. Waiting. I was sure that's all she was doing. Hoping. Probably no longer taking shelter in the cellar.

The pounding in my heart began to slow to a steady yet hard beat. I came to the corner, checked it, then continued on down the street that had little damage. I poked my hands in my pockets, hung my head, passed beneath balcony after balcony. A boy in a dark wool jacket, blond hair. I wouldn't, I knew, be that hard to pick out, so I turned off the street and wound my way on.

I started running, my imagination dripping red. Heinrich's wrath at my escape would be as foul as it would be great, and I feared for us all. A salty, rancid taste crept up my throat, blotted the back of my mouth. I clicked my tongue, tried to swallow the worry but couldn't. Someone, I was sure, was about to die in a manner most gruesome. I had to warn Joe and Loremarie.

I hurried down a street of refugees pushing prams loaded with clothing and clocks and children and potatoes. I heard Polish, noticed an old man leading a horse and cart that held his daughter and grandchildren. A babble of round faces and blonde hair and staccato language. Some of the lucky ones, I thought, to have a horse. Smart ones, too, squeezed from the east, fleeing the Russians.

The remains of the *Pension* loomed above the bar like a ghost standing boldly over a grave. I slowed near a hill of bricks and twisted metal, then sank behind a rusty mass of steel. The street was empty except for one young woman in a black coat and pants and hat, her face quite serious. She carried a small valise in one hand and a purse in another. Had she, I wondered, been bombed out, or was she heeding the warnings, fearing the stories, aware that nice young girls like her were mere fodder for the approaching hordes of Ivans?

I scanned the street, saw no lingering men in lengthy coats, no soldiers either. Had I made it back here first, or could Heinrich and his men be already hidden about or even down below in the bar?

The young woman approached, and I motioned toward her.

"*Bitte*," please, I began, "Have you—"

Her icy stare froze my words. She gave me the once over and read, I'm sure, that at the moment my fear was greater than hers, that right now her hold on life was stronger than mine. All this she did with a severe, glum face, that of a person who learned to depend on no one because everyone always died.

She spoke quietly, softly. Without stopping. "I've seen nothing."

Which told me as much as I needed. At least there wasn't a truck of troops about, and I turned, hugged the ruins, made my way as cautious as a cat. My eyes hesitated on the remains on the *Pension*'s top floor. The big room with the curving balcony—was this Dieter's private lair? His hide-away where he indulged his sexual preference? Was that why Mother would never go up there?

I waited a moment before pressing on and entering the ground floor of the ruined building. I slipped into what remained of the original cafe, then moved through and out the back side. Entering the courtyard, I paused, looked and saw no one, then headed for the door that led down to the bar. Nailed to the heavy oak wood was a piece of cardboard announcing that our establishment was closed. I glanced about one more time, reached for the handle.

Suddenly the door was hurled outward, exploding in my face. I stumbled back, certain that Heinrich and his men had caught me, would push me into a bloody death. I screamed, turned to flee. Just as quickly, a large arm reached out of the darkness.

"Willi!"

I swung around, ready to battle any soldier, but instead saw a large, familiar figure.

"Tante Lore!" I gasped.

"*Mein Gott*," she said, flushed with worry, "where's your mother?"

How much should I say? "There . . . there was some trouble."

"Oh, *Gott*, what? What?"

"The Gestapo and—"

Her face blanched. "What happened? Is she all right?"

"I don't know." I knew it now. Of course I shouldn't have left her. "There were gunshots."

"Oh!" Loremarie's eyes darted around. "Come on, we shouldn't be out here."

She pulled me in, locking the hefty door behind her with a big iron key. Rushing down the stone stairs, we were greeted by one of Dieter's tunes. A truce of sorts had been declared, and Dieter was at the piano, cigarette in mouth, brown bottle of beer on a ledge. Joe sat off to the side, sipping a cup of coffee. At the sight of me his face blushed simultaneously with relief and worry.

"Where's your mother?" he asked, rising to his feet.

Clicking her tongue, rubbing her head, Loremarie then said, "The Gestapo has her."

At that, Dieter shrunk from the keyboard. "What happened?"

I told them everything, how I'd followed Mother to that building and waited in the bakery, how the two of us were later discovered and I'd been shot at and forced to run.

Dieter asked, "You say it was a blond man? Sharp features?"

"*Ja, ja.*" With punch, I said, "Heinrich's his name."

Dieter flinched, then shook his head and offered a disgusted groan. "Oh, Eva . . . you've brought us real trouble now."

"That's right," said Joe, "because this guy's the type who won't stop at anything."

I stared up at Joe. How did he know what Heinrich would or wouldn't do?

"Oh, *Gott, mein Gott!*" gasped Loremarie. She bit her lip, looked down at me with that big face of hers. "Willi, are you sure he heard about the passes? And Anton's name? He heard that?"

I muttered a faint, "*Ja.* Everything."

"*Scheisse!*" cursed Dieter, banging the piano with his fist.

I understood now. I looked from Loremarie to Dieter, and from the sickened expressions on their faces it was all clear. Immediately Loremarie was turning, charging out of our subterranean chambers, muttering and crying, both cursing the heavens and praying to God.

"Where are you going?" Joe called.

Dieter took a swig of beer, and said, "Back to her house. If it's not already too late, she has to warn Anton and get him out of there. Heinrich won't let that tip drop. He'll squeeze Eva until he finds out everything." Rubbing his face, he added, "I imagine that means we'll all have to abandon this place. For a while, at least."

"Loremarie, wait!" said Joe, grabbing his coat.

"We're dead. All of us," proclaimed Dieter. "Once Heinrich and his crew find Anton and his forgeries, we'll all be done in. You know, hiding a Jew, false identification and ration cards." A cloud of beer belched out of his body and he laughed. "I'm sure they'll come after me at least. Hell, Eva's probably already told Heinrich all about my exploits."

I stared at Dieter, fearing that he might be right. Closing my eyes for a moment, I had that vision again, the bloody, drippy one in which one of us was killed in a most awful way, and at once I was bounding across the stone floor, up the stairs, and after Loremarie and Joe.

Chapter

21

The three of us didn't speak as we rushed down the block, fear driving us along. And we didn't check for a *Streife*—a patrol—either. No. We couldn't be slowed by caution. We had to reach Loremarie's house as quickly as possible. If only we could make it there before Heinrich, then we could warn Anton, perhaps even destroy his hidden den. Running down the street, I fantasized about a huge fire, one that would totally gut Loremarie's house. That's what we needed to do. Set Anton on the run, then light a fire in the basement of her house, which would destroy all the evidence.

But would Anton even be there? My mind whirled. We'd buried Erich just this morning. With any luck, Anton would still be in hiding near the cemetery. He'd said he'd take it slowly, perhaps not return to Loremarie's until dark. Now it was late afternoon. Would Anton's life be saved by a stroke of good fortune? I prayed that he'd been forced to hole up somewhere. If he'd found the streets empty, however, he would have proceeded on. Which meant he could already be back.

"Oh, *Gott, mein Gott,*" Loremarie mumbled over and over, again and again.

Leading the way, she half-walked, half-ran, as she steered Joe and me up one nearly untouched street, then around a corner. And here everything was gone, huge buildings bombed and burned into piles of rubble. We headed north, directly from the Schöneberg district toward the Tiergarten. Rushing, running, our hearts beating, lungs puffing, images torturing us, we circled Wittenbergplatz, cut across the road and through a human train of refugees. Loremarie plowed right through, using her weight and force like a bulldozer to run over this string of weakened people. I glanced back, spotted the monolithic KaDeWe department store, a charred block of Swiss-cheesy openings for windows.

We pressed on, block after block, across Kurfürstenstrasse, into another once-elegant district. I looked up into the sky, saw that it was pristine, a soft late-winter blue. But, unfortunately, no silvery triangles. What we needed right now, I thought, was tonight's forecast: clear skies, massive raid. Absolutely. A thousand British and American planes that would come and shit death right down on Heinrich. Something at least that would slow him down, keep him from reaching Loremarie's first.

"My house is just around this corner," said Loremarie, quickening.

Her body was puffing for air, her face beaded with sweaty worry. She broke into a trot.

"No," said Joe, catching her by the arm and pulling her back. "Just in case."

"But—!"

"Joe's right," I said. "If Heinrich's already there, we can't let him see us."

That made sense to her, and she let Joe cautiously lead the way up to the edge of a corner house. He made his way past a wrought iron fence that was only half standing, past a wall with all its stucco blasted off. And froze.

"*Nein!*" came a distant scream, a hoarse cry that scratched its way quickly down the deserted street.

I knew that voice of course. It was Mother, giving us our answer, broadcasting that Heinrich had indeed dragged out the truth and perhaps even Anton. Everything horrible I'd ever heard or seen rushed to the front of my mind.

Something charged past me, a large desperate figure, a bundle of fur about to get herself killed. I lunged but missed her. Joe turned around, though, spread out his arms, caught her head-on.

She begged, "Let me—"

Just as quickly Joe plastered his hand over her mouth and threw her to the ground. As strong as she was determined, Loremarie bucked and twisted as everything she'd feared came rushing to reality.

"Quiet!" hushed Joe.

"But Anton!"

I knelt by her, whispered, "He might not even be there, Tante Lore! He might not even be back yet!"

Joe's face flushed red with nervousness. He said, "And if you go out there, you're dead for sure!"

She quieted herself, eyes looking up, down, as she realized there might still be hope.

Joe added, "The only way you can help Anton, now or later, is if you're alive and free. You can't let them see you, right?"

Defeated, she gasped, "*Ja . . .*"

No sooner had she spoken than my mother's voice came curling down the street, at first laughing, then crying. In response I was on my feet, rushing back down toward a hole in this corner house. What must have once been a servants' entrance was now a cavelike gap, and I darted in. Clambering into the burned-out guts of this place, I was shaking. Mother. I feared what Heinrich had done to her. Would do. And suddenly my mother was innocent again. Absolved of any wrongdoing. Guilty of only wanted to stay alive. On my hands and knees I crawled up a half-flight of something that must have once been stairs, around a pile of fallen ceiling and wood, over burned floors. I feared for my mother's life, and I wondered if a friend—perhaps even a good friend—of Loremarie's had once lived here. Maybe Loremarie herself had spent hours in this house, drinking port wine and laughing.

Heeding a grand hole in the floor of what was once the main salon, I made my way up to the shattered front window. Slipping close, I spied out the now crude rectangular opening and nearly screamed at what I saw. Past a spindly, stubbly bush, beyond a small yard of bricks and clutter, and sitting in the blasted road was a vehicle, an army one of some sort, pulled right up in front of Loremarie's house. Two soldiers held my mother, pinning her arms behind, and she hung from them as if from a crucifix, coat ripped wide open, her little fur-trimmed hat slipping off her head. Heinrich was the wild card, pacing back and forth, and brandishing his pistol like a real American cowboy.

"Mama . . ." I moaned.

A hand clenched my shoulder, kept me hidden behind the wall. Loremarie. She and Joe were behind me. And it was only her tight grasp that kept me from leaping out the window and across the rubble yard.

Heinrich commanded, "Give her more! She always talks when she's drunk!"

One of the soldiers, a boy-man in helmet and drab *feldgrau* uniform, lifted up a bottle. Brandy. I could tell by the smooth shapes of the brown glass. Mother twisted away, but the other soldier grabbed her by the chin, then reached back and squeezed her jaw. He must have been from the country because he was doing it all as if Mother were a calf and he needed to force down some medication. And sure enough, she grimaced and her mouth dropped open. Immediately, the first soldier began pouring a stream of golden colored booze into her mouth. Mother gagged and sobbed and spit out a large plume of liquid.

Heinrich stepped up to her, held his pistol to her head, and said, "Drink, *Liebchen!*"

As soon as the bottle was back at her lips, she was indeed like a calf, an orphan one, sucking at the bottle, guzzling down the booze. But she could only drink so fast, and the brandy came bubbling up and over, and she twisted away and began hacking.

"Now, Evchen, be good and tell me about this Anton," said Heinrich, his voice syrupy sweet. "Evchen? Evchen, is this the house where we can find him?"

Waves of coughs hammered her body; obviously the two soldiers were all that kept her upright. But this seemed to only further encourage Heinrich, and he gave the signal and the bottle was crammed back into her mouth. She swallowed, I could see that through my tearing eyes, but after just a few gulps the brandy came shooting back out like petrol from an overfilled tank.

Heinrich grabbed my mother by the hair, lifted up her face. Clenching the pistol in a metal-hard fist, he struck her chin.

"Tell me!"

She mumbled something, her words all garbled. He struck her again, and she swirled and teetered on the edge of passing out. Heinrich cursed and ordered the soldiers to release her. My very own mother dropped like a sack to the ground, and I watched as Heinrich stood above her, aimed his pistol at her head, readied himself to execute her on the spot.

I opened my mouth to scream, flexed my muscles to charge out there. No! No! I wanted to explode from this hiding spot, fly across the yard, and tell Heinrich I knew where to find Anton! Yes, and I'd take him and his soldiers there if only they'd leave my mother alone! This I'd do, and I jabbed my foot in the wall, took hold, and—

A hand was over my mouth, that ball of fur over my body. Loremarie stifled me, and then Joe and she pinned me against the wall. I twisted and kicked, wanted to scream, to damn the world I'd been born into. But their grips were so tight. Didn't they understand? Didn't Joe and Tante Lore realize that in spite of everything Mother had done I'd gladly give my life for hers? In fact, that was what I wanted. Erich and bombs and Gestapo and firestorms. I was electrocuted with rage, and I just wanted peace. Permanent peace in the shape of a bullet in my head.

Joe said: "She's all right, Willi! He's not going to hurt her!"

At last still, I heard a quick high-pitched cackle roll from outside. The oddness of it all shot me with silence. Of course. That was all part of Heinrich's technique. The gun to her head was all part of the plan.

Loremarie and Joe released me, and I peered out between several boards. Heinrich was caressing my mother like a lover, holding her, warming her.

"That's right," cooed Heinrich. "You just show me where to find Anton, and I won't hurt you."

Unmoving, my mother dangled in the hands of her executioner.

"You don't want me to hurt you, do you? I could kill you, Eva, if that's what you'd like."

Slowly, her head moved from side to side.

"Of course that's not what you want, Evchen," Heinrich said like the most benevolent of grandfathers. "Now, is this the house? Is it? You just show me where I can find this Anton and I'll get you a nice warm bath and a nice clean bed."

What could she do? What? She was caught, trapped. She loved Anton, I knew that, finding him a gentle soul, something wonderful, like the last precious tin of food. That's how she really felt, and that's what Anton really was. Preserved goodness. But what way did she have out? What choice did she have? I closed my eyes. Oh, God, I wanted to turn and run as far away from here as I could get.

"Stay with it, Willi. You'll be all right."

I spied out again. Mother had no choice, that is not if she didn't want to end up in her own puddle of death. Which, I suppose, was why she let Heinrich lift her to her feet. Then again, who knew. Her body was so sodden with brandy, toxic with confusion.

"Oh, *Gott*," prayed Loremarie behind me, "please don't let him be there. Please!"

Supported by Heinrich, Mother led him and his two young soldiers up and across Loremarie's front yard. As she stumbled along, I heard my drunk mother sobbing. Crying as she mounted the front steps, passed through the portico, and disappeared into the blackened house, leaving behind an eery trail of quiet.

In back of me, Loremarie muttered, "Oh, *Gott, mein Gott*, if Anton is home, oh, if anything happens, then I don't know what I'll do to that drunken bitch!"

My confusion and anger turned to a rigid board inside me. I was paralyzed. My own Tante Lore talking so horribly about my own mother? But . . . but Mother didn't mean to be bad. I knew she didn't! Oh, God, I thought, my head spinning. I hated this. Hated living in a world where everything was pushed to the edge. Alive one moment, dead the next.

They were gone so long, and Loremarie, Joe and I stood in concealed, chilled silence. If Mother had led them directly to the hidden room in the cellar, then they should have been there by now. Perhaps Mother had rallied, tricked them, led them into the dark, wet cellar and lost them. Or perhaps Mother had fled out the back, thinking that Heinrich wouldn't really kill her. My hopes buoyed. It was taking so long because Mother hadn't taken them to Anton's secret den. Or if she had, then Anton wasn't back yet. That would mean that we might be able to stop Anton before he returned. We could catch him as he sneaked back, then Loremarie and he could escape somehow. Perhaps, I thought, we could all disguise ourselves as battered refugees, I as their beleaguered son. Of course. And we could slip into the line of souls stumbling from the east, flowing through Berlin, and on to the west. That was good, that might—

Several shots cracked the sunny day, and with them were shattered the last of any wishful thinking I would ever have. This was essentially an evil world. Evil prevailed now and forever.

"I'm sorry," whispered Joe, clutching Loremarie's hand.

But the shots were only the beginning of a most gruesome end. From the depths of Loremarie's house came a long, pained howl.

Quietly, Loremarie cried, "Anton!"

Joe held her. He clutched her as much in sympathy as to keep her from exposing herself in the window. Anton was killed or would be momentarily. For having hid him, Loremarie would be next on the list. And then Mother and me. Dieter, perhaps. Joe, of course.

We heard more shouting. Heinrich's voice trumpeted and blared with victory. I peered out, saw Mother kicked out of the house, shoved off the front of the portico. She toppled onto a pile of wood, raised her head, her face a twisted mask of horror and pain. Cheeks lined with watery streaks. Mouth open in one long, huge scream all of it silent. Next came Heinrich. Behind him, hanging from one of the soldiers like a butchered scarecrow, was Anton, blood pouring from each of his legs. So he was alive, but hobbled. My stomach turned. Shot in both of the knees so he couldn't escape.

Heinrich shrieked Jew this, Jew that, filthmonger, traitor and spy. It was as if a dial on the back of him was being slowly turned up, cranked to full hysteria. He waved his gun around, set off a shot. Crazed. Absolutely. Anton was the reason Germany was losing the war. No great army could defeat the Bolsheviks with the likes of Anton the Jew doing evil in the home camp. Therefore the Jew had to be exterminated. Here. Now. On the spot.

Heinrich marched down to the street, ordered Anton and my mother dragged front and center. Heinrich jerked her head up, aiming her face at Anton, who hung so limply.

"We don't need this kind of rat in the *Vaterland!*" he screamed. "You're going to see every bit of this!"

Mother sobbed, begged for mercy, cried for forgiveness. I should have turned away. Or closed my eyes at least. But I couldn't. I stood hidden with Joe and Loremarie in the house across the street, and I stared.

Behind me, locked in Joe's protective arms, Loremarie chanted, "Be quick, be quick!"

Heinrich screamed, his voice rising and crashing, as if he were the one on the edge of death. And as he raved like a bedeviled preacher, he took Anton's right hand and wrapped it around the end of his pistol.

"See what we do with his kind?"

He squeezed the trigger, and the palm-piercing bullet left a spray of blood as it rocketed into the sky. Anton moaned, but only slightly, stoic in his sacrifice. Then Heinrich snatched Anton's left hand and blasted that, too.

Loremarie was on her knees, eyes closed, hands clasped in prayer. From her lips poured a stream of mumbled words, pleas and hopes for Anton's hereafter.

Legs pierced, hands drippy red, Anton swooned. Finally

a cry erupted, long and high, operatic in its clarity. But he still stood, propped up by a soldier. He had, I thought, staring at him from my hiding spot, expected this all along, waited for this moment. That was why he looked so unsurprised, so calm. He'd already left Berlin, flown out of here, abandoning this mutilation.

"Chain his feet!" ordered Heinrich.

My eyes and my heart glazed over as I watched one of the soldiers wrap a chain around Anton's feet, then attach the other end to the back of the small truck. They couldn't, they wouldn't, I thought. But this is war and the world is crazy, and that man is among the craziest. And indeed this mad dog of humanity ordered Anton dropped, allowed this stick man to tumble to the ground. Next he commanded his men to board the truck. To start the engine. To prepare to drag this scum to his filthy end. Then they would return and pull the Jew-hiding owner of this house to a similar fate.

"And you!" he shouted at Eva. "I'll deal with you later!"

As the engine coughed, then roared, Loremarie twisted on her knees, pushed herself upward, and raced to the window. Joe and I held her again, though, keeping her hidden and tackling her desires: Take me now! Kill me too! Let us die together!

We grappled with her, and then she was still, lost in the hopelessness of it all. Veiled by the ruins, she spied her Anton, a mere bloody rag on the street, and her body shook with swells of sobs. It was over . . . or would be within moments.

No sooner had Heinrich taken the front seat, then Mother cried out: "Anton!"

She hurled herself toward him, touched his black hair, sought to pull him into the warmth of her lap. The calmest of all, he gazed at her, my mother the betrayer, and offered a smile. A gentle smile, lips thin and relieved, as if he were pulling into a station after a very, very long ride.

"*Du sollst leben!*" Live on, he called to my mother.

No sooner had he spoken than the truck lurched forward with an awful, bone-wrenching jerk. And then off went the tattered and fading body of Anton, bouncing amid the rubble, mopping the streets of Berlin with his death.

Chapter

22

Live on, I thought. It sounded like a curse. Live on and suffer through all of which is to come. Suffer for the rest of your life. Was that what Anton meant?

I pushed myself up and off the furry-coated ball of my Tante Lore, and stood in the window. In the street my mother had collapsed, shaking quakelike, clutching her body, clinging to herself because there was no one else. Her mouth opened and that golden voice of hers let out a perfectly pitched shriek that pierced the neighborhood. Then her head toppled forward as if it were barely attached and she screamed into her lap.

"And what about you, Willi?"

I stared out at her, my face streaked with slow warm tears. Erich fried. Anton dragged to pieces. Horror had shackled my imagination, made me witness to things worse than I could ever have dreamed.

My fingers started moving first, clutching at lumps of plaster and pieces of wood, then pulling me up and out the window. I jumped, tumbled forward, landed on my hands and knees, and was up and running over bricks and headless cherubs. I ran into the street, looked to my right. Heinrich and the truck were gone, but the road was swabbed and dotted with blood and flecks of Anton. Down the way I saw a big block of bricks, a clump of a dozen or so blasted into the street, now all warmly covered by a shimmering shawl of blood. I wanted to cry, to vomit. I wanted the shock to rush from my sickened body and dirty this place and time. But I couldn't. I was too numb.

"Willi!" cried Mother upon seeing me.

She reached out to me like a crazed beggar, arms and hands outstretched, face pleading. I ran to her, wanting nothing but her warm embrace and shelter and denial. She threw herself at my legs, clung to me, sobbed her stinky, drunken breath. I stared in disbelief at her pathetic face, grotesquely twisted beyond recognition. This was my mother? This weak, needy thing? No, I thought, my entire being recoiling. She had to be there for me, to love and comfort me, me, me!

I heard someone charging, heavy feet pounding over rubble. I flinched and turned. Joe was running toward us.

"We've got to get out of here!" he ordered.

He was right, of course. For all we knew, Heinrich might only be out for a quick death spin. He could just be circling a block or two, and return any moment. And then what would it be? What lengths would he go to for details of Anton's forgery operation? I looked at the blood splashed down the street. We had to disappear, this second. That is, if we wanted to stay alive.

As Joe neared, Mother lunged toward him, crawling across the sidewalk, grabbing him, clutching his legs as desperate as if she were drowning.

He asked, "Are you all right?"

She flailed one hand in the direction Anton had disappeared and a garbled wail erupted from her wide mouth.

"I . . . I!"

Just then I heard the distant grumbling of a truck. Joe was right. There wasn't any time for this. Then came another huge scream, and I saw Loremarie charging us, her face red and wet, hands outstretched, ready to rip apart, kill. A buzz saw of anger, she cut a direct path of fury toward my mother.

"Bitch!"

I understood that she really did mean death, and that right here and now she would shed blood. Mother's. That was who the countess wanted to rip apart.

"You drunken whore!"

Joe jumped up, caught her and the brunt of her attack. Loremarie tried to push around him, but he caught her and her flailing fists. I backed away. Loremarie's force was as large as her anger, and she twisted and kicked, desperately struggled to reach the object of her venomous hatred.

"It's all because of her! Because of her!" she shrieked. "She killed him!"

I couldn't move. A horrible realization crept into my mind. Would any of this have happened had I not followed Mother, then stopped her in that burned-out bakery? Wasn't this all my fault? Wasn't I the one who should be dead?

"Stop it, Loremarie!" shouted Joe.

"No!"

All her rage came beating out on Joe, fist after fist, scream after scream. He shouted at her, shook her, finally hurled her back and to the ground. Joe then grabbed my mother and pulled her to her wobbly feet.

Turning to me, Joe said, "Take Loremarie and get out of here. I've got your mother."

I froze. "But—"

"We can't all go together!"

He was right, of course. We had to disappear as quickly as possible, and we wouldn't make it ten meters with both

Mother and Tante Lore. So we had to split up, then meet later and formulate the next step. Burrow in Berlin? Attempt escape to the countryside? It seemed hopeless, all of it.

"Willi," began Joe, trying to move Mother along, "we can't go back to the bar. We'll . . . we'll meet you back by the Schulenberg's, okay?"

My voice pecked: *"Ja."*

I envisioned the ruins of the apartment building from which Joe and I had barely escaped. And the piano. Frau Schulenberg's piano clinging to that ledge. That was a good place to meet. Easy to find. Only steps from our little hidden room with the metal door.

As Joe led her away, Mother cried, "Willi!"

I stared after her but didn't know what to say. I love you, I hate you, I'm sorry? Overwhelmed with confusion, I turned away, went to my *Nenntante* and helped her to her feet.

"Hurry!" shouted Joe as he dragged my mother off.

We had to be quick, all of us. And invisible. When Heinrich returned we all had to be long gone, melted into the ruins. Especially Loremarie. If she were caught, she would be shot at once. No. Tortured and questioned for having hid Anton, for her knowledge of the submarine Jews lurking beneath Berlin.

Taking aim at my mother, Loremarie screamed, "You're nothing but a drunk whoring bitch!"

I bit my lip, tugged on Loremarie's arm. "Please!"

She turned on me, the evil side of her charging forward. "Your mother was always right on the edge, flirting, you know, doing awful things! Stealing and more! She's a real whore, you know, and—"

I was crying but I didn't let go of Loremarie. Mother was all of that and more. I knew it, yet each of Loremarie's words pierced my heart. Stabbed me with pain.

"We have to hurry!" I pleaded.

I dragged her along, finally making it across the street. I glanced back, saw the last of Joe, my mother's sober crutch, leading her behind a house.

Loremarie said, "Your mother will pay for this, you can be damned—"

I froze, as did Loremarie. An engine was grumbling, biting its way toward us. *Mein Gott.* A large engine, that of a truck. I spun from side to side, saw nothing, but knew that Heinrich would reappear any second.

"Come on!"

Grasping Loremarie's hand, I tried to rush off. But in that same instant all the fight and anger fled from Loremarie, leaving her lost and vacant. I tugged on her, but she barely moved.

"Anton . . ."

Whatever was left of him was probably still chained to the truck. And it was obvious that all Loremarie wanted was to wait here so that she could gather up his remains and weep.

"Anton's dead, Tante Lore!"

She gasped, and I pulled harder, leading her around the corner, past the burned-out house where we'd hid. To another street, and into the ruins of an apothecary. Parking her in a corner behind some boards, I went back and checked the road. Animallike truck noises filled the neighborhood. Brakes squealing. A short trumpet of a claxon. Then equally gruff voices. Peering carefully out, I saw no one, but knew Heinrich was out there somewhere having a tantrum of a fit. He'd come back and Mother was gone. I only hoped Joe and she had made a clean escape.

Loremarie was pale and quiet, eyes glassy, breathing short and quick. As if it were deathly gas, I could practically see the shock seeping over her. She looked like any of the bomb victims I'd seen wandering the streets after a raid, and I knew now there would be no more resistance.

"Come on," I whispered, taking her hand again. "We'll go out the back."

"Dieter."

"What?"

"Dieter was always nice to Anton." She looked at me, blinked once. "We have to go back."

"But Joe said—"

"We have to get Dieter."

She was right. In spite of Joe's instructions, we at least needed to warn Dieter that Heinrich was on the rampage. At the same time, we could take what we could—some food, clothes, and, hopefully, Mother's American dollars.

"Okay," I said, "we'll go by the bar and then to the Schulenberg's."

"*Ja.*"

We made our way around some smashed counters, through a little back hall, and into an interior courtyard. I looked up, saw blue sky hovering over us, a partly smashed building. Then we squeezed through a wrecked door, down a little hall with dingy yellow paint and a lamp with a fringe shade. Soon we emerged on another street, found it empty, and then passed ghostlike right through the center of that block and yet another one, too. As we moved along, a steady stream of tears began to drip from Loremarie's wide face.

After almost an hour of painfully weaving our way back into the Schöneberg district, we neared our bar. We slowed, slunk into a faceless building. I looked around, studying shadows, odd shapes. There were no vehicles, no soldiers. A trap?

Loremarie wiped her eyes, squeezed my hand, then spoke for the first time since we'd left the apothecary.

"Here, let me go. It doesn't matter if Heinrich catches me."

With that she was off, a large elegant figure wrapped in a battered fur coat. I watched her traipse along, then slip into the ruins of the *Pension* above the bar. She didn't come back. Minutes passed. No one. I began to stir. Was Heinrich there, after all? Or had Loremarie simply collapsed in her misery? I started to—

Her head poked out, her face a moon of misery. Cupping a hand, she scooped the air, waved me to come, which I quickly did, rushing down the edge of the street and to the hotel.

Leading the way through the ruins of the original cafe, Loremarie said, "No sign of that bastard . . . yet. According to Dieter, a couple of people tried to come down for some schnapps, but that's all."

She pulled open the oak door to the bar and ushered me through. Then the two of us stood on the top stone step, pulled the door tight behind us. I locked the door with the big iron key, then we dropped three boards into place, one at the top, middle, and bottom. Designed to bolster the door against bombs and the hurricane force of firestorms, the security measures would certainly slow Heinrich.

We curled our way down the cool steps and entered the dark bar. Dieter sat at one of the oak tables, a cigarette propped on his lower lip, his crutches leaning on a stool. Just how much, I wondered, did he know about Mother and her relationship with Heinrich? How many, if any, had he informed on?

He asked, "*Ist Anton . . . ist er tot?*" Is Anton . . . is he dead?

My eyes on the dazed Loremarie, I slowly nodded. "*Ja*, and we're supposed to meet Mama and Joe near the Schulenberg's."

He shrugged, took a puff of his cigarette. "Of course we can't stay here, but God knows where we'll go. I suppose we can try and make it out of the city tonight. If there's a raid . . ." He cut himself off. "If? If?" Shook his head. "We might escape in tonight's confusion. Then again, if the Gestapo doesn't get us, the bombs probably will."

Still we had to try. We couldn't just wander the streets. The only way to escape Heinrich was to escape Berlin itself.

I said, "We need to take some food and money."

Dieter blew out a cloud of smoke. "I think cigarettes. You can buy almost anything with them now."

"Mama has some American dollars," I said, matter-of-factly.

Acknowledging that, Dieter said, "Oh, *ja, die Dollar . . . die bring' ich.*" Oh, yes, the dollars . . . I'll bring them.

From up above came a harsh crack and a screaming voice. A flash of fear shocked my body. That wasn't someone begging for a beer. No. That was Heinrich and his men. With what sounded like rifle butts, they pounded on the door, stopped, and waited for a response.

Loremarie looked upward, hatred pinching her eyes. "I'll make sure they don't come down."

Dieter puckered his face in a hopeless grimace, pulled himself up on his crutches, then headed toward the back room. From his mouth flowed endless curses, long German ones with a billion words all strung together, and he ordered me after him. Following him into the back chamber, I passed the cot where Joe had lain when he'd first arrived, saw the tin plate that had held the greasy potatoes. I heard my brother's giggles, and my memory surged and heaved.

Within seconds, Dieter and I had pushed aside the chest and were in the hidden cavern. Hands grabbing, snatching, pushing, we crammed cigarettes and Reichsmarks and American dollars and coffee and silver trinkets into three leather valises. Tinned meat and candles and matches, too. Glancing over, I saw Dieter smash open a small wooden box and grab a handful of watches as if they were slippery herring. He crammed them, a bottle, and candles and matches into a leather rucksack. Then balancing on one leg, he stood, a black pistol in hand. He checked the barrel, loaded it and shoved the remaining bullets into his pocket.

I gasped. Even though I was sure I'd never seen it before, for some reason I recognized the gun. And staring at it, I knew that I must rip it from Dieter's hands, that he must leave it behind. That gun, I was completely certain, would do a lifetime of harm, and I had to—

"No, Willi, you can't change what is about to happen."

Out loud, I said, "But—!"

Dieter turned, looked at me oddly, then shouted out the hole and into the bar. "Loremarie! Loremarie, let's go!"

I heard glass shattering, the dull smashing of wood. Certain that Heinrich had broken through our meager door of defense, I charged out.

"Tante Lore!"

As manic as she had been angry before, Loremarie was hurling chairs and stools up the stairwell. On top of that she was throwing clothing and towels.

"The mattress from the cot—bring it out here!" she snapped like a *Wehrmacht* colonel.

I dashed into the back, ripped the old cottony thing from its frame, and dragged it and several blankets out. Then together Loremarie and I stuffed them into the stairwell as well. I smelled kerosene, saw the shards of a broken lantern and a stream of liquid slinking down the steps, across the stone flooring, beneath my feet, across the room and . . .

She turned to me, her face red with glistening sweat. "I will live to kill this man!"

Up above, a machine-gun wave of death riddled the heavy oak door. It would be difficult to blast through, but Heinrich was certain not to give up.

"Tante Lore, come on!"

Lost in black delight, she ran to a side table, grabbed the

last spirit lamp and lit it. Almost with a grin on her face, she hurried to the stairs, took aim, and heaved the lamp. The whole thing broke neatly on the wall, and there was a gentle rush of flame, both up and down the stairs and all around the broken chairs and mattress.

She screamed, "Throw those stools up there!"

I did as she commanded, began to take hope in a wall of flame and smoke that might actually be stronger than a door of oak. And as I worked, Loremarie ran into the little kitchen, next emerging with the spirit stove. Racing back, she hurled that into the growing fire, and there was an explosion, a perfumy ball of fire as the container of eau de cologne burst. From up above came a constant chattering of bullets. Unfazed, Loremarie rushed across the bar, took hold of Dieter's accordion, and tossed that into the growing blaze. No, I thought, there was no going back. Ever.

"Tante Lore!" I shouted, waving the smoke from my face.

Once again I grabbed her by the arm, now steering her toward the small back room, to the hole, and into the candlelit cave. Together, Dieter and I then dragged the chest of drawers back over the opening. He shoved one of the valises at me, the other two at Loremarie, and strapped the rucksack to his back. As Dieter grabbed his crutches, I noticed the pistol clutched in his right hand.

"Willi!" he said, motioning toward a flashlight on the cavern floor.

I took the thing, shook it until there was a sleepy beam, then led us through the small tunnel and into the blood-filled sewers of Berlin.

Chapter

23

"Joe?" I called into the crystalline night.

A bright moonlit evening was just beginning, and my eyes searched, begged, for a familiar figure. There were only odd shapes, however. Broken walls. Fractured beams. Ghosts of a civilized world.

"Joe?"

Having tromped through the war filth of the sewers, my feet were still soaked, and with each step they gathered more and more dust and dirt. But that didn't slow me. Dieter's dying flashlight in hand, I was desperate to find Joe and my mother, desperate to learn if they'd really escaped Heinrich. Somehow I was certain they had, yet in the half block since I'd left Loremarie and Dieter—left them huddled in the shadows of the squashed Schulenberg apartment house—there was no one. A deserted neighborhood.

It had taken nearly thirty minutes to escape the sewers, then we'd been forced to hide for over an hour in some small cellar as Heinrich and his men swooped back and

forth. Finally they'd moved elsewhere as the day faded
away, and we'd been able to push on. But we were hours
late. If Joe and Mother had made it over to this neighborhood, had they since given up, taken shelter somewhere
else?

A catlike moan, deep and devilish and horrid in intensity,
swept across the rubble, swirled around my ankles. I stood
motionless as ripples of chills crawled up my spine, as I
tried to tell whether that was human or indeed animal. It
came again, at first deep and low, then rising not into a hiss
but a plea.

"Oh . . ."

I spun to the side. "Mama?"

I aimed the light at the remains of a corner building, saw
a black hole for a door, two more for windows. At once I was
clambering over clods of brick and wood. That had been a
person, hadn't it? But was it them or perhaps just some
poor buried-alive slob?

"Mama, where are you?" I whispered, "It's me, Willi."

Nothing.

"*Hallo?*"

A chorus of giggles rattled my heart. Of course I knew
that voice, even amidst this setting of destruction. I kept
the flashlight on the ground, followed the trail of light up
and over and around and to the doorway of a groundfloor
room that really seemed more like a cave. Rough stone
walls. Filth floor. And black. So black. I swept the beam
from corner to corner, stirred up dirt in a gray beam.

She lunged out at me, grabbed me by the arms. The
flashlight dropped, smacked on the ground, and long waves
of hair flowed across my face and little girly laughs pierced
my ears.

"*Hallo, mein* killer diller baby!"

A cloud of booze blew in my face, fumes so strong that
they seemed flammable. Just as quickly, Mother began to

fall, and I had to grab her, hold her by the waist. She swooped down and planted a big wet kiss on my forehead.

"Want some cognac, Willichen?" she said, waving her silver flask at me. "This is all I got left."

Anger surged within me. *"Nee!"*

She smelled both so sweet and so biley, and my stomach flinched with disgust. How could we flee with a drunk like this in tow?

My eyes searched the cavelike chamber. "Mama, where's Joe?"

"Oh, around," she laughed, flinging an arm outward.

I lowered her to the ground, helped her prop herself up against a wall. I reached for the flashlight, shook it until the beam jittered back to life, then turned it on her. My heart jerked and I nearly jumped back. Red eyes, sagging eyes. All watery. Her face all soft and jowly. Hair that hung limp and ratty. I stared at this disgusting, boozed-up woman who was supposed to be my mother, and I didn't want to have anything to do with her. All at once my darkest desire, the one I'd been trying to run from for months, now rushed forward, catching me as if by the ankle and pulling me down.

"And what is that, Willi?"

I couldn't help but want it, think it: I wished she'd die. I wanted this hideous person to topple right over and never rise!

Footsteps scruffed against rock. I spun, saw a large, dark figure approaching.

"Joe!" I said rushing from my mother and out the opening.

He grabbed me in eager embrace. "Willi, what happened? I've been looking for you."

I looked back into the hovel. Yes, if Mother were gone I could stay with Joe. If Mother disappeared for good she'd never look at me with those red eyes or breathe that stinky breath on me again!

"Are you all right?"

What could I say? How could I explain? *Mein Gott*, I hated my mother!

"Willi, what happened?"

Trying to shake the evil thoughts from my head, I said, "We . . . we went back to the bar. Tante Lore said we had to, and . . . and . . ."

In the distance I saw two desperate figures hurrying down the street. It was Loremarie and Dieter—she carrying all three valises, he crutching himself along—charging as if pursued.

In a whisper I called, "Tante Lore!"

Behind them daggers of light started poking into the ruins, and I heard the deep rumble of an engine, too. Heinrich, I thought, tensing with fear. Joe and I rushed down to them, grabbing the valises from Loremarie.

Her panic barely contained, Loremarie said, "There wasn't anyplace to hide back there!"

Joe asked, "Is it Heinrich?"

"I . . . I don't know," replied Dieter.

Hurrying off the street, we charged up and into the room where my mother sat. As we threw the valises behind the wall, Mother pushed herself up, looked brightly at the excitement.

"What's all the commotion? Why—!"

"Shut up!" snapped Loremarie as the lights neared. "There's a *Streife!*

"So what?"

In the shadows, I saw Loremarie spin, ready herself to dive on my mother. At that last moment, Joe caught the countess by the arm, shoved her back.

"Get down! I'll take care of Eva!"

Loremarie shouted, "If they don't kill her, I will!"

"Get down!"

The sounds of the truck grumbled nearer, and a search-light speared the building across the street and probed its innards. Joe hurled himself over my mother, forced her to the ground, and I dropped next to them.

Mother said, "What—?"

Joe clamped his hand over her mouth. "Shut up!"

I saw her squirm and wiggle beneath him before growing still. Seconds later the large truck lumbered right out front, shooting spotlights everywhere. Above the clanging of gears, the deep churning of the motor, I heard thin voices and laughter, too. Those were boys out there, I realized. Soldiers perhaps, but boys first, who really weren't that much older than me. Perhaps they'd been sent by Heinrich. Perhaps not. Fortunately they weren't that thorough, for their lights flicked only briefly over our hideaway, then prodded on. Within minutes they were gone altogether, the latest of dangers having flown haphazardly by.

I sat up, brushed myself off. Mother, one cheek all dusty, began groping madly about, content only when she found her little flask.

Dieter said, "The sooner we leave town, the better."

"Leave?" gasped Mother, unscrewing the flask.

"Good God, Eva, stop drinking!"

She took a swig. "We'd never make it, you know. We don't have any papers because . . . because . . ." Giggle. *"Unser Jude ist weg!"* Our Jew is gone!

Loremarie flew through the air and dropped like a lead cloud on top of my mother. She screamed and shouted the coarsest of obscenities as she drove fist after fist into Mother's ribs and face and head. Mother curled up like a fetus and howled helplessly. As quickly as I could, I lunged at Loremarie, grabbed her. She was much stronger than me, though, and hurled me back almost without effort. Then

Joe was grabbing her in a desperate attempt to pull her off my wailing mother.

"For Christ's sake, stop it!" shouted Joe.

He peeled Loremarie away, spun her around and shoved her toward Dieter, who caught her and pinned her arms behind her back. As they struggled, I heard a clatter, looked down, saw Dieter's pistol swirling around their feet. Staring at it, I wondered just when it would go off, who it would kill.

"Let me go!" demanded the countess.

"Ah!" moaned my writhing mother.

Joe swooped down and seized Mother, forcing her to her feet. She cried and moaned as he hurled her about, shoving her outside. Of course he had to get her out of there. I glanced back, saw Loremarie now trying to lunge downward for the gun.

"Willi!" shouted Joe.

Caught in a beam of confusion, I stood paralyzed. Oh, my God. I didn't want anything more to do with her or this. Didn't want to go forward into death.

"Willi!"

Flashlight in hand, knowing I had no choice, I stumbled out. The defeated, drunken figure of my mother hung in Joe's two arms, and another wave of both repulsion and fear swept through me. Leave her, get rid of her, drop her in the ruins!

"Willi," snapped Joe, "where's that place—the room with the metal door?"

My eyes were wide and white, trained only on my nearly passed-out mother. I couldn't move, couldn't think.

"Willi!"

I pointed the beam along the front of the building, then started following the faint light. Of course we couldn't just stand out here. Another patrol or Heinrich himself might appear at any moment. And so I slipped along. Lugging my all but unconscious mother, Joe trudged after me, leaving Loremarie's curses and threats and sobs behind us.

I headed toward the Schulenberg's bombed building, turning a corner and climbing over tossed bricks as easily as if I were a mountain goat. I glanced about, saw no one. The neighborhood was gone, killed by the bombs, and I thought how I was guiding Mother and Joe right into a similar black abyss. The raid. Picking my way along, I realized that it was brighter out, and I shuddered. Joe's predicted raid could be upon us any second, yet we no longer had our bunker to shelter us.

Leading Joe along, the flashlight struck what seemed a familiar block of stone. It was the beige color, the floral carving. A portal. Certain that I had seen it before, I looked up at the shell of a memory. This had been the building where my mother's grandfather had lived, in an apartment right beneath the Schulenberg's. My breathing came quick and tight. This very building had collapsed around Joe and me only a few days ago. So much had happened since, so many had died. I felt as if I were walking directly into a deadfall, a deathly trap that would collapse on me, pin me in this place and time forever. But still I tromped on, leading Joe and Mother right over the massive collapsed pile of brick and wood, right through a canyon of towering walls. Right over the giant grave of the two Schulenberg boys. Like a clairvoyant, I knew what I would see when I lifted the flashlight upward: an upright piano that sat on a cliff-like ledge some four floors up. I wondered if anyone could climb up there, make music that would rise above this time, this place. No, only my mother could have done that. She was too drunk, too far gone, though, and somehow I knew she would never sing again.

Behind me, the body cradled in Joe's arms moaned, "Oh . . ."

"We're almost there," he reassured her.

Through and around, beneath a beam. As if I'd gone over and over this path, I didn't hesitate at all. We skirted a crater, passed a wall with a window, came back around and stood in front of a rusty sheet of metal. I stopped dead. The last time we'd passed through the makeshift door there had been two Gestapo agents waiting for us. Could there be someone smoking and lurking in there again? No, I thought. Those two thugs were killed and Dieter, who'd undoubtedly told of our location, was back there with Loremarie. Still, I was afraid, as if one or more of us would enter this hovel and never emerge again.

Wait here, I whispered to Joe in the darkness.

I touched the sheet of metal, found it as cold as a guillotine. Just as quickly as a slicing blade, I pushed it back and dove into a sea of darkness. I didn't flounder, though, using the flashlight to cut a path of sight through the room and to the back wall. I crossed to a column at the back, bent down and found another sheet of metal, this one smaller. I shoved it aside, revealing the rucksack Mother and I had stashed here months ago. Pulling it out, I dug into it, clawed over a blanket and socks and papers and more clothing. Found matches and a candle, a thick one, and lit it. Yes, this was our hideaway, a crude shelter that was supposed to protect us from Gestapo or SS or even Russians. But friends? Mother had never said anything about a war amongst our own.

"Okay," I called in English.

Carrying my mother like a forlorn lover, Joe stepped into the glow of the fat, creamy candle. She had her arms around his neck now, and nuzzled her face beneath his chin, murmured something soft and sweet.

I dripped some wax on a rock, stuck the candle down, then pulled out the dark green blanket and opened it out over rock and dirt. Joe knelt down, spread my mother over the blanket as lovingly as if on a featherbed. I watched as he brushed her silky hair from her face, and as her hands lingered on his neck in a sleepy, lustful clasp. These two were like magnets, repelling each other one moment, desperately drawing each other together the next. And forever confusing me. What really had happened between them back before the war? A union that had produced me? Was I really all that terrible?

Her arms tightening, I saw my half-conscious mother now trying to pull Joe down on top of her. She murmured something, and her legs shifted, widened beneath her skirt. Joe glanced at me, embarrassed by the truth so graphically demonstrated. Of course I understood. I was Willi, after all, and I had incestuous insight.

Joe uncurled her fingers from his neck. "You need to rest, Eva," he cooed in her ear while at the same time reaching into her coat pocket. "Don't worry, everything's going to be fine."

He tugged half the blanket over her, wrapped her in it, then pulled back and stood. I stared up at him. I'd thought this big, broad man was an angel tumbled from the heavens, come to save us. But could he? Could anyone?

"We'll figure out something," he said to me. "Can you stay and watch her?"

I didn't respond because I honestly didn't know whether I would strike my mother or embrace her if she woke.

He started for the opening, anyway, saying, "Don't worry, she'll be all right. I won't be gone long. Just shout if there're any problems." He stopped. "If she asks for this, tell her I have it," said Joe lifting the silver flask he'd taken from her coat.

His shuffling steps faded into the night, and then I turned back to Mother. Staring down at her long, lush body, I thought how she was like Berlin, broken and ruined, something great gone terribly wrong. As if I were looking at a corpse, it struck me that I couldn't see her future, couldn't picture her tomorrow or the day after. I wasn't able even to imagine her out of this hole in the ground. My God, I sensed my hateful wish was about to come true, and I started trembling, maggots of fear starting to munch through my body and up into my mind. I had to get away from her and all this. I had to run as fast and as far as I could, not stop until I reached a place where I'd never see anything ugly again. I tried to push myself up, but my body gave out. I tried again, but couldn't rise. I had to flee but I had no strength! My arms were useless, my legs, too. I could barely move! Surging with soured emotion, I stared at Mother, knowing I was chained to her, our fates bound by an invisible cord that could never be severed. All I could do was sit there and cry. Oh, Christ, when would I be free? When would I find peace?

In response I sensed a ghostly presence reach out and take my hand, cradle it in reassurance, and then heard, really heard, a very distant voice say: "*Soon.*"

Chapter

24

Like Mother, I fell into some deep state, a trance of sorts. Jarred by her stirring, I woke and found her shaking, the coarse wool blanket tugged up under her chin. With each moment her trembling grew more exaggerated, and yet she said nothing. She just lay there shivering before me, and I thought how it seemed like another night. My anger was gone, having burned off, evaporated into the cool night like unwanted steam. Now studying her in the candlelight, I felt something just as strongly but altogether different: pity.

I reached out, touched her on the leg. "Are you all right, Mama?"

She looked as pale as the waxy candle. So helpless. I knew it was up to me, that I had to do something. Make her warm again. I thought of hot coffee and fried potatoes. If only we had what Loremarie had earlier prepared. That's what Mother needed. Sustenance. Something solid and hot.

Catching me and knocking me down like an unexpected

wave, Mother gazed over at me, worry warming her face, and said, "Willichen . . . I'm so sorry."

"Mama, no, I—"

"I've disappointed you, haven't I?"

It frightened me that she knew the truth and stated it so boldly, yet nothing could have encouraged my love or soothed every fear more quickly. It was like she was coming back, the mother I cared for, the one I wanted, who could look so pretty and sing away war. Studying her, I caught a glimpse of that parent, the one who could see what I needed and offer it automatically. She just needed a little more rest and something pure and clean to flush away the toxins, and then everything would be the way it should!

"I'm going to get you some water. And . . . and then I'll go get Joe."

"I'm so cold," she mumbled, chattering beneath the blanket.

"I'll be right back," I said, a bizarre sense of hope rushing my heart.

Flashlight in hand, I scrambled out, sliding the door of metal back in place, sealing Mother in, just to make sure she was hidden. I'd get her water and bring back Joe, and somehow we'd revive her. We'd get her back on her feet, help her walk. There had to be some food nearby. That would give her strength. Yes, with the cigarettes we could get bread and maybe some *Bockwurst*. Coffee or tea, too. Better yet, soup.

I charged through the remains of the Schulenberg building. Bucket. I had to find a bucket. Or cup or bowl or even an old bottle. Quick, Willi, I told myself. Be quick!

I crossed what remained of the street, found the arched entrance to a *Hinterhof* and ducked into the long courtyard. I climbed a tremendous pile of rubble from the collapsed buildings. My foot hit something. I pointed the light at a pot and picked it up. Poked two of my fingers through a rusty hole. No good, but that meant there might be a kitchen nearby. Or what was left of one.

The front of the apartment building gave way to smaller houses packed in the center of the block. Spotting a door in a brick wall, I charged in. A rotting divan and a shattered rocker. I rushed into the next room. There. The rusting hulk of a coal stove. I swerved the beam back and forth, illuminating broken plates, a shoe. A fork. My heart leapt. A bucket! I seized it as if it were gold, checked. No holes!

Rushing out, I was certain now. We could make it. I had a bucket so there was a chance after all! I even knew where to find water. Emerging on the street, I thought back to that night when Joe and I had been nearly buried alive and this neighborhood nothing but flames. I'd found a rag and soaked it in water. I turned right. The pipe was only meters away, and it was still bubbling and gurgling with life. Just wait, Mother, just wait! Everything's going to be all right!

Entirely proud of myself, I held the bucket and let the water rush in. There'd be some for Mother to drink, and even enough to let her wash. Perhaps we could even heat some. Build a small fire or something. I had to tell Joe. He needed to know that Mother was awake, that I'd found water, that we could be on our way within minutes. Perhaps it was best if just Joe, Mother and I went. The little happy family. Loremarie was much too mad at Mother and . . . and so she and Dieter could go off. Do what they wanted. But the three of us, well, under the cover of darkness, we could travel far, make pretty good progress. Perhaps even make it to Potsdam tonight.

Lugging the pail, I looked up. The sky was dark, a deep, rich navy blue. I saw stars, bunches of them spread across the vast sky like handfuls of glittery sand. It was completely clear, not a cloud spotting the sky. And the moon—I craned, couldn't see it. No. Nothing to the right, to the—

It hung just between two buildings, big and white and heavy, a huge orb straining to rise over Berlin. The size of it shocked me, the biggest moon I thought I'd ever witnessed. Or perhaps it just looked that way because it was so low, the atmosphere magnifying the distant planet, fishing it out of the heavens and into the next block. At the same time I realized this was indeed the most perfect of bomber moons, offering the ideal night to wipe out the city, to blast its broken carcass into smithereens. Gazing up into the clear, still air, I imagined that a pilot could probably even see me down here, a kid running along with a clanky pail of water and a weak flashlight. We had to be fast.

As I neared the ruins where Joe and the others were, angry voices rushed to greet and slow my pace. I heard Joe shouting, Loremarie screaming back. Dieter cursing and muttering. Only ten or fifteen meters away, I saw the windowless chamber flicker with candlelight and hatred.

His voice charged with anger, Dieter said, "What are we supposed to do? Sacrifice our lives for hers?"

"Of course not," replied Joe.

Something terribly cold and sharp hit my chest, pierced my skin and went deep into me. As if I'd been punched in the stomach, I lost my breath, came to an immediate stop. Water sloshed out of the bucket and onto the ground. They were talking about my mother. Of course they were.

"She's a slut and liar!" shouted Loremarie.

I stood there, struck, by the disgust boiling in her voice. But . . . but . . . Mother was awake now and . . .

"Believe me, since you left, Joe, she's slept with every dog that's come along. God forgive me, but she should be shot! And it's not only because of what she did to Anton, but Erich, too!"

"What do you mean?" asked Dieter.

"I mean there were bombs falling all around us and she let go of her child's hand!"

Joe moaned, "Good Lord . . ."

"*Scheissdreck*, the stupid bitch dropped her flask and she let go of him so she could pick it up! I saw it! And after that, Erich was lost!"

So that's how it had happened. Of course. The countess was right, I knew she was because I'd also witnessed Mother in the smoke, stumbling, lurching, and . . . and . . . I felt sick and scared. Mama had let go of my little brother and lost him in the chaos, and he couldn't run for shelter because of his leg.

"Dear God," cursed Dieter. "She's gotten to be too much. Just too much."

He said something else that I couldn't hear. Without thinking, my hand lowered the bucket of water, placed it on the uneven ground. I was like fog, slithering silently over bricks and toward the room. I had to hear what they were saying, what they were planning. A quick disposal of Mother? Perhaps a bullet in the head? And what about me? Guilty by association?

I turned off the flashlight and crept up to a hole in the wall. And thought: I have to find out what they're going to do . . . can't let them hear me. No, mustn't let them know I'm out here because Dieter has a gun.

Joe said, "I know she's out of control, but . . . but . . ."

"Believe me, this time she's gone too far!" said Dieter. "Next time I'll be the one she betrays."

"That's right!" exclaimed Loremarie. "First Anton, then you!"

Joe pleaded, "But she won't last a week if we leave her!"

"Good!" replied Loremarie.

"But what will Heinrich do?" asked Joe. "You know he's not going to stop looking."

"Of course he won't," shouted Dieter. "And when he gets his hands on her, he'll twist her until she tells him every little sordid detail about Loremarie . . . and me, too! And that's not to mention you, Mister Joe."

Loremarie started sobbing. "Oh, if only he'd butchered her instead of Anton. We just have to forget about her and get out of Berlin—the sooner the better!"

Dieter groaned. "That's right. We have to leave her. She's too dangerous."

"But . . . but what about Willi?" asked Joe.

Loremarie shouted, "I don't care about anything having to do with that bitch Eva!"

But . . . but I wanted to go, too! I had to go! Before the next raid and before the Russians. I couldn't just wait here! I bit my lip. My Joe and my Tante Lore and my Onkel Dieter wouldn't all abandon me, would they? Oh, *mein Gott*, I thought as the truth slapped me. The only way I could go with them was without Mother. But even though I'd thought it before, I really couldn't leave without her. Or could I? No, I could only leave if she were—

"Dead," sighed Loremarie. "Just admit it—we'd all be better off if she were dead, wouldn't we?" The pain caught, ripped like a run in a stocking, and she started crying. "I know I would. Anton loved her so much and . . . and she betrayed him. Give me your gun, Dieter, and I'll solve our problem right now!"

"Loremarie!" protested Joe.

"Come on, Dieter, just give it to me. Aren't you sick of having her wipe her feet all over you? Aren't you sick of worrying when she's going to let something slip?"

"Stop it!" demanded Joe.

Loremarie's laugh was as big as it was witchlike. "You're still in love with her, aren't you, Joe? Well, she'll never love you, not after what you did to her!"

"What I did to her?" he replied. "What about what she did to me?"

Then Dieter started shouting, going on about how he should have stopped it before it began, barking at about how stupid he'd been to let them have that room. They all three started yelling about Joe's long-ago visit to Berlin. But I didn't need to hear anymore. The danger was quite immediate and quite clear, and I turned to get away. If they saw me here, they might shoot me right on the spot. Ask no questions, just pull the trigger. I had to get back to my mother, didn't I? Didn't I have to tell her what they'd said? Warn her? Yes! I was her son and I had to warn, save her from these people who once were her friends and who now wanted to kill her! I had to be quick, so quick! There was no time. I looked up at the moon, so big and white and innocent. Oh, *mein Gott*, hurry, Willi, hurry!

I clambered along, right over a pile of rubble. So quick, so quiet, until . . . until my right foot smacked into a big hard brick. Struck it and sent it tumbling end over noisy end, smacking and finally breaking to pieces. Shattering, it seemed as loud as a bomb. I snatched up the bucket of water, taking it in my hand and bolting as quickly as I could. Behind me, I heard voices, tight and quick. Then steps. I glanced back and saw a huge dark figure emerge from that little chamber and aim a gun in my direction. Was that Loremarie? Joe?

"Who's there?" demanded a deep voice.

I couldn't let them catch me! My spine tensed, certain that a bullet would spear me any second, prevent me from warning Mother. But nothing happened, and I darted to the right, around a corner, only then turning the flashlight back on. I had to race back, beat them back to the room where my mother lay, help her up. And then the two of us had to run, hide from Joe, Loremarie, and Dieter as well as Heinrich. We could do it! I'd take care of Mama!

I looked up, saw that stupid piano up there, sitting on that ledge where no one could reach it. That's when I heard it. My mother's voice. It rose high and loud in the night like a powerful song. I stopped dead, froze right there atop the ruins of the Schulenberg apartment house. Mama? But that wasn't a song. And if not a melody, what then, a laugh or a cry? There was something shrill and unfamiliar about it. I closed my eyes, tried to catch my breath that wanted to run away from me. I looked behind. There was no Joe or Loremarie or Dieter. So, perhaps—

Mother's voice rose again, this time higher, longer. I could almost see it rise into the cloudless, moon-filled sky, and at first, for just a second, I was awed by its beauty. The clarity of the tone, its richness. I was momentarily happy. For an instant I was amazed by Mother's ability to create a sound so pure. But what was that? Laugh, cry, plea or what? What had happened?

The realization hammered me, punched my gut with fear. A scream. Mother was in trouble and she was calling out, pleading for her life! Dear God, someone had her, was hurting her! Maybe Heinrich had found her, perhaps some slob was robbing and beating her! Or . . . or Loremarie had taken Dieter's gun, come back via another route and now she was going to shoot my mother!

"Mama!" I cried.

I darted over the Schulenberg rubble, down toward the room where I'd left her. Water sloshed back and forth, up and out, over my pants and on the ground. Cutting the route short, I climbed through a window with no glass, jumped through to the other side. The bucket caught on a nail, and I let it drop to the ground, where it struck brick, crashed like a cymbal, tipped and clanged its way down the slope.

"Mama!"

I shouldn't have left her. I was supposed to be the good son, the little soldier, there to protect. But I'd left and now someone was hurting her. I heard her voice again. a scream? No, weaker, more like a moan. Oh, God, had some-one struck her or stabbed her? Was she lying in a pool of blood? Mama!

The metal door was hurled to the side. I rushed in. Empty. The dark green wool blanket had been thrown back, crumpled to the side. The fat candle burned steady and unblinking. Off to the side a cigarette sat perched on a rock, burning calmly all on its own. A cigarette? Mother didn't have any cigarettes, did she? So whose was that? Who had been here?

What I heard next frightened me more than anything: a moan of delight. My mother's. Her voice cooed with plea-sure, oozed desire. She was nearby, quite close as if we were back in the *Pension*, separated by only a thin wall, and I were listening to her and some soldier kissing and more. No, I realized, she wasn't in danger. There was too much delight in what I heard. All that was missing was the crinkling of fresh white sheets and huffing of a downy featherbed. At first I couldn't move, but then I started fol-lowing the groans as if they were a tantalizing scent waft-ing from a bakery. Tears were flowing from my eyes. My mother was a thief, a terribly clever burglar who'd slipped into my heart and stolen my youth.

Flashlight dangling from my hand, I made my way out of the hideaway, back outside, then right. They were in the neighboring ruins, Mother and some man. I heard his beefy grunts, his deep moans. Who? Who this time? Tiny beams of light squeaked through some boards. I peeked in, saw a lantern set on the ground of a large space. And mother. Coat dropped at her feet, she was locked in the embrace of some man, and her dress swirled and danced as she was pawed with passion. I moved past the boards, down a brick wall. I heard my mother's breathy words. I couldn't turn back, run away, pretend that I didn't see this when I'd seen it all. I couldn't be quiet anymore, either. I'd witnessed every one of them. I had to tell my whore-mother that, so I moved to a door, slipped in. Before me was a vast space, half cellar, half ground floor, now gutted by fire, walls charred, ceiling scaling with peely black scabs. And there in the middle, near a kerosene lantern, stood my mother, locked in the ravishing embrace of some man, his coat also thrown on the ground and his back to me. She tilted her head back, and he was kissing her neck, nuzzling down, lunging toward her breasts. I'd caught her just like I could have any number of times. Only now I'd let her know.

"Mama."

Her eyes popped wide. She looked about, saw me standing there.

"Willi!"

She pushed him away. Broke his lock and shoved him and his wet mouth back. Despite her surprise at seeing me, I recognized the booze on her. It hung from her face like a thick haze, eyes droopy, cheeks flaccid. And the upper eyelids a little bit sleepy and not quite in control, pulled just over the top of the eyeballs like lazy window shades. Drunk again. I glanced at the floor, saw a bottle of something—brandy or cognac?

His back still to me, the man lunged for Mother, wrapped his arms around her. A desperate man, eager for love in a time of hate. But she twisted, would have none of him in front of me for she was embarrassed, her face having flushed white to crimson.

"Let go of her!" I shouted.

The light-haired marauder started shaking. No, laughing and swaying. More drunk than Mother, he roared from the bottom of his lungs, blasted this burned room with his glee. My body locked rigid while my heart seethed with fear. What did he know that I didn't? He turned. Full of pride, this man with the pinkish skin and sharp features shot his amusement right at me.

"*Hallo*, Willi," said Heinrich. "Glad you could join us."

My horror flicked from him to Mother and back. What was this? How could she? This was the man who'd dragged our Anton to another world! This was the man who'd been trying to kill my Joe!

"Shocked, little boy? Really?"

I muttered, "How . . . how did you find us?"

"Come on, don't look so shocked." The victorious jokester, he cracked. "Your Mutti and I have met here lots of times."

I charged right at him, flashlight held back like a huge club. I ran across that room and hurled myself at him, hitting and beating him with the flashlight. I was going to scratch his face to shreds, pull his tongue from his mouth and chop it to bits! I threw myself at him, and he grabbed me by the shoulders, tried to shove me away. My left hand locked on his belt, the other pelted him with the flashlight. I was screaming and kicking, and then I heard my mother begging, felt her trying to push me away.

"Willi, stop! Stop!"

More furious than ever, I kept on battling, even as an awful realization came to me. Mother was on his side. Right here, right now, I was the wrongdoer. That meant Heinrich was telling the truth. Mother was indeed this man's mistress, on call to his wishes. And that meant I'd been wrong. Mother wasn't an informant. At least not a very active one and certainly not a very good one. That's not how she obtained the booze for our bar. No, I thought, kicking and fighting all the harder. In exchange for wetnursing his desire, Mother was supplied with an unending flow of brandy and cognac, schnapps and Schultheiss beer and more, more, more. That was how he took care of her. Of us. I felt sickened. We'd basically been fed and clothed by this man? No. No!

A thick black object tumbled from Heinrich's waist and

landed with a thud in the dirt. A pistol! Desperate, I lunged to the side but couldn't reach it. He had me by the right arm, was shaking me and beating me on the head. I reached out with my left hand and my fingers just grazed the barrel. Please! But then Heinrich saw what I was begging for and as quick as a bolt of lightning he jerked me up. He caught me with both arms, cocked me back, and then sent me hurling like a human cannonball. I screamed out as I spun through the air, saw Mama reaching, crying after me, those big, sad eyes of hers opened wide and scared.

"Willi!"

But she'd switched sides too late. I went tumbling through the air until I struck a column, my shoulder hitting it first, then my head smacking it with a bright, sharp crack. Like a bird that had flown into a window, I dropped to the ground, stunned and unable to see. I lay there, eyes open, nothing but blackness before me. Too shocked to cry out.

"Blödes Gör!" Stupid brat, snapped Heinrich.

Behind him, Mama's wail came big and round. I blinked, saw an edge of light encircling a large spot of darkness. Then suddenly behind me, from the street, I heard desperate steps, a board being ripped and hurled aside. And heavy breathing. I looked toward the opening, could only make out the shape of a big, strong figure, but knew it was my never-acknowledged father. I blinked again, my sight daring to seek more, and in his hand I spied a gun. Dieter's gun.

"Joe, no!" screamed my mother. "Get out of here!"

He stood there, unmoving. "This is like old times, isn't it—just the three of us."

I twisted on the ground and noticed Heinrich eye the gun that lay only a meter or so from his foot.

"And it looks like," Heinrich said, "we're about to finish what we should have back then."

With that, Heinrich dove forward and scooped up the gun, racing on toward me.

"Joe!" I cried.

Mother screamed.

As Heinrich charged closer, I looked over, saw Joe trying to take aim on the running figure, saw his gun pointed right over my head. Shoot, Joe! Shoot! I curled into a ball. I wasn't in the way, he wouldn't hit me! Heinrich ducked behind me, then emerged on the other side of the column, taking fast sight of Joe and firing his weapon. Quick and sharp, a noise blasted the room and magnified with each second.

My mother's voice cut the night: *"Nee!"*

I looked across the chamber, saw Joe thrown backward, struck by some invisible, deathly force. He looked at Mother, disbelief gripping his face, and then he started crumbling. The gun dropped from his hand, and he collapsed to his knees, a red circle rapidly spreading across his chest.

"Joe!" I cried.

"Oh, *mein Gott, mein Gott!*" sobbed my hysterical mother, biting her own hand and not moving.

It had happened so fast, and I was up and running, my hands out, begging for Joe's life. He glanced at me, eyes open and sad. No, sorry. He looked so sorry, and then he tumbled over, landing right on his face.

"Joe!" I shouted, rushing to him.

I dove to the ground, brushed aside Dieter's gun and grabbed Joe's hand. His fingers tightened on mine, clutching desperately, then weakening just as quickly. Piercing his back was another hole, this one uglier and cruder, the place the bullet had burst from his body. I stared helplessly at him, saw blood, so much blood, pouring from him.

Behind me I heard booted steps. Heinrich had done this.

He'd shot my father and . . . and killed Anton, too, and . . . and . . . my fingers wormed through the dirt, encircling the handle of Dieter's gun. I felt the still-warm grip in my hand and spun. Heinrich was tromping toward me, Mother now right behind him, and he froze the instant I pointed the gun at his hated face. He was shocked, I think perhaps even confused, because he smiled. Little boys weren't supposed to do this kind of thing, but I would and I did. Real quick, almost without thinking. There was an explosion in my hands, a burst of fire so strong that it sent me hurling back on top of Joe. He groaned beneath me but didn't move, and in the same instant I saw the right side of Heinrich's face expand and burst into a cloud of liquidy red. His hands clawed out, and he screamed long and hard like one of the animals at the firebombed zoo. He stumbled back, screeched. Then caught himself and turned toward me. The shattered cheek of Heinrich seemed to dissolve right before me, yet he continued toward me, tromping in hate, blood spurting everywhere. Above it all Mother screamed. But Heinrich didn't stop. If only the monster had, but he didn't! I knew that he would leap upon me, rip my heart from my body and bash me to pieces. I lifted the burning-hot gun again. I wasn't even thinking. Just reacting. I swung the gun around, I had to stop him before he killed me. I lifted the weapon up, pointed it at his face again and started squeezing the trigger. And only then . . . it was too late . . . but only then did I see my mother, grabbing him from behind, sinking her hands into him, jerking him to the side. My mother—she was like a crazed lioness protecting her cub. Protecting me! She was trying to keep him away from me, to save me but . . . but instead she threw Heinrich out of the way and the bullet that was supposed to kill Heinrich and stop him forever instead struck my mother, hit her right in the forehead, and I didn't mean to,

I didn't mean to! I thought I'd wanted her dead, but I really didn't! I didn't mean to shoot my mother!

"No!" I cried.

It was an accident because she pushed Heinrich out of the way and the bullet hit her and burrowed its way right into her and killed her almost instantly. She tumbled forward, staring at me as she fell—her two blue eyes and that red jewel of death I'd sunk right in her forehead! She toppled onto Heinrich, and the two of them landed just short of my feet. I sat there unable to breathe. Mother dead. Dead because I shot her! I gasped for air. I couldn't move, the horror clutching me so tightly, twisting my heart and mind. And then I noticed something squirming. Fingers. Curled appendages clawing in the dirt. I followed the hand to the arm to the body of Heinrich. His face all muddy and drippy with blood, he strained to push himself upward. As if returning from the grave, he then heaved himself from beneath my mother's body, lunging out and grabbing my ankle.

"Get away!" I screamed.

I kicked myself free, snapped my ankle out of his weak grasp. I bolted to my feet, tore a glance over my shoulder. The right side of Heinrich's face was hidden behind a pulpy flow of red, but he had his gun, was taking flimsy aim. He fired. A bullet exploded just to my side. I tripped, fell on my hands. In the dirt was a sliver of a mirror, and I saw my murderous image.

"No!"

Mama was dead and Joe would be soon, and I wanted only to stop, run to them, curl up and die with them, but the disfigured, blood-drenched Heinrich was sitting up. Now struggling to his feet. So I ran. I ran as fast as I could, as far as I could, leaving my parents back there, escaping that horrible Heinrich and that horrible nightmare. Then finally the air raid began. The huge one that Joe had been promising all along. The Allies came, thunderstorming Berlin with bombs and ribbons of fire, and I crawled in a hole while the world exploded around me. Me, wishing, hoping that just one bomb would land right in my lap. I sobbed and shrieked, but nothing came to kill me, and I lay there in the dirt while everything was blasted from me, I mean the memory of what happened back there. I think I lay there for several days, actually, until someone came along and peeled me up like a piece of rubber. I couldn't talk. I didn't speak, not for the rest of the war. They said it was shell shock, but it wasn't really.

"*Ten. Nine . . .*"

I just couldn't talk because I was afraid to remember, afraid that it would all come pouring back out. And that's really why I didn't speak when I came to America. It wasn't because German was banned in the house. I just didn't mutter a word—

"*Eight, seven. With each count you feel yourself returning to the present.*"

I didn't speak a syllable until one day I realized I could pretend that Willi Berndt of Berlin was dead at last and that Will Walker now existed. I became someone else and imagined that I'd never seen how dark a world it really was.

"*Six, five. It's all right, Will. You're going to be all right. Four . . .*" Long pause. "*Three. When you open your eyes, you will be in Chicago. You will be your adult self, able to recall all that you have seen. And you will find strength in my presence and in the knowledge that I will help you process all you've remembered.*" Deep breath. "*Two.*"

Suddenly I was out of Berlin and at the bottom of a mucky pond, hooked and being tugged to the surface. I was fighting it, my mind twisting and flopping. God, I didn't want to come back. I just wanted to sink in the dark mud and never rise again. But this thing, this voice, kept yanking at me, pulling me up and up. It was all so lusciously, gravelike black before, but now my world was growing lighter. I pinched my eyes shut. Keep me in the dark, don't let me rise to the top!

"And one."

Chapter

25

Alecia said, "You can open your eyes now, Will."

Despite every effort of my own, my lids rolled back and my eyes were blasted with horrid fluorescent light. I blinked, shielded my face with my left hand. Shit! I was back. Through my fingers I saw the outline of Alecia, beautiful Alecia, sitting there surely hating me.

"Do you know where you are, Will?"

"Chicago!"

"Are you all right?"

I shook my head. My right hand groped down the side of the La-Z-Boy, jabbed the lever back and forth until the contraption folded back into itself with a quick swish. End of trip. End of trance. I threw myself forward, head in my hands, elbows on my knees, so I wouldn't have to look at her. Oh, Christ. Now I not only knew the truth, but someone else did as well. Tears streamed from my eyes, slithered down my wrists, slid down my nose, fell and splattered on the floor. How could I be back here? How?

"I killed her!"

251

"I know," she calmly said. "I've thought that's what happened."

"What?" My chest heaved. "But I didn't mean to. It was an accident! Heinrich was coming after me and I wanted to stop him. I had to! He'd killed Joe and . . . and . . ." A sob plunged me under, pulled me down. "Jesus Christ, I'm sorry! If only she hadn't been trying to push him aside, then she wouldn't have gotten in the way! Mama, Mama, Mama! I didn't mean to!"

I heard the rustling of clothes, several soft steps, and then Alecia was kneeling down next to me. Gently, she lifted my hand from my head, took it in both of hers. As if she were plugging into me, a surge of energy shot through my body. I looked up. Her eyes were red, her cheeks streaked with tears.

Alecia said, "I know you didn't, Will. I know it."

"But . . . but . . . I wished her dead! I thought about killing her! And then . . . then I did it! I shot her, put a bullet right in her forehead!"

Alecia clutched my hand, squeezed it, tried to press everything she knew into me.

"There's a difference, Will. Believe me, there's a fundamental difference between the two."

I stared at her. A difference? What was she talking about? Dead was dead. I'd killed my mother!

She caught her breath. "At some point every child gets so mad that they wish their mother or father would die. They . . . they get so angry they think they could kill them. My God, I even said it to my own father. I said, 'I hate you! I could kill you!' "

"And that's exactly what I did!" I breathed in, smelled that alcoholy breath. Saw those hooded eyes of my mother. "She drank so much!"

"I know it. She hated the war and how it had ruined her

life and everything she'd dreamed of. Booze was how she coped with that. Your mother was an alcoholic, Will, during a time when people didn't see that truth." Alecia rubbed my knuckles in her hand. "Will, you have to understand that that's the part of her you wanted to kill because it was not only killing her, but you, too."

"I loved her."

"Of course you did. Otherwise you wouldn't have cared what she did with herself. Otherwise you would have run away and left Berlin months earlier."

I blurted: "I just wanted her to hold me in her arms and rock me and sing to me." I shook my head. "Instead I—"

"That was an accident. Can you see that?"

There was something right out in front of me, taunting and teasing me. Shrouded in a cloak, it danced around just out of arm's length.

"What do you mean?" I asked.

"I mean you've been very confused by two separate things—the frustrations and needs of a boy, and a horrible accident. It's completely understandable that you're so upset. Anyone would be. In fact, I don't know if I would have had the strength to cope as well as you have." Her tone soft and almost admiring, she said, "Will, you survived the war and a number of awful things, and you need to give yourself great credit for just that."

But I wished I hadn't survived. Living was a curse, Anton's curse. I looked up at beautiful Alecia. Couldn't she see that I wanted to be blessed with death?

Alecia added, "Will, every child has had the same thoughts that you did about your Mother. But these thoughts are just frustrated musings—irrational feelings and impulses—and they hardly ever come true. That yours did is a tragedy almost beyond comprehension." She smiled. "We'll work this out. Believe me, you hurt terribly now, but you can overcome this and leave that pain behind. This is what we'll be working on. It's going to take a while, but trust me, Will, you'll make it."

I searched her face but couldn't see what she did. Hope? No, that was impossible. The only way any of this could get sorted out was to punish me. Send me to jail, put me to death. Was there anything more needed beside this awful confession?

"Don't . . . don't you have to report this to someone?"

She smiled and shook her head. "No. What happens between us is entirely confidential. Besides, Will, it was so long ago."

So long ago yet a wound ever-festering. Looking around this silly little room, I still found it difficult to believe I was here. And that I was Will, an adult. A man. No, part of me was still that boy. Willi lived in me, burned in me. He gave me energy to push in my career, to dream things beyond a normal imagination. And fuel to hate myself.

"What time is it?" I asked.

She checked the silvery watch on her thin wrist. "Almost eleven."

"Oh, my God. I'm sorry I—"

Crashing through my words came the sound of shattering glass. With an explosion of disaster, a window or door or something large burst into pieces. Alecia and I froze, turned toward the door, then stared at one another as distant shards cracked and finally fell into silence. It came from just down the hall, perhaps as close as the reception area. My heart recalled Berlin and bombs, then immediately started galloping forward. Flushed with fear, I turned to Alecia, my shrink, for direction.

"George." She rolled her eyes and laughed nervously. "I wonder what he's done now."

Of course. George, the janitor. "What did he do—throw a garbage can through a plate glass window?"

"I better see if he's all right," said Alecia, slowly pushing herself up.

As she moved toward the door, Berlin pulsed through my body, my mind, and I thought of all who were dead. And who might be alive and could be here; someone from then who might have recently tried to run me over and later hurl me onto the subway tracks.

I saw Alecia's hand on the doorknob and jumped up, shouting, "Wait!"

Dancing in my mind was a faint vision of the face I'd seen behind the wheel of that blue car and again outside on Wabash Avenue. That present-day memory began to merge with faces I'd just seen in my trance, faces from Berlin, 1945. Now I knew who'd died and who'd lived, and I thought, oh Christ, it couldn't be.

"Alecia, I . . ." My breath was coming short. How would we get out of here? "I think I might know who's been after me."

She gazed at me as she flipped back through my story, and then her face tensed, tripping on the same thought. I slipped up next to her, hit the lightswitch—finally, at last, killing those obnoxious lights—then carefully turned the knob. Silently opening the door a crack, I peered out and saw a chair just a few feet away. My God, that hadn't been there before, had it? No, which could only mean that someone had been sitting right out there in the dark, listening to my entire Berlin confession. My face surged red and hot. I stared down the lightless hallway. Was all this George's doings, or was someone else here with altogether different intentions?

I nodded to Alecia, and she called, "George, is that you? Are you all right?"

Her question passed down the hall and returned unanswered. I looked at Alecia. So maybe George was hurt or maybe he'd broken something and had gone for a broom.

Or perhaps there was indeed another person. I opened the door further, looked, could see nothing. We had to find out. I took a breath and felt a calm sensation suffuse me. Was this the final confrontation I'd been waiting for all these years? Of course it was. My past was about to join hands with the present.

Holding a finger to my lips, I led the way into the dark corridor, careful to stay close to the wall. Alecia followed right behind, and she reached over, took my hand. That alone should have been exciting, but I was too preoccupied trying to imagine what or rather who might be waiting ahead. Silent step after step, we eased through the faint light, reaching another office door. I tried the handle, found the room locked, then continued. The next office was locked as well, and we stopped there, listening, trying to glean something, anything. But there was nothing, and so hand in hand with my shrink, we made our way around a corner and toward the reception area.

I stopped, pressed Alecia against the wall. Up ahead moonlight flooded into the waiting area, and in the gentle, bluish light tiny pieces of broken glass sparkled across the carpet. And on the floor just past a desk lay a body.

"George!" shouted Alecia, rushing forward.

I hurried after her. Ran right behind. Expected a bullet, prayed that I would be hit first. Eyes darting, I saw phones, file cabinets. Chairs. Leafy plants. But no lurking figure. I glanced at George, who was lying face down in a bed of glass that had once been the window onto the elevator lobby.

Alecia dropped to his side, pressed two fingers into his neck, and said, "He's alive!"

I suppose we should have run for help. Charged out of there as fast as possible. But I couldn't. There was someone I had to see. Just once. Once before I was killed. I only hoped the bullet—if it would be that—wouldn't strike me in the back, denying me this vision.

"Stay down!" I ordered Alecia.

My eyes swooped up and down, over and around. A couch. More plants. Drapes concealing a figure? No. And then I spotted it. The dark folds of a figure leaning against a tall file cabinet.

My native tongue had somehow followed me back from Berlin, and I said, *"Sie sind aber alt geworden."* You must be old by now.

"Alt? Ganze acht-und-sechstig Jahre alt. Ich war ein paar Jahre Jünger als sie." Old? Altogether I'm sixty-eight. I was a couple of years younger than her. *"Oder,"* he said, employing Marlene Dietrich's famous line, *"haben Sie vergessen?"* Or have you forgotten?

The figure dragged match over flint, sparked a light, lit a cigarette. Sauntered into the middle of the office. In the faint light I saw the patch, big and black. And then that nose. So sharp. And the skin. Now more ruddy than it was pink. Yes, this was the one who'd been after me. Even in the dim light I could tell that he was trim, had retained most of his hair, and had generally aged well.

"Hallo, Heinrich."

"Guten abend, Willichen."

So this was it. Him, standing there in the ghostly light. The thing, the person, who'd chased me out of Berlin and my past. As if I'd just lost a very long race, I took a deep breath. It was a relief, almost comforting. So there really had been someone after me, pursuing me through the years and dreams. So I wasn't crazy after all.

"Have you come to kill me?" I asked in English.

"Gut geraten." Good guess, he said. A small gun in one hand, a folder in the other, he continued in harshly accented English. "After I lost you in the subway, I went to

your apartment. When you didn't return, I figured you'd come running back here like a lost puppy." He smiled "It was a very interesting confession—and mostly true, by the way. I heard most of it until I was interrupted by this fellow," he said, waving his gun at the unconscious George.

Staring at Heinrich, I said, "I always knew you weren't dead."

"The intuitive one—that's what your mother used to say about you, anyway." He shrugged. "I, on the other hand, thought you were long gone. You know, it wouldn't have come to this if you hadn't written that letter to the adoption agency. A contact of mine notified me."

"I'm glad you're here."

And I really was. This was the past incarnate, something real that I could not only see, but touch. And hopefully kill.

"*Dankeschön.*" Standing in the faint light, he touched the patch over his right eye. "You shot out part of my face back then and I lost my eye, but you saved my life. Isn't that ironic? You wanted to kill me, yet you saved me."

I didn't want to hear this. My jaw clamped tight, mashed my teeth together. If only that second bullet had struck him, erased him forever!

Smiling, Heinrich continued, saying, "I bandaged myself and then a stranger managed to get me to a hospital. They admitted me, and then there was a raid and the hospital took a bomb." He laughed. "I passed out. I was unconscious for a week, they told me, and when I woke I'd been evacuated. Thanks to you I escaped Berlin and the final onslaught and those stupid Bolsheviks. I was taken to a village, a little town captured by the Americans. All my papers and everything had been lost in the bombing, and so I just made up a name and . . . and . . . well, here I am, ever so grateful to you, Willichen." He asked, "How's my English?"

"Very good."

"It should be. I helped the Americans, you know. Helped them identify the last bits of Nazism." He took a long drag on his cigarette, sucking it until it glowed a fiery orange. "Alecia, you can stand up—I know you're back there behind the desk. I did so enjoy your file on Willi—it was me who stole it. You're very perceptive, I might add."

She rose, pushing herself up and immediately punching him with her shrinky logic, saying, "If he saved your life, then why do you want to kill him?"

"Because, my dear, as you wrote in Willi's file, his main goal is to reveal everything that happened back in Berlin. And although that might be nice for him, I'm not about to let him ruin my life. We were all crazy during the war, you see, and Willi here is the only person alive who witnessed any crimes I may or may not have committed." He smiled. "I've become quite successful—I own a chain of furniture stores, have a wonderful family, grandchildren even—and I won't let Willi jeopardize all that by spreading stories about my killing a Jew. No, I won't." Turning to me in the faint light, he said, "I wanted to marry your mother, Willi, and I think she would have agreed after the war. But then . . ." He lifted my file. "Alecia says right here that she knows you're quite attracted to her, so perhaps I should kill her first. That would really hurt you, Willi, wouldn't it? Then you'd know perhaps how I felt when you killed your mother."

"Shut up!"

"Oh, but you would find this file very interesting. She summarizes you very well, and I really think it's quite clear how much she admires you and is even attracted to you, too, and—"

The ceiling exploded with light, an entire plane of white fluorescent tubes burning with operating room brightness. I ducked, shielding my eyes.

"Will!" shouted Alecia.

She'd hit all the switches by the front door and was bolting out. In an instant I saw Heinrich—gray and wrinkly—fumbling with his cigarette and the file and the gun. I dug my foot into glass, bounded over George. Hurled myself after my dear Alecia. As I reached the door, I heard a snap, a sharp explosion. Heinrich fired his gun, and I flinched, expecting to feel the dull thud of a bullet slam and burrow into me. Instead my hopes were dashed as the piece of death went racing past and slammed into a wall. So Heinrich, aged and missing the eye I'd shot, wasn't the marksman he'd been when he'd shot Joe. I darted around the corner. Alecia was halfway down the hall, holding out her hand. The elevator. She'd struck the button, found the elevator still on this floor. And now she stood, desperately begging me to run to the shelter of this little chamber. Yes, we could probably jam it between floors. Yes, we could probably hit the fire button, use the phone to call for help.

But I stopped.

Safety was just up there in the elevator and perhaps in the arms of Alecia. But I was so tired. I'd been running for thirty years and I couldn't run anymore. I had to stop, face Heinrich, deal literally head-on with my Berlin past. And so I threw myself up against the hall wall. I heard Heinrich, his charging feet crunching over glass. I listened to him race after me, and I clenched my fist. I knew he was expecting me to be down the hall by now, perhaps in the elevator or the stairwell or in an office. Someplace where he might trap us. He hadn't thought at all that I'd be right around the corner. His expression of gross miscalculation told me that much, that eye and even the black patch rising up with the lines of his brow in astonishment. I hurled my fist forward, stuffed my bound knuckles into his soft stomach. The gun went off. A desperate attempt. But a failed one, sending another bullet to another harmless end. I punched him and knocked the old man right off his feet.

Threw him back, ripping the gun from his hand. My file that he somehow still clutched went flying.

And within the split of an instant he was on the floor and I was atop him, straddling him, my knees pinning his arms down, and my two hands pressing the gun to his chest. When he'd hurled me through the air in that Berlin ruin, I'd been just a boy, weak in comparison to his manly strength. But now I was about the same age as he'd been then. Only I was much stronger than this worn, heaving, breathless body beneath me. I could blast him inside out. For Anton. For Joe. And, yes, for my own mother. I positioned the gun over his heart. In just one second I could—

"Will, no!" screamed Alecia, rushing up behind me.

"Get away!" I ordered.

"Don't!" she begged. "Please, Will, don't!"

"Stay back!"

I was staring into the face of a ghostly devil, and just the sight of him sent me back to my *Vaterland*. Jerked me back faster than even the La-Z-Boy and Alecia's chants. Here was proof that the past had existed and died just as I'd so recently revealed. And for Heinrich's part in it, for all those I'd loved who'd been killed, I would grant him a grisly death.

"This is from all of them!" I said.

But as I went to squeeze the trigger, the body trapped beneath me began to shake. At first I thought he was panicking, that he couldn't catch his breath. Then I thought he was having a heart attack.

"Will, no!" shouted Alecia from behind.

I realized he was laughing. Heinrich was staring up at me and death and once again he couldn't have been more amused. Chuckling just like back then when he'd revealed that Mother was his mistress.

"Don't . . . don't worry," he struggled to say through thick, perverse amusement. "He won't do it."

A fury of blood swelled my heart. "Just watch!"

He looked right up at me. Stared right up and smiled and shook his head. It scared me, this eery confidence of his.

"Oh, no, you won't." As if declaring trump, Heinrich offered a devilish grin, and said, "You can't kill me, Willi-chen, because . . . because I'm your father."

Nothing could have disarmed my fury more quickly or thoroughly. Father? This eel? It couldn't be!

"What? No! No, Joe was my father!" I shouted.

He stared up at me, pixieish amusement stretching his old wrinkle-lined face. "Wherever did you get that notion? Your mother? Joe?"

My mind flashed to our little bar. To my huddling, eaves-dropping on Joe and Mother. I'd overheard what they'd said, witnessed my mother's bitterness. But, dear God, I'd never actually been told the precise words.

"What do you mean?"

"I mean . . ." Heinrich gazed up at me, glanced over at Alecia. *"Mein Gott,* this is like confessing on one's death-bed." He took a deep breath. "I mean, I knew your mother and Joe long before the war."

My head swooned. Hadn't Joe seemed to recognize Hein-rich as we spied him and his two thugs outside the bar? Yes, and my memory echoed Joe's voice later when he'd held the gun at Heinrich in that pit of death and said how it was like old times. It hadn't made any sense back then. Neither had Heinrich's words about how they were about to finish things at last. But it all did now, giving horrible credence to Heinrich's present story.

"Ja, ja, ja. We three were almost inseparable during Joe's first visit to Berlin. That was just when the Nazis were starting to come on strong, just before I signed up. And those were the last wild days of Berlin. Oh, *Gott,* I think we must have hit every bar and cabaret in town. We drank so much—every night, you see—and . . . and . . ."

I couldn't believe this. My mind, my body was shutting down, and I started backing off him. No, this couldn't be!

"Well," continued Heinrich, "finally Joe took me aside and told me how much he wanted her. I mean, cousin or not, Joe could barely contain that youthful American physique of his. I smiled when he told me, for I'd seen it all along. He didn't know, though, that I also thought Eva was the most beautiful creature I'd—"

I whipped the back of my left hand across his foul mouth, ripped his bottom lip, brought a trickle of red from his mouth. He was lying! I knew it!

Heinrich dabbed his tongue, licked at his own blood. "Believe me, it's true. Joe begged me to take them somewhere—a hotel, a bordello. Anywhere."

"No!"

"Oh, but yes. So I took them to some awful little place and got a room. But Joe kept on drinking and drinking—he was quite nervous, after all—and the first thing he did was go into the bathroom and pass out!" Heinrich grinned. "I'd been about to leave, but then I helped Eva undress and get into bed. And then, well, let me tell you, I slipped in with her, and even though she was almost as drunk as Joe, she was more wonderful than I could have ever imagined."

"That's not true!"

"Of course it is. I had her. I spent half the night with her—I'll never forget our first time together."

"No!"

"Of course that's true. How else do you think it all started between us?" He added, "But then . . . then somehow Eva's grandfather found out where she was. He came over that morning and discovered Eva and Joe in bed—obviously after I'd left Joe had woken up and crawled in with her. Who knows if they actually even did anything—he was so drunk I don't think they could have—but, oh, *Gott*, her grandfather was so furious. He beat Joe and threw him on the first train, then kicked Eva out for good. That's when Dieter took her in."

"You're lying!"

I threw the pistol to the side, grabbed Heinrich by the collar and started shaking him. He was not going to take the last wonderful thing from my life, and I whipped his skinny neck from side to side. His patch twisted and slid off. A thick, hideous scar and an eyeless mound of flesh stared up at me.

"You're not my father!"

I banged his head against the linoleum, smashed it down over and over again. I had to beat him to death, crush this horrible person and his ugly lies! Heinrich cried out and writhed, but I was much stronger and determined. I beat him against the floor, then wrapped my fingers around his neck and squeezed, feeling dry flesh worm in my hands.

"Will! Stop!" shrieked Alecia, rushing around.

No, I had to kill him!

"Stop or I'm going to shoot!"

It was like she'd knocked the breath out of me. I looked up. Alecia was standing in front of me, legs spread, arms out. And she was training the gun on me. I lost all my strength and dropped Heinrich, gasping, to the floor. This wasn't possible. Alecia? No, she wouldn't harm me! She couldn't!

"Will," she said, her voice shaking, "I don't want to hurt you—I'm your friend! I just want you to stop."

Stunned, I stared at her and the pistol. Now I knew the truth. A whirlwind of hysteria began to twist within me, and I started shaking, sweating, because Alecia had been pretending all along to like me. That much was clear. She'd just been acting, faking everything to gain my confidence so that she could hear my awful story. That's all she wanted. Not me. She'd faked everything, and now that the real me was fully revealed, so was her real feeling for me: contempt. It was obvious. She despised me for what I'd done to my mother. That gun she aimed at me was proof. Everything else had been a lie.

"Now just get back, Will. Get off Heinrich and go sit against the wall. Go on!"

My body was shaking, waves of tremors rolling over me. I'd been horribly deceived, and I wanted to run away, to cry out, but instead I did as she ordered, and started pushing myself up.

"That's good. That's good," she said. "I'm your friend, Will. Do you understand? I don't want to hurt you. I'm just trying to prevent any trouble."

Bullshit. She was no friend, and I froze. Sweat poured from my head, dripped all over Heinrich. Staring at the gun, I realized Alecia should shoot me. She knew what had happened. She knew that I'd killed my own mother. And my shrink should be the one to punish me. I deserved to die, I wanted to die!

"Will, please!"

No. I wanted this to be all over. Mistake or no mistake, I wanted to pay for what I'd done. My eyes clenched shut.

"Just shoot."

Nothing happened and I opened my eyes, saw Alecia lowering the gun. I'd won while wanting only to lose.

Grabbing Heinrich again, I demanded, "Shoot or I'll strangle him!"

"No."

She didn't even lift the gun. The determination and the fright had passed from her face, and she just stood there, defeated. No, stood there, catching her thoughts. Then she looked up, having searched her arsenal of reason.

"Heinrich, where was that hotel?"

"Wh-what?" he gasped beneath me.

"The hotel you and Eva and Joe went to—where was it!"

He rolled his head on the floor, twisted to see her. "I don't know."

"Think!" she demanded. "Was it in Schöneberg?"

"No." Totally confused, he closed his eyes, then said, "On the Ku-damm. A little place right on the Kurfürsten-damm."

I stared at Alecia. What was she talking about? Why was she asking? None of this made any sense. Alecia had to kill me or I had to kill Heinrich. That's all there was. That was the only choice left. No other way out. Weary, my fingers clasped Heinrich's collar. A slow death. A painful one. For him or for me. I didn't care which.

"Will," began Alecia, "if you release Heinrich and just sit on the floor over there, I'll tell you something. I want to show you the real truth about your father."

My fingers clenched, then began to relax. I stared at her. Heinrich? No, there wasn't anything more, was there? There couldn't be.

"Will, do you want to learn who your father really was?"

I knew that tone, soft and luring. The glint in her eye told me Alecia saw a greater truth. Something looming that I was blind to. And she wasn't going to just tell me. No, Alecia could never make it that easy. She was going to make me work for it, force me to discover it myself. Yes, she knew something very important, something that neither Heinrich nor I was even aware of.

Without thinking, I loosened again my grasp on Heinrich. Slid off him. Defeated, I pushed myself away. Crawled across the linoleum, over bits of broken glass. From the office I heard someone moaning. George. He was coming to. Forget about him, I thought. I just wanted to die. As quickly as possible I wanted to be punished and banished from this life. But not without learning about my father.

"Good, Will. Very good." She waved the gun at Heinrich.

"Now you, you sit over there, against the other wall. You can be sure I'll shoot if you so much as move."

The gray-haired man slowly pushed himself up, propping himself on one arm. He caught his breath, wiped the blood from his mouth and forehead. Sheepishly, he did as he was told, leaning his tired body against the wall opposite me. He was so different now. Not at all the fierce image I'd kept alive all these years. So this, I realized, is how we all shrink.

"Now, Will, I want you to do something."

Oh, Christ. I knew that voice, too. That was the beginning of her chant. No, I thought. No trance. Not now.

"I want you to go back," she said, staring at me.

"But—!"

"Will, you heard something else. That last night when you overheard Joe and Dieter and Loremarie arguing, they said something about this, didn't they?"

"I . . . I don't know."

"Of course you do."

I rubbed my eyes, and the answer that I didn't know was there popped forward, and I replied, "Yes, I guess so."

"Of course you did. Now if you want to know the truth about your father, then you have to go back and tell me what you heard."

Heinrich groaned, said, "Oh, *Scheisse,* how ridiculous."

"Shut up!" snapped Alecia, waving the gun nervously at him. "Or I'll permanently regress you!"

My left arm crossed over my chest, and I bowed my head and suppressed a smile. She'd do it. I was proud of her because she'd really do it.

"Okay. Will, take a deep breath," she began, cueing me with her own breathing.

Like a circus dog, I almost couldn't help myself. I sucked in all the air my lungs could hold, then let it trickle back out.

"That's good. Will. That's very good. Now roll your eyes up and slowly, very slowly—"

"But don't you do a trance, too!" I said. "He'll jump you if you close your eyes."

"I won't. I'm watching him. Now just breathe easily, fully, and roll your eyes up. Good. Very good. Now slowly close your eyelids. Good."

In spite of or perhaps because of the intensity of the present situation, I felt hypnosis rush into my body and mind. This had to be quick and sharp. No messing around. There and back. I felt myself lunging for that bit of a trance that was beginning to appear, grabbing at it and throwing it over myself like a big blanket. I had to duck into Berlin, learn something, and fly back here with that knowledge.

"Now, Will, you're going to go back to that night in Berlin when you heard Joe and Dieter and Loremarie arguing. You can return as an adult, able to see this all like a film. You will see your young self, Willi, sitting on those rocks, spying on them and listening."

Yes. Everything around me was gathering speed. I had to hurl it forward, rush to get there.

"And you can . . ."

A great gust seemed to sweep over my body, lift me up and out of windy Chicago. Go back, back to Berlin. Yes, there was something more. They were shouting, saying all this stuff. I wasn't really listening, but I heard it. Those voices. They were so far away. But not really. I could go back quite easily, right to that ring in the tree of my life.

". . . *you can recall everything that was said.*"

"I'm on my way."

"*Good.*"

As if I were flying from O'Hare, the lights of the Loop swirled beneath me. The John Hancock tower, the Standard Oil building. And that stupid, vast grid of orange street lights. Lake Michigan. Big and black. Behind me I heard voices, and I turned and gazed down. Now Berlin was down there. I was up in that moon-filled sky and what was left of the city was crumbled like bread crumbs beneath me. Oh, my God.

"It's nothing but a shell. Everything . . . everything's ruined. The whole city."

"I know. Just tell me what you hear. Tell me what else they said."

Voices rose from one area, and everything started swirling, sucking me down. In a giant whoosh, I fell out of the sky and into the remains of a Schöneberg neighborhood. Willi. He sat outside a windowless window, crouching in fear.

"I was so afraid."

"Of course you were."

"And so skinny."

"Now look at Willi sitting there, being worried and afraid. While he was trying to think how to help his mother, the three people inside got in an argument. Tell me what they were saying just before Willi ran away."

"Loremarie called Dieter a doormat."

"She did, didn't she? And what else?"

"Dieter was mad at himself."

"Why?"

Just as Alecia said, I left Willi sitting on the rocks, and turned my attention to the room. As if I were merely turning up the volume, their voices came clear and sharp and I focused on them.

"For the same reason Mother wouldn't forgive Joe."

"Go on."

I heard the three of them arguing and yelling, throwing curses back and forth. Suddenly Loremarie slapped Joe. Oh, shit. She poked him with hot, seething accusations. Oh, Christ. And what was Dieter now saying? What? What did he say? My God. I had to—

"Alecia!"

"I'm right here."

Alecia! I had to get to Chicago, had to tell her what Loremarie said and Dieter, too! With every bit of energy, I twisted and shouted. I had to break this trance, snap myself right out of Berlin!

"Alecia!"

I punched through. Huffing and sweating, I ripped open my eyes and found myself sitting back on the floor. Heinrich across from me, Alecia standing just beyond him. I looked from one to the other. I understood it all. What had been said in those ruins was the last of the pieces to complete the huge puzzle.

Staring at Heinrich, I said, "Dieter cursed himself because . . . because he should have stopped them but didn't!" Little dribbles of things I'd caught here and there suddenly all fit together. "He should have stopped them the first time. He was talking about Mother and Joe. They . . . they went to the *Kneipe* at Dieter's *Pension* back in 1934 or whenever, and it was there in the bar that Joe confessed his love for her." Yes. That room with the curving balcony was where all the illicit love took place, Dieter's as well as Mother's and Joe's. "She loved Joe, too, and they got a room. Dieter gave them a room at his *Pension*. He knew they were cousins, but Berlin was Berlin, and he gave them his most special room, the one on the top floor with the balcony. Later . . . when Mother's grandfather threw her out, Dieter took her in. He needed her, sure. She was a convenient alibi. But he also felt a little bit responsible." I added, "Mother only hated Joe because he abandoned her—he left Berlin without her. Yet I think she really loved him."

"I do, too." Alecia looked right at me. "But her grandfather didn't find them at Dieter's, did he?"

"No. No, he didn't."

I heard Joe and Mother echoing in my memory. He: Once should have been enough. She: But it wasn't, was it?

"He didn't find them there because . . ." I stared right at Heinrich. "Because that was the first time Mother and Joe made love. Grandfather didn't find them until the second time . . . at that little hotel on the Ku-damm!"

Heinrich's face flushed red. Shaking his head, he cursed and muttered.

"No, that's not true!" He grew deep red. "Besides, even if it were, it still wouldn't prove anything. You could still be my son!"

I studied him, this ugly man, left over from a terrible time. He'd quickly done away with Joe and Anton, but had taken years to ruin Mother.

"No," I calmy said, knowing deep within that I could never be the offspring of such a person. "My father was Joe."

I glanced at Alecia and could almost visibly see something strike her. With a rush of excitement, her eyes opened as a chorus of insight blossomed in her mind, illuminating both past and present.

"Of course!" She turned to Heinrich, pierced him with her eyes. "You're the one who told Eva's grandfather where they were."

"No!" He waved his head from side to side, lifted his hands, palms out. *"Nein, nein."*

"Yes, you did."

The great seer, Alecia was calm and direct, flying on pure intuition to the only sensible point. Sure of herself, she smiled victoriously. Finally she had the prize, the very thing all shrinks want: complete understanding of all the relationships, which in turn made everyone's actions all quite logical, even sensible.

"You wanted Eva all to yourself. That was the competition between you and Joe, and you were afraid that Joe was winning, that somehow Eva and he would run away together. And . . . and so you called her grandfather—no one else would have—knowing full well that he'd chase Joe out of town!"

Oddly Heinrich lowered his hands and then sat quiet, gazing at the floor. So it was true. Heinrich had phoned Mother's grandfather and told him where in all of wild Berlin to find his two incestuous grandchildren. That had been the start of Mother's long slow fall in which she lost family, lover, cabaret dreams. And me.

It happened so quickly. I didn't think Heinrich had it in him. Nearly as fast as a lashing whip, he hurled himself over and grabbed Alecia by the ankle. Using all his force, he jerked her right off her feet and she screamed and came tumbling down, smacking hard on the linoleum. He scrambled right over her, pawing and clawing, lunging for the gun. I threw myself forward, but I wasn't fast enough. Glass. Lots of it beneath my feet. I slipped. Oh, Christ! He was going to kill her!

"Alecia!"

I jumped over her, grabbed at the gun she was still struggling to hold, at the weapon Heinrich was trying to rip away. And somehow we all three came up on our knees. Bobbed to the surface, the gun a wild bomb between us that we were all struggling for but could not control. Caught in our tangled mass of hands, the pistol tilted barrel-up right toward Alecia's head. I thought of trances and hypnosis and a power of concentration stranger than I could ever conjure on my own, and I pictured my body a single, hard muscle. In an instant the gun snapped into my control and the thing was pointed right at my throat.

His face now crimson with fury, his brow bulging with wrinkles and veins, Heinrich shouted, "I . . . I want to haunt you for . . . forever!"

He jerked his head back, then hurled himself forward. His forehead dug into my temple and ... and my head exploded with pain. As my grasp weakened, Heinrich wrenched the gun toward himself, heaved himself up. And wrapped his lips around the barrel. With a simple twitch of our collective fist, it was over in an instant.

Epilogue

I thought it would be an impossible knot to untie, but now, six months later, I'm beginning to sense this thing loosen. Alecia tells me I'm making great progress. I don't know. Everytime I see an article about a hunting accident, I clip it out. Awful things continue to happen, and it's comforting to know that I'm not alone in that hellish boat.

The police wanted to know every detail. That was the hardest part. The same questions, over and over again. I couldn't have made it those first few weeks without Alecia. She ran defense, telling them that Heinrich had come after me because I had witnessed him killing a Jewish man during the fall of Berlin. They bought it, of course, as did the *Tribune*. Nazis still get ink. There was no mention of Mother.

Alecia made me a new tape right away. I saw her nearly every day for that first month and when I wasn't seeing her I was listening to her voice and floating off into never-never land. It was sort of like being pickled, but it worked. I'm still alive.

The big news is that I've taken a break from work—Dear Agent has politely called it a sabbatical—and last month I went to Berlin. Went there physically, I mean. Via Lufthansa. Alecia wasn't sure I could handle it, but I packed the tape and off I went. I had to. I needed new Berlin memories. I flew into Frankfurt, then took the train across East Germany, passed through *die Mauer*—The Wall—and arrived right at Zoo Station. As we pulled in, I noticed that the Zoo Bunker was gone. Don't ask me how they destroyed something so staunchly fortified, but they did, blasting that monolithic pile of concrete into a dusty memory.

I stayed at a little *Pension* on the Ku-Damm itself, right near Uhlandstrasse, a cozy inn on the top two floors of a five-story building. A bordello occupied the floor beneath, and I couldn't help but wonder if possibly, just maybe, this was where my great-grandfather had burst in on his two grandchildren. I had every intention of asking the management if this had indeed been a *Pension* before the war, but somehow I couldn't bring myself to inquire.

The very first thing I did there was go out walking, and my feet had a memory of their own and took me right into the heart of the Tiergarten district and to one particular house. Tante Lore's, where a large headstone with a Jewish star on it now dominated the front yard. The former aristocratic townhouse had been rebuilt and divided into apartments, and I climbed to the top floor, took a deep breath, and knocked. Somehow I was sure she'd still be alive, heavy with years, that Aryan blonde hair all gray. But she wasn't. Instead a fair-haired woman about my age answered the door, and when I asked after my Tante Lore, this woman hesitated, then informed me that her aunt—her brother's sister—had died not long after the war. By the name of Marianne, Loremarie's niece was quite pleasant and very attractive—high cheekbones, long, slender body—and she invited me in for tea. She'd heard of Eva, Joe, Dieter and me, but assumed we'd all died during the fall of Berlin or the first horrible years of defeat. Dieter had, anyway. She knew that for a fact, because Loremarie had told how he'd saved her from a Russian and in turn been executed.

I stayed only for a while—I really didn't recognize the house, it had changed so during restoration—and next I went to the cemetery where we'd buried Erich. When I couldn't remember where we'd placed him in that vast space, I did a short trance, took myself into hypnosis until I saw a tree and a wall. Then I opened my eyes. The wall with the hole was repaired, of course, and that tree long gone, but I found the approximate site and spread out a bed of flowers. *Mein kleiner Erich.*

I crossed The Wall and visited shabby East Berlin only once, but I spent several afternoons at the zoo, which was all rebuilt and was totally amazing. Inquiring at the zoo office, I learned that my elephant pal, Siam, had survived the war and the beginning of the peace, nourished by cabbages Berliners had grown all around the zoo. But he'd passed away, I was told, in 1947. However, Knorke, the hippopotamus who'd survived the firebombings in his tank of water, was still going strong, still siring an endless line of little hippos named Bulette, Jette, etc. I found him, and for hours I stood by his pen and stared at that big, ugly thing, and cried and laughed.

As for Dieter's *Pension* . . . it was no more. Occupying most of the block was a very plain, very brown apartment building. A big structure without a single balcony.

On my last day in West Berlin, I met Marianne for coffee and torte at a *Konditorei,* and she presented me with an envelope of old black and white photos. They'd been in a trunk with the last of her aunt's things, she said, puffing on a cigarette, and she wondered if my mother might be in one of the pictures. I flipped through only three and would have screamed when I saw the fourth if all the wind hadn't rushed from my lungs. I couldn't believe it. There were the two of them, Loremarie and her Evchen, embracing by the Brandenburg Gate. My God, Mother was as beautiful as I remembered. Full of hope, I shuffled through the rest, and some twenty pictures later came across one of Loremarie and Dieter, this one obviously taken after the war because they were standing next to a jeep emblazoned with an American star. It wasn't a good photo, the faces and figures all blurred and foggy, and I held it closer, studied these friends from my former life. Oddly, in the background I noticed the shape of a boy and a tall man, the two of them walking as if they were about to join Dieter and Loremarie. My heart squeezed, then jumped. That was me, wasn't it? Absolutely. I'd know those knobby legs anywhere. That was me with some stranger. But who? I couldn't tell because the man's head was turned as he looked back down the street. It looked like Joe, it really did, but that of course was impossible.

Actually Berlin was quite inspirational, and I feel better and more secure than I think I ever have. At last I possess a picture of my mother, and whenever I want I use hypnosis like a record player to hear her voice. That city was inspiring, though, because although it was smashed and ruined, then cruelly broken in two, its healthier part managed to not only rebuild itself but regain its true character and even thrive. Like the island metropolis of West Berlin, I'd lost huge chunks of my life, and if it could move on, so could I. It's going to take time, but I'm willing to work. Besides, my love and admiration for Alecia continues to deepen, and I get to see her a lot. And she is dressing better these days, not that that really matters.

Who knows. The whole process'll probably take years, but maybe one day I'll be out of therapy. Maybe then I'll be able to actually ask Alecia out on a date. Something simple.

Like a lost tropical island or a remote mountain village in the Himalayas. She actually did let something drop about the two of us going sailing out on Lake Michigan, which I guess I'd settle for.

Yeah, right, dream on, I keep telling myself. I'm nuts. I admit it. Alecia and me , shrink and dink, off into the sunset . . . when hell freezes over or . . . or the Berlin Wall comes tumbling down.

Then again, there've been greater miracles.